Her Perfect Twin

Sarah Bonner

HODDER studio

First published in Great Britain in 2022 by Hodder Studio
An Imprint of Hodder & Stoughton
An Hachette UK company

This paperback edition published in 2022

1 3 5 7 9 10 8 6 4 2

A CIP catalogue record for this title is available from the British Library

Paperback ISBN 9781529382747
eBook ISBN 9781529382723

Typeset in Sabon MT by Manipal Technologies Limited

Printed and bound by in Great Britain by Clays Ltd, Elcograf S.p.A.

Hodder & Stoughton policy is to use papers that are natural, renewable and
recyclable products and made from wood grown in sustainable forests. The logging
and manufacturing processes are expected to conform to the environmental
regulations of the country of origin.

Hodder & Stoughton Ltd
Carmelite House
50 Victoria Embankment
London EC4Y 0DZ

www.hodder.co.uk

To Mum and Dad
For making me believe I could do anything xx

Part One
Megan

Chapter One

I have no memory of my husband taking this photo. It shows me lying on our bed in my underwear, eyes closed, a private smile on my face. It is definitely our bed, with the padded leather headboard I have to wipe constantly because otherwise it accumulates so much dust you'd think I hadn't cleaned for a year. The white bedding with the little blue forget-me-nots is the one I bought in the January sales last month and the flowers perfectly match the electric-blue bra and knickers I am wearing.

I do not own electric-blue underwear.

Chris is still in the shower; he's humming some god-awful soft rock song as he splashes water around the en suite. Keeping an ear out, I dig through the top drawer of the dresser, spilling plain black and flesh-coloured knickers to the floor as I hunt for the more risqué items at the back. I find a red lace set that hasn't seen the light of day in. . . well, probably a year? I don't know, it can't be that long, surely, although it's been a while. But there is nothing blue. Stuffing things back in, I sense someone behind me and turn to come face to face with my husband, wet from the shower, hair hanging around his face.

'I always liked the red.' He smiles lazily at me, holding the towel around his waist with a dangerous casualness, like he could drop it to the floor at any time. He raises both eyebrows, gives me an almost imperceptible wiggle of his hips.

I blush and look away, trying to ignore his presence behind me as I carry on stuffing everything into the drawer, the feeling of his eyes on the back of my head.

'Were you looking for something?' he asks.

Still facing away from him on my knees in front of the dresser, I shake my head. 'Nothing important.'

'It never is,' he says with a sigh, scooping his phone from the bed and sauntering towards the little dressing alcove.

There was a time in our marriage when I would have reached out and grabbed the towel. When I would have slipped into the scraps of red lace poking out from the humdrum sea of black and tan microfibre/cotton blend. Chased him around the house.

Instead, I pick up my phone and begin scrolling through my own photos. I take a lot of pictures to help me remember. To confirm. Documenting every outfit helps me by linking my memories of what I was doing to the feel of certain fabrics against my skin: if I was wearing cotton or silk, or a slightly scratchy jumper like that mauve one I bought last year and still wear even though it gives me goosebumps if I move too quickly.

I scroll back through the album dedicated to shopping: the last week, then the last month; but there is no sign of electric-blue lace. I definitely did not buy these. And surely I would remember wearing them? Remember lying on the bed with a little smile and one finger jauntily hooked into the waistband waiting for him to take the picture.

There is a chance that Chris bought the set and then I put it on for him, too caught up in the moment and the fact that my husband had finally paid me enough attention to go out of his way. But we've been together for four years and he's only ever bought me underwear once. A virginal white set for our wedding night. Since then, nothing.

Unless he's trying to fuck with me. Again.

He thinks he's so clever, but I will catch him out eventually. His 'concerned husband' act is starting to wear thin, the edges fraying. I know he's behind at least some of my 'forgetful episodes', even if I can't prove it yet.

I can hear him in the kitchen, making coffee in that irritatingly precise way of his. All carefully measured and exacting, like he's a chemist in a lab. He always looks horrified when I scoop some instant granules into a mug and slosh on some boiling water. Even worse when I top it up with cold water just so I can drink it faster. I begin to paw through his drawers. He is tidy and so I am slow, careful not to leave a wake of mess behind me. No blue lace. But something so small would be easy to hide and I don't have time to take the house apart.

Did he want me to find the photo? Did he leave his phone deliberately, right there on his pillow while he had a shower, knowing I wouldn't be able to resist having a little peek? And knowing I wouldn't be able to confront him either, not after I'd made such a thing about privacy last week. Fuck him.

I abandon the search and pad down to the kitchen, hoping that I might catch a glimpse of whatever he is up to. He is making pancakes – little American ones with their bubbly surfaces, light and fluffy – while he hums a song, one I know from somewhere but can't recall the name of: a vague memory of singing along in a car, feeling wind whipping at my hair. The air is salty, cool. 2002. The summer Leah and I went to Dublin on a school trip, hours and hours on a cramped coach, desperate for a pee. The second night, Leah had met these boys who took us for a ride in their dad's convertible, driving us out of the city and over the wooden bridge towards the long sandy beach at Dollymount. Leah had gone off with one of the boys and left me with his friend – or possibly brother, I don't really remember – trying to make polite conversation while I tried not to imagine what my twin was doing behind the men's swimming shelter.

'You don't fancy. . .' the one I was left with had said to me with a gesture towards the shelter.

'I have a boyfriend,' I'd replied, prim and proper, waiting for the perfect boy and the perfect time.

Chris has laid the small table in the corner of the kitchen, a French press of coffee alongside a few white flowers in a narrow vase. The one I bought at the same time as the forget-me-not bedding, along with a pair of soft grey cushions for the living room and a bale of new towels. I have a photo of each. Chris wasn't impressed with my choices, but then I hadn't expected him to be. We'd had a row about the towels. His mother had bought us some for a wedding gift, ones I had to throw away because I accidentally covered them in hair dye but hadn't been brave enough to tell him. I had thought I was replacing like for like, that I could shuttle them into the airing cupboard and he would be none the wiser, but he had noticed immediately. Of course he had; he always notices when things are out of place. Ever since we moved in together, I have painstakingly tiptoed around him, going to great lengths to ensure that everything is just so. I even make sure the toilet roll is the 'correct' way in its holder and load the dishwasher per his exacting specification, knowing that he would notice the second anything was out of place, out of line, out of the order he imposed on the world around him. He'd accused me of being slovenly. Forgetful. A disaster. *Just like your mother.*

The Pattersons have a curse. But I will not let it take me, will not succumb like my mother, will not let it wash over me and drown everything like she did, to leave me and my sister to flounder while she sank away.

As I pour a coffee, I watch Chris stack pancakes on a plate and drizzle some maple syrup over them. He has that spring in his step he normally reserves for special occasions and he puts the pancakes down in front me with a practised flourish.

'Ta-da!' he says. 'Pancakes for my beautiful wife!' He kisses my cheek and grins at me. The grin grows wider as he pulls some napkins from a drawer and unfurls one into my lap. It is a brilliant electric blue. I watch him as I take a mouthful. It is like glass in my mouth. He watches me back, a flicker of something at the corner of his mouth. He is goading me. Again.

'Are you OK, Meggie?' His voice drips with concern. 'Something wrong with the pancakes? You've hardly touched them.'

The pile in front of me seems to shimmer in the weak sunlight coming through the window. The glass in my mouth dissolves into ash; am I imagining the taste of almond on my tongue?

'I'll eat them if you don't want them,' he says, hovering his fork over my plate. I push them towards him. 'Worried about seeing your mum?'

No, of course not, I want to scream at him. Why would I possibly be worried about seeing Mum? Who doesn't have any idea who I am and who calls me Leah every single time I can face visiting her in that place? Instead I smile and whisper, 'A little.'

'I'll be with you, Meggie. We've got this. Together.'

Mum lives just outside of the village of Wotton, near Dorking. The house is gorgeous, with the North Downs behind it, large grounds full of fruit trees and hidden nooks of shade, perfect for summer reading. It would be idyllic: except for the other residents and the truth of why they live there. Sometimes I can imagine everything is fine, that we are just meeting up for a pot of tea in the grounds of an old stately home, like some of my friends do with their mothers, a lovely day out somewhere special. But most of the time our visits to the Jonas Institute are punctuated by the screaming of the woman in the next room, normally set off by the man who likes to rap on her window just to scare her, or by the man who likes to strip naked and run around the grounds irrespective of the weather until he is caught and bundled back into the warmth by the harried-looking staff.

'What's the racket, Leah?' Mum will ask me, confusing me with my sister. Sometimes I just go with it, let her think that I'm Leah and reminisce with her about the past. I wonder if Leah does the same when she visits? If she visits at all.

I just wish I could talk to Mum properly. Tell her that I'm terrified I'm turning into her and that all I have in my future is a room right here, in this place that smells like stale piss and overcooked cabbage. Or that I think there is something very wrong about my husband.

'You should call her,' Chris says as we drive home.

'Hmmm?'

'Leah. You should call her.'

We always have this conversation after visiting Mum, her confusion over which twin I am leading Chris to once again suggest

8

a reunion. I haven't seen Leah for a long time. Although, of course, I keep tabs on her. It isn't stalking. Stalk – that's a strong word, bringing to mind some dirty pervert in a mac watching through the window as the pretty girl takes off a roll-neck sweater with the light playing exactly right in the background. No, I wasn't stalking. I was just checking in, making sure Leah was alright. She's always made the worst choices, after all. Has always had terrible taste in men, looking for those who will treat her like shit, worse even than Dad did to Mum. She needs me to keep an eye on her. Even if my own romantic judgement hasn't exactly turned out to be so great after all.

***

I don't know which of us was born first, but Leah always maintained she was. The hospital had attached a little band to each of our scrawny, wrinkled wrists, our skin the colour of uncooked chicken in the glare of the delivery room lights. Our bassinets were similarly labelled with Baby Girl One and Baby Girl Two. But the bands were taken off in favour of a different colour of piping on our onesies as we were prepared to be taken home. Our dad wasn't around, and Mum had forgotten which colour represented which twin in her struggle to take two tiny babies home on her own. Dad had found Mum in hysterics, not knowing who was Megan and who was Leah. He had looked from the tear-streaked mess of his wife to the identical faces of his twin daughters and made a rather worrying decision. With a needle and a broken BIC pen he tattooed a tiny dot on to Leah's ankle. Two dots on to mine. Yes, my father tattooed us. When we were just a few days old. It was the only way he could think to tell us apart. Of course, once Mum had calmed down a bit, she told him he could have just used a marker pen or something, but by then it was too late. We don't know if he was right, either; perhaps I was actually the elder and had spent the first few days of my life being called Leah. We will never be certain.

When we were about five, I remember we tried to get away with a swap. We swapped all the time, of course we did. Twins always do. Especially as it's harder for parents to discipline both of you for a crime committed by just one. But normally we were just trying to avoid the punishment for minor transgressions: a stolen biscuit, spilt milk on the floor, a little bit of felt tip bleeding through the paper on to the wooden kitchen table and leaving a small stain. This was a little more serious, involving a football and the next-door neighbour's greenhouse. We got away with it though. My father hadn't counted on the ingenuity of the rather precocious children we were. Children with a permanent marker to ensure we both had two little dots on our ankles.

When we were fifteen, we lied to a man on holiday in Turkey, convincing him we were eighteen – it was an ill-advised ruse and one he really shouldn't have believed – and he tattooed a little matching flower on to each of us, obscuring the baby marks for ever. No one could tell us apart then. That was the summer before everything started to change. Before Leah began to look at anything that was mine and want it for herself. Until we were sixteen things had been ours: our toys, our clothes, our bedroom with the bunk beds and the weekly fight for who got to take the coveted top one. When Dad left the second time – or was it the third? I don't quite remember – Mum had swapped rooms with us, taking the smaller one for herself so we could get rid of the bunk beds and have two divans side by side. I bought a curtain and used it to divide the room down the middle.

Nothing was safe from Leah's sticky fingers: my make-up pillaged, clothes bought with saved-up wages from my Saturday job stolen and ruined, books destroyed. But her greatest pride came in stealing away my friends. And, of course, the occasional boy who looked my way. I had begun to shrink away into her shadow, and she seemed to draw strength from watching me suffer.

'You definitely should talk to her sometime.' Chris has been speaking without me listening for the past ten minutes.

'What?' I reply.

'Jeez, Meggie. Have you been listening to anything I've been saying?'

We are only five minutes from home; the past forty minutes have shot past without my recollection. Stoke Park appears on our left, home to the County Fair where, last year, Hannah – my best friend, who can be a little ditzy sometimes – had got pissed and ordered a hot tub from a very nice man she had been trying to chat up. Then Burger King and the retail park on the right. Chris and I had once eaten the world's biggest whippy ice creams there as we debated spending a fortune on a pair of sofas for the living room. Amazingly, a sugar high is almost like being drunk; we'd ended up buying a sideboard and a new kitchen table at the same time.

'Sorry. I was miles away.'

'Which affront to your life were you obsessing on this time?' He sounds tired. Like he's bored of me talking about the issues with Leah even though he is the one that brought her up again. Did he always do this? Needle me to talk about something and then act like a dick when I did? I've noticed it more and more recently.

'I wasn't obsessing.' I sound like a child. I feel like a child. I wish I could have a tantrum and scream and shout and generally just make a fucking scene. How cathartic that would be. But I don't. Because. . . well, adults don't get that opportunity, do we?

'You need to let things go and move on. She is your sister, after all.'

'You wouldn't understand.' He's the very spoilt oldest child of wealthy parents who are still together. His idea of dysfunctional is laughable – the worst skeleton in the Hardcastle family closet is his Aunt Louise who didn't marry until she was nearly thirty-nine and almost missed the boat to collect her trust fund. I've never had the heart to tell him that his dearly beloved aunt is living a lie to keep up appearances, the marriage a sham to ensure her eligibility for the inheritance that demanded she be married, and the 'friend' she always talks of is undoubtedly the true great love of her life. Well, I do have the heart – I would love to see the look on his face when he realises his aunt isn't quite so prim and proper as he imagines – I just know he wouldn't believe it. And, of course, if he *did* believe it, he would make Louise's life difficult, possibly even try to have her disinherited or something awful. But she knows that I know, and we have a lovely time exchanging cards and gifts that are increasingly unsubtle. My last birthday she had signed the card from Louise and Bella instead of Louise and Tony. Not that Chris had noticed.

Anyway, in his ignorance, Chris assumes all other families are like his. He is wrong. Mine is a disaster, a car-crash lurching from one catastrophe to the next. I forgave Leah so often growing up, as time after time she would beg my forgiveness and promise that she wouldn't do anything bad again. 'Cross my heart and hope to die,' she would say. But then she did something that I couldn't forgive and will never forget. That was before Chris and I got together. He has never met my sister. He has no idea what she is capable of.

After we get home, I pour myself a huge glass of wine, right to the brim, catching the overspill in my mouth before it sloshes on to the floor. Chris looks at me and then sighs and heads to his man cave in the spare room, leaving me alone with thoughts of my sister and our mum and all the shit that has come to pass.

Instagram sends me a notification. Leah has posted some new pictures. What did people do before social media? I mean in terms of keeping tabs on each other? I have not spoken to her for five years now – ever since the book was launched – but I still know exactly what she ate for breakfast yesterday, who she has been dating, what days she goes to yoga. And now I know that last night she went 'out out' with a gaggle of girl-friends, wearing a very low-cut black dress. An electric blue bra peeking its lacy face from her décolletage.

The same electric-blue bra that I don't remember wearing as I lay on the new duvet cover in my bedroom and my husband snapped a little photo.

Does Chris think it was me?

This time I *will* fucking kill her!

Chapter Two

Michael was my first proper boyfriend. I was sixteen when we met, a few months away from doing my GCSE exams, stressed and comfort-eating chocolate in the library as I struggled to revise for Maths. Michael was in the sixth form, with a crooked smile and floppy hair. He had asked me nervously which one I was.

'Megan. Sorry.'

'I'd hoped so,' he had replied as he slid into the chair opposite me.

From then on, we had been inseparable. I was infatuated by this boy who had finally chosen me. Who had looked at me and my twin and decided I was the one he wanted. Up until then, I had only ever been considered the consolation prize by the boys Leah rejected.

Michael and I waited until after my exams were over. Mum was working that special evening, pulling an extra shift at the care home because Dad had messed her support cheque up again and we were in danger of slipping behind on the rent. Leah had agreed to go out and leave us to it. When I'd told her the previous week that I wanted to finally 'do it', it had felt like the old times again, lying side by side on one of the beds in our room, sharing secrets into the darkness as we waited for the sound of Mum's key in the lock to mark her return home. I had told Leah I was scared. Worried that I wouldn't know what I was doing and that he'd laugh at me. Or, worse, that he would tell everyone at school and *they* would laugh at me. She'd soothed my fears, told me that as it was his first time too, he'd be worried about the same things.

But on the evening of the 'deed' – as my year had come to call it, assuming our parents would have no idea what we were up to as long as we were at least a little oblique about it – I had to deal with a crisis at work. I had a job at a restaurant in town, working the swing shift to make sure that everything ran smoothly as we transitioned from serving afternoon teas to evening dinner. I had to wait for one of the other waitresses – some girl who Leah knew from theatre club – to finally turn up. She was almost an hour late and I was frantic. I had told Michael to meet me at my house at seven, but my phone battery was dead, and I couldn't tell him I'd be late. Just after eight, I let myself into the house and ran up the stairs two at a time to find my charger and plug my phone in to call him. He was already in my room. In my bed. In my sister, as he whispered my name in her ear.

She stole my first time with the boy I loved. I had wanted to kill her that night, to drag her out of the bed and scream in her face and smash her head against the floor.

Michael had thought she was me, assumed I was nervous and that was why I wasn't quite 'myself'. But as he had turned to look at me in the doorway of the room, dressed in the uniform I wore to wait tables and serve drinks, with my name badge as clear as day pinned to my blouse, I witnessed the light of his love die immediately as shame and anger and a whole host of things I've never been able to describe crossed his face in an exquisite moment of pain and betrayal. He had pulled his clothes back on and run. Leah had sat up, letting the duvet fall away to show her nakedness. She looked me in the eye – 'He wasn't worth it, Sis' – tossing her hair back and laughing to herself. The anger boiled hot and bright. Luckily for her, Mum had come home early and had dragged me off my sister. We had both been grounded, Leah for putting out and me for planning to. For two weeks we weren't allowed to leave our room as we considered our morality. My anger cooled and my desire to kill her abated, and I had begun to plan how I would get away from the girl who would stop at nothing to take everything from me.

Well, she wasn't going to take Chris. Even if I wasn't sure I wanted him anymore.

I can't stop looking at the picture on her Instagram. The picture in the slutty dress with her blue bra on show was taken on the pristine steps of her home. I recognise it from the pictures featured in an edition of *Writing Magazine* four years ago, after she had celebrated twenty weeks on the *Sunday Times* bestseller list by buying an overpriced white stucco property in fashionable Belsize Park. An area filled with attractive women in Lycra, holding personalised eco-friendly coffee cups as they strolled towards their Bikram yoga class. Or was it aerial that was trending now? No doubt Leah would be into it, whatever it was. The article, entitled 'How the other half live', showcased the excessive wealth of the handful of authors who had hit it big in the last few years. Leah's house was valued at around two million pounds. Almost seven times the pokey little maisonette I had scrimped to buy, burdened with a huge mortgage and sense that something major was about to go wrong, like the ceiling caving in, or the water tank spontaneously bursting. Leah had paid cash and her place was in perfect condition. The article was published three days before Chris suggested we move in together, pool resources to buy something nicer. I had jumped at the chance.

The book Leah wrote was an exposé about our lives growing up as twins. The book we had promised we would write together. It was going to be the way we mended things between us. I had quit my job and we hunkered down in a cottage in the middle of nowhere for the winter: writing all day; drinking all night; existing on a diet of baked beans and the occasional roast dinner served in the local pub. But the money we had saved for this adventure ran out faster than we had thought. And so I reluctantly went to find a job, leaving Leah in that little cottage to put the final touches to the manuscript and begin to woo an agent. But as I worked my arse off doing the accounts for a lumber company in Reading, living in a damp houseshare so I could keep up the rent on the cottage and send Leah care packages, she had a different plan. Instead she wrote the story we had promised not to tell, took my name off the project and sold it solo. She made millions from the book. Stories of identical twin antics and the double life my father had lived had broad appeal.

We – as in Leah, Mum and I – were my father's 'second family', the dirty little secret kept hidden from his 'real life' with his pretty wife and two rugby-obsessed sons. Mum didn't officially find out until we were ten. Although I suspect she knew far earlier. The book drove Mum over the edge though, and I'd had to find her a place in the home a week after she read it. I guess ruining the lives of those around you was something we Pattersons inherited. My father's legacy.

My mother's legacy, however, is a combination of self-denial and delusion. She spent the first part of our lives deluding herself that everything was fine and the second convinced that someone, or something, was coming for her, looking over her shoulder at every sound and shadow. She had been struggling for a while but had just about managed to keep her head above water. Until the book came out and the press camped on the little patch of scrubby grass Mum called the front garden as they waited for a glimpse of her. As the 'second wife', she had been the one whose life and morals were raked over the coals in the court of public opinion. My sweet little mum, who had met Dad when she was only twenty-three, had fallen head over heels in love with the man who promised her the world. When had she begun to suspect who he really was? When they got married? When she told him she was pregnant? When he failed to be there for the birth of his twin daughters? When he was never there for birthdays and holidays and Christmases? When he told her he didn't have any brothers, or sisters, or aunts, uncles, cousins? When he told her both his parents had been killed when he was a boy, without even a shadow of emotion crossing his face?

The gutter press, with their zoom lenses and insatiable desire to paint her as the enemy, had hounded her over her lack of intuition that something wasn't right with the man she married. They said she should have seen it, and that because she was blind she was therefore just as culpable as he was. So easy to demonise, to point a finger at someone and say it must have been their fault. To ignore that she was young and impressionable and in love, and a sudden mother of two tiny twin girls who needed nappies and wipes and onesies and who she could never dream of supporting on her own. They painted her as a hussy and burned her at the stake. I remember the headlines, the ones that called her a harlot. And a particularly vicious article, accompanied by a poor-quality photo in which a scarlet letter 'A' had been photoshopped on to the breast of the white sundress she wore.

That fucking book and those fucking journalists. And my fucking sister who took my mother's last shreds of sanity and threw them to the wolves so she could buy some fancy house. I wish I'd killed her then.

In the one conversation we'd had since she released the book, she'd told me it had nothing to do with the money. That the amount she had made was just as much a surprise to her as it was to me. It had been an accident, our meeting that day – she'd been standing in a queue for coffee at Kew Gardens, wearing skinny jeans, tan ankle boots in leather as soft as butter and a simple white T-shirt, hair tied back in a sleek ponytail. The epitome of the laid-back casualness I could never get right, even though she was my mirror. Actually, she's not my mirror. Some twins are real mirrors: one left-handed and one right, a smatter of freckles on the right cheek for one and the left for the other.

But Leah *is* me.

My perfect twin.

Although we are so different in how we think and act and choose to spend our free time. Yet despite being so different in our tastes, we have always ended up with the same haircut. In an act of rebellion after the Michael incident, I had cut mine into a bob. At the same time, across town in a different hair salon, Leah was having exactly the same thing done. She had said it was to prove to me that she wanted people to tell us apart, that she would never again cross the line like she did with Michael.

Did Chris think it was me in the blue underwear?

Surely my own husband would have known it wasn't me? Surely Leah wouldn't be able to pretend to be me to the man I had married? To the man who had promised to love me to the moon and back in front of everyone?

But if he knew it wasn't me. . .

Why would he have done it? And how? They had never met, my husband and my twin. I met Chris a few months after the book was released. He had approached me on the train as I travelled home after work.

'Are you who I think you are?' he had asked. I'd shaken my head and turned away to continue to sip a slightly warm gin and tonic in a can. A treat to myself after a hellish week.

'Are you the other one?' he had asked, ignoring my obvious signals for him to leave me alone.

Eventually, I had acquiesced and looked at him. At his chocolate brown eyes and the little creases around them as he smiled. I had been about to say something rude, but suddenly I was scraping around my head for something witty as my traitorous mouth inched towards a smile at the stranger. 'Guilty as charged,' I'd said, wincing at how ridiculous I sounded.

'Of not wanting to drag your family through the tabloids?' He slid into the seat opposite, digging one hand into the backpack on his lap to fish out two tins of a slightly more salubrious brand of gin and tonic. 'Beverage?' He waggled one at me. Chris has this habit of grouping things together with a common word: so any alcoholic drink is a 'beverage', although which drink he is referring to is denoted by time of day, location and company; conventions strictly adhered to but known only to a select few. 'Snacks' is the common name for any savoury – they must be savoury to count – item consumed in front of the TV. Any meal containing bacon is 'breakfast', irrespective of the time of day the meal is consumed, unless it's a burger with bacon because that is obviously not breakfast. We have added to his dictionary over the years. 'Telly' is anything mind-numbing that you can watch without attention, 'hols' the kind of trip where the location is less important than the presence of sun and cocktails. I thought this one was endearing the first time: walking hand in hand through the terminal at Gatwick, dreaming of our swim-up room at an all-inclusive resort in Turkey, as he sang a song about how we were going on 'hols' and all the fun we would have. Now the word kind of makes my skin crawl, if I'm honest.

Anyway, Chris had been well stocked on that train ride and, by the time we pulled into the station at Guildford, I was three double gins to the wind and a little fuzzy. I have hazy memories of dinner in a small Italian bistro at the top of the high street and a chaste kiss at the door to my flat. He had asked if he could come in and I had feigned mock horror before exclaiming that I wasn't 'that type of girl'.

For the record, I wasn't any kind of girl, not consistently anyway; I'd had my fair share of spontaneous and ill-advised trysts over the years. But something screamed at me through the gin and the wine not to let him into the flat that night.

In the morning, head pounding, I had found a handful of texts from him, begging to see me again. At the time, I had thought that inner voice was my guardian angel making sure

I followed the three-date rule. Thought that perhaps this man would be 'the one' and I shouldn't jump into bed with him so quickly or he would think less of me, or some such bullshit.

Or perhaps it *was* my guardian angel. Screaming at me to NEVER let him into the flat.

Chris graduated from train stranger to boyfriend, then fiancé, and eventually husband. He never pushed me to talk about my family or demanded he meet any of them, except Mum. He knew what a crazy fucked-up group of idiots they were and let me leave them to it.

So how had he met Leah without me? How long had they known each other? How many times had she been to my house, sat on my sofa, lain on my bed? I say 'on' rather than 'in': Chris is not an under-the-covers kind of guy; he is a full-lights-on-and-fingers-crossed-there's-a-mirror kind of lover. At first it was hot. Now I feel like a performing seal who just wants to go to bed with a hot chocolate and read a book about other people's hot romances.

Had Chris tracked her down just to mess with me? Or had Leah been the hunter? There is a part of me that always wondered what Leah would do to eventually bring my world down. I need to find out the truth.

Her Instagram is full of pictures of brunch, and the interiors of black cabs, and her peering over a pair of glasses – most likely fake as I assume her vision is as 20/20 as mine – with hashtags like *#workinggirl*, *#gottamakealiving*, *#business-bitchesthatbrunch* and a whole load of other banal shit that I absolutely detest. I struggle to find a way to break up the string of letters into sensible words. My twin, however, has made a living from this. When she says 'business bitches' she is literally meaning other women, like her, who swan around not actually doing any work at all. But still, from the sound of it she is tired and strung out and *#inneedofheadspace*. Her last message is signed off with an apology that she is taking a few days out, to *#decompress* and *#findherself*, and that she won't be posting for a while. *#homeiswheretheheartis*. That's her last status. I know exactly where she will be.

Luckily, I am able to leave the office at a reasonable time for a Monday afternoon, but the drive to the cottage still takes over two hours with the traffic. I am seething and irritable, constantly cutting up other drivers and swearing when others do the same to me, my mood getting worse and worse. I play the scene where I will confront her in my head a hundred times and each time she is more infuriating, more smug, more of a bitch, until she is a parody even of herself. I finally pull off the main road and find the small National Trust car park. I will leave my car here and walk the rest of the way, give myself a chance to calm down a little before I confront her.

I told Chris that I was staying up in London tonight, so he won't be expecting me home. We agreed when we got married that we wouldn't be 'one of those couples', couples who feel they have to check in constantly and always need to know where the other one is. We make sure to let each other know if we won't be home for dinner and check in if we get held up. Plus we make sure to have a 'date night' every other Friday. It works. Particularly as we both travel a lot for work, although I spend a fortune on a data plan to be able to FaceTime regularly. The one time Chris couldn't make it – his colleague was having major surgery and he had to cover for him at a conference – he apologised so profusely I thought he might give himself an aneurysm. We were so smug about it all, especially in our first year as Mr and Mrs Hardcastle.

But there was always a little part of me that wondered if I gave him too much opportunity to cheat on me. That I was too laissez-faire about the nights he spent alone in soulless hotels with little to do but drink too much on expenses. I have never cheated on him. Despite the number of times I've had the offer of a little 'comfort' or 'distraction', or whatever other buzzword someone could think of. The only time I had ever even considered it – considered only, I never acted on it – was with a guy who just laid it out in black and white.

'Come to my room, we'll order room service, drink the minibar and do the deed.' His accent was similar to mine.

'I'm guessing you're also thirty-two?' I had asked him. We had been in the same year at school – although in different Wiltshire towns – using the same oblique word to hide our activities from our parents. He had nodded and laughed. 'Would it help if I offered to. . .' He made the motion we had used for oral sex.

I'd turned him down, but we'd sat at the bar for a while, reminiscing about school and the toys we had as kids, the films we watched, the music that had been our shared soundtrack to adolescence. Perhaps I shouldn't have turned him down. Maybe then my life would have turned out differently. Maybe then I wouldn't be walking to the cottage to confront my sister about how she's been fucking my husband.

I say cottage, but it's barely a shell now. We found it when Dad took us camping when we were about eight. An abandoned old homestead with a little hearth and a tree growing through the centre of what would have been the living room. A well in the garden had been boarded over, the wood rotten enough to give me palpitations if I walked within two feet of it. Nightmare visions of falling over, tripping on a rock or a branch and careening head-first towards the decaying wood, hearing it splintering around me as I plummet to the depths of the dank tube of the well. Leah ignored my fears and declared it 'home'. We had set up camp in the little walled garden that Leah promised one day we would renovate, put in a door like in *The Secret Garden*. A haven for two little girls who weren't always quite sure where they belonged.

'We belong here,' my twin had told me. 'Together.'

She had bought the ten acres of woodland, within which the ruins stood, about three years ago. There was a small lake and she had built a cabin on the shore, with a huge wraparound deck that jutted out over the water.

The cabin was bathed in soft light as I approach. She looks like she's alone, judging by the legging-and-hoodie ensemble she's wearing: hair scraped back into a messy top-knot, face free from the make-up she tended to slather over herself. For once she was dressed like me. I'm crouched in the bushes as I watch her dump two share-size bags of chocolates into a bowl and slug over half a bottle of white wine into a huge glass. Definitely alone.

I hate to say that Patterson genes are skinny genes. We can eat and eat and always stay the same weight. Please don't hate us for it. We have shit hair that costs us a fortune to keep the march of grey, which has plagued us since our late teens, at bay and a monobrow that won't quit no matter how often we pluck it, if it's any consolation. It is freezing now I've stopped walking and I'm desperate to be on that deck, where she has one of those lovely patio heaters like in a nice beer garden, even though I know they are terrible for the planet. But I force myself to wait until she has settled into the large wicker sofa, has pulled the blanket over her legs and is about to reach for the glass of wine, before I walk out of the shadows.

She doesn't start, or flinch. Merely lifts the corner of the blanket so I can slide in, and hands me the glass. Two bags of chocolate in one bowl. Two measures of wine in one glass. 'I wondered how long it would take you,' she says.

I take a large gulp from the glass and pass it back to her. 'You knew I'd come?'

'I knew you'd check his phone and find the picture.'

'Does he know?'

'That I planted the picture?'

'Who you are?'

'That I'm really Leah?' She giggles, not a shy-girl-flirting giggle, but an oh-you-don't-know-the-half-of-it giggle. 'How long have you been married?'

'Three years.'

'You think he wouldn't realise? Jesus, he's your husband for fuck's sake. He'd notice if you were a whole different person.'

I nod. Of course Chris knows. This isn't a nervous teenager, blind to everything else on the cusp of his own first time. This is a grown man I have been to bed with for four years. 'Why, Leah?'

She takes a gulp of wine and then grabs a fistful of chocolate, shrugging her shoulders as she scarfs the whole lot as if she is inhaling rather than eating. She shuffles her body round to face me directly. 'There's something. . . I don't know. . . off about him, Megs.'

'So you thought you'd shag him? Just to. . . what?'

'You're my baby sis—'

'By three minutes, Leah. Probably.'

'Definitely. He came on to me, Megs. I swear. We were staying in the same hotel. He didn't tell me, at first, who he was.'

'Oh, please! You never looked at my Facebook? Saw a photo of my wedding?'

'I didn't realise. I'd had a glass or two and he's extremely attractive. I think there was a little part of me saying "Hey, I know this guy" but I never put two and two together and came up with my estranged sister's husband. He knew who I was though.'

'Of course he fucking knew! We have the same exact face, for fuck's sake.'

'It's not my fault that your husband is a cheating shit, Megs.'

'When did you realise who he was?'

At least she has the grace to look a little sheepish as she says, 'He called me Megan.'

I groan and take the glass from her, swilling down a huge amount.

'It was a cock-up. From him. The second it slipped out of his lips he stopped and just kind of froze, like a dog who's been caught trying to steal from the cat's bowl, just froze with his hands on my hips and waited for my reaction.'

'Which was, I presume, to slap him round the face and run away to immediately phone your twin and tell her that her husband was a cheating shitbag? Only, I don't remember getting that call.'

'I. . . He. . . I. . .' She clears her throat. 'He told me you were having troubles. In that department, I mean. And that it didn't really count as him cheating. He'd seen me in the bar and thought that it would be like you and him. Like it used to be before you got all weird and uptight and frigid.'

'I'm not frigid.'

''K.'

'K. I hate it when my sister says that. 'K. Like we're still little kids. 'K. Like she didn't fuck my husband.

'He's weird, Megs.' There's something in the way she says it. I know what she means.

'He pulls you in.'

Yes, yes, he does. I feel it too, even as I try to swim away from him. She continues, 'Every ounce of me wants to run away from him, but I just can't.'

I know, my life is in perpetual motion. 'He's my husband, Leah. Not another boyfriend to steal.'

'Do you love him, Megs?'

'I don't know.' My voice is quiet, muffled by the trees behind us, refracted by the moonlight on the lake.

'He loves you, Megs. You know that don't you?'

I nod. That is what I'm afraid of.

'Really loves you.'

I know. He terrifies me.

'What would he do, do you think? If he knew that you knew?'

I swallow. I don't know. I don't want to know.

'Shall I tell him?' She is reaching for her phone. 'Give him the heads-up that his wife knows about his little dalliance and that she might be a little bit pissed at him. That she might consider packing her bags and leaving him.'

Her phone screen lights up the darkness around us. My heart is in my mouth as she scrolls her contacts for his number.

'Oh, Chris. Here it is.'

The heavy wine bottle swings in a clean arc. I'm surprised when it doesn't shatter into pieces as it makes contact with her skull. Instead the deep 'thunk' reverberates in the night air. The phone drops from her hand and clatters between the wooden slats of the deck, plops into the water.

There is more blood than I would have expected. Not that I ever expected to kill my sister. However many times I had wanted to.

Chapter Three

How do you get away with murder?

It's not exactly something you can Google.

I need a plan.

Shit, shit, shit.

My phone vibrates in the pocket of my hoodie: *Where are you, Meggie?*

It's Chris.

A cold sweat breaks out down my back and I look around me, searching for a sign of him. But of course he's not here watching me.

He's just doing his usual: checking up on me, pretending to be the concerned husband. Making sure I'm not out with some other guy. I close my eyes to try to catch my breath, but inexplicably his face swims in my vision. Not Chris, that guy from the hotel.

What if I *had* just said yes that night? Gone up to his room and slept with him.

It is easy to think in what-ifs.

What if Chris hadn't slept with my sister?

What if she had been the nice, normal twin I'd so desperately willed her to be for all those years?

What if she had loved and supported me instead of trying to rip my world to shreds at every available moment?

What if she hadn't tried to tell Chris that I knew?

What if I hadn't killed her? Right there on the deck of her cabin.

What if I had any idea of what the hell I was meant to do now?

I need to buy myself time. To make some space in my mind to be able to think this through. I text Chris back with some bullshit about work. He never questions my work. Thank God for small mercies.

There is a tiny droplet of crimson blood suspended in the glass of wine in my hand. I watch it float idly around the glass without a care in the world. For a moment I imagine the sensation of being suspended in cold liquid right now. I could just step off the deck into the murky water below. Float to an icy oblivion. It's February, it would be so easy. Instead, I drink the wine. Blood of my blood.

Some people sail through life, an instinctive road map laid out in their DNA to offer them up the right answers whenever they need them. I am not one of those people. I need time and calm and space to think. Free from distractions. My dead twin is a distraction. It is hard to ignore her lying there on the wicker sofa, the blood pooling from her head, eyes glassy in the flaming light of a hurricane lantern. She looks like a Madame Tussauds waxwork. Perfect, but not perfect. Every detail of her face captured but still your brain can tell something isn't right. Something your conscious mind can't name, but your lizard brain screams danger like a beacon. Tells you to run and never look back.

I can't run. I have nowhere to go, nowhere I can hide. No one to help me to figure out this mess. I need to buy some time. Or at least find a way to slow things down.

Our dad was a fisherman. Not an out-at-sea-salty-dog kind of fisherman, but a sit-on-a-comfy-chair-with-a-few-rods-in-the-water-and-perhaps-I'll-catch-a-single-carp kind of fisherman. When Leah built the cabin, she had assumed she might occasionally rent it to men like our dear old dad. Perhaps she had even thought to entice him to spend some time here, to mend some bridges or something. She had always held out hope that one day he would apologise for what he did and decide he did want to be a father to us after all. But even the lure of a share of the money she ended up making hadn't drawn him out. Although he had made some money selling his side of the story to the tabloids, dragging Mum through even more shit, as if he hadn't hurt her enough already. Anyway, the cabin has a side store attached. A small outhouse that could be used for all manner of angling paraphernalia.

My panic swells as I search the cabin for the outhouse keys, eventually finding them in a little bowl on the mantel next to a picture of Leah smiling at the camera as if she hasn't a care in the world. I stifle a sob; there's no room for that, not yet. I stumble out of the patio doors and back on to the deck, eyes deliberately averted from her prone body, and head towards the outhouse. Please, please, please. *Let there be one.*

There is. In one corner stands a huge chest freezer, just like the one Dad had for bait. The gentle humming is reassuring, like the lull of white noise on an aircraft. There are only a couple of small bags of bait at the bottom. I think you can tell where this is going?

We've all seen enough crime series on TV to know that rigor mortis sets in fairly quickly and so I know I don't have time to waste. But even so, it's tricky to manoeuvre her. I'm grunting and sweating as I half drag and half carry her across the deck to the outhouse, praying that the noise I'm making doesn't attract some early dog walker. Lifting her into the freezer takes the last vestiges of my strength. I smooth her hair from her face and close her eyes before I lower the lid.

Out of sight, out of mind. But she will never be out of sight, will she? I see her everywhere I look, reflected in every surface, in every mirror. She will haunt me always. I don't deserve any less.

Just please, please, please don't let Chris find out what I've done. I say it over and over again in my head.

What would he do if he did find out?

The sun rises over the water, huge clouds in the distance streaking the sky with reds and pinks like the underbelly of a farmed salmon. There is a smear of blood on the deck, now viscous and sticky black in the grey light. I need to clean up. To make sure that anyone passing by would have no idea we were ever even here. Not that anyone does just pass by, but you never know if a rambler will go off-piste and think they could eat their picnic from this deck with the fantastic view over the lake.

I scrub and scrub, the scent of bleach burning my nostrils. I lock the storeroom, checking it is secure over and over. I don't look inside. Don't peek into the chest freezer. What to do with her. . . That is part of the plan I haven't worked out yet. Satisfied with my cleaning job – perhaps I should thank Chris for being such a perfectionist, at least I know how to make sure I haven't missed a bit – I walk the mile back to my car. I'm almost there, the glint of the rising sun bouncing off the roof of my sensible hatchback, when a tiny flash of inspiration ignites the early embers of a plan.

Could I possibly pull it off?

I hadn't seen her for years, not properly at least, unless. . . It wouldn't need to be for long, a few weeks, maybe a month. And it's not like I haven't studied every inch of her Instagram life, lapping up every tiny detail like a deranged fangirl.

I get in the car and drive a mile or so down the road to a different National Trust car park used frequently by dog walkers. My drive up yesterday has left splashes of mud up the sides of the Ford Focus and it blends beautifully in with the other grubby cars; no one will notice if it's here for a few days.

I trek back to the cabin through the forest. It is almost peaceful in the frigid air of the dark winter. This is my favourite time of year. When it feels as if the winter may last for ever, like time is suspended and will stretch on for eternity. Days and days of endless grey in which to cocoon yourself from the outside world and the normal sense of constant change and flux.

Plenty of time to figure this whole mess out.

My plan is to simply be both of us. At least for a while. Until I can think of something better. I'm trying not to panic, not to think of the hundred and one ways this could go wrong. My professional life hinges on my ability to be cool and calm under pressure, to step back from the cliff edge and think things through properly. I'm good at my job as a management consultant, running workshops to turn around the fortunes of failing businesses. Even though I know my career choice has a bad reputation, that the companies I work with hate me, that their staff talk about me behind my back and probably disregard everything I recommend the second I leave their offices. But still. I have a nice salary. Lots of travel. The promise of a career trajectory most can only dream of. It will be helpful. I need the time for two lives now. For a month perhaps. Yes, a month should give me enough time to figure out what the hell I do next.

Can I really do it? Be both of us? After the mess I've been making recently of being just me? But there is no option now and I've always been better under pressure. You can do anything when your liberty depends on it. Or your life.

No one can know I killed her. Especially not Chris.

Leah and I are exactly the same height. The same weight. We have the same length arms, legs and torso. So why the hell can I barely reach the pedals in her car or see out of her rear-view mirror? It's like she drives sitting on the edge of the seat, holding herself up by gripping the steering wheel. This may be why she's had two minor car accidents – both her fault, she even admitted as much on Facebook – in the past two years, along with two speeding tickets. I'll need to make sure I drive like a model citizen in her BMW coupé to ensure the police don't pull me over. Would her fingerprints be in a database somewhere for those minor transgressions? Better to be safe than sorry, I suppose. I will have to go back up to the cabin by train in a few days to collect my own car; I add that to my growing mental list of things to do. I wish I could write everything down in that borderline obsessive way I make lists about my life, a nice detailed document of how I might manage to keep hold of all the strands. But I won't risk it. What if Chris found it? I just have to trust myself that some things are too important for even *me* to forget.

I park the coupé in her garage and let myself in through the back door. The house smells like home. Like the house we grew up in. We had shared a tiny room for almost eighteen years and now I am met by the familiarity of her sweat, her vanilla candles, and something else that is so unmistakably her. It slaps me round the face, and I stagger against the wall.

I killed Leah.

Vomit streams from my mouth, spattering her polished wooden floor.

Even after everything she has done. Every part of my life that she tried to take for her own.

In the end it was me who took hers.

Suddenly, there is a blur of grey launching towards me. I scream and take a few steps back before realising it's just a cat. A very fluffy, very happy cat who is now mewling and rubbing herself against my legs as if she hasn't seen anyone in months.

Actually, it's a he. I remember now, Leah had posted hundreds of pictures of him when she first adopted him about six months ago. His name is Earl. Because he's grey. Earl Grey. Get it? Leah thought it was hilarious, she promised to get him a sister one day and call her Lady. She'd barely mentioned him for the past couple of months, though. I'd wondered if she'd got rid of him, or if something tragic had happened. But no, I guess she just got bored and moved on to the next exciting thing, replacing her affections with yoga or kombucha or whatever the new exciting trend was.

I'm more of a dog person if I'm brutally honest. Cats generally don't warm to me; but Earl is acting like I'm the only person he would want to be close to in this moment. I pick him up and he squirms on to his back so I'm holding him like a newborn human, his purr vibrating across my chest. I swear there is a self-satisfied smile on his face.

In the kitchen I find one of those cat auto-feeder things and a water fountain that appears to give him a constant river of fresh water. All the mod cons can't make up for human inter-action though. That's why I wouldn't let Chris get a puppy; we're just not home enough to take on an animal. I'm going to have to find someone to give Earl a proper home.

I walk around Leah's house, taking a measure of her life, of who she had become. Perhaps, if I can prove – irrevocably prove – that she was a terrible person, I can justify what I did. To myself at least. Or if not justify it, then find a way to live with it. Her house is full of the hallmarks of a life lived well, a life lived fully, of fun and laughter. At least that is what you would think if you were a visitor. A wonderfully cultivated veneer.

A huge bookcase dominates the living space, wall to wall and ceiling to floor, filled with thousands of books. Leah does not read. I inspect the volumes: a wall of thrillers; another of Book-er and Pulitzer winners; volumes of poetry, essays by influential writers, non-fiction about philosophy and politics and popular technology; classic novels and plays. The spines are broken on most of them; they sit in a slightly lumpy fashion, a few on their sides as if they are being read. There are gaps. A few books sit on the coffee table in front of the sofa, a pair of glasses balanced on top. I pull one of the books from the shelf, the spine broken in three careful lines. The pages are pristine. The cover spotless. No one has ever read this book despite it being made to look like someone has. This entire library is a backdrop. A carefully curated and effort-filled prop in the life of a woman who cared too much about what strangers thought and not enough about what those who loved her felt.

Her laptop sits on the desk, carefully positioned so the bookcases fall symmetrically behind her when she does a video conference. It's a fancy model with a rose-gold cover. Far prettier than the boring black model I have for work. I cross my fingers as I lift the lid and it blinks into life.

Couldn't find you. The message on the screen blinks in time with the little red light of the camera. *Move closer to the camera. Couldn't find you.* I begin to panic. I need to get into her laptop. How can the camera not think I am her? I know that facial recognition is flawed for twins. I had a client once who made a huge deal of me being a twin and insisted I had tri-factor security installed on my work laptop so it really was only me who could use it. Retina, fingerprint and facial recognition. We took it off when the commission ended though; far too much hassle and too prone to glitching.

As my panic mounts, I begin to gurn. Twisting and contorting my face in an effort for it to recognise me. I see my reflection in the laptop screen and pull myself up. No way would Leah pull faces to unlock this thing in public. Deep breath. Then I turn my body forty-five degrees, push my chin up, widen my eyes, allow a glimmer of a smile to tug at the corner of my lips. Leah's press pose. The screen unlocks immediately. I'm in.

Her desktop is perfectly ordered, another curated piece of her flawless public life. A picture of the two of us from when we were little forms the background. I thought they had used this picture on the front cover of the book, and tried to sue for the use of my image without my permission. But it turned out that the publisher had got round it by carefully knitting together two pictures of Leah so it merely looked like both of us. I'd received a letter from her lawyer that Leah had very obviously dictated and insisted they send:

As you will see, this image does not contain your specific likeness. While we apologise profusely for the similarities you bear to our client, these similarities are insufficient to warrant grounds of restricting the image of our client. Restrictions of this nature would be tantamount to not allowing Billie Piper to be photographed on the red carpet because Sandra from Wigan bears a passing resemblance to her. You will understand the farcicality of this kind of request.

Leah had chosen Billie Piper on purpose. I always said I wanted her to play us if there was ever a movie made about our lives. When we were writing the original first draft of the book, we'd spent a lot of the time watching reruns of *Doctor Who* in the evenings and drinking the cheapest wine known to man.

My first job is to order a new phone. Leah's is lying at the bottom of the lake, underneath the decking. I nearly have an issue when the lady on the help desk asks for Mum's maiden name and my answer doesn't match what she has on file.

'Ermmm,' the nice-sounding woman says. 'That's not. . .'

Of course she wouldn't have used the real one. I chastise myself. I didn't use Mum's real maiden name myself. It would be far too easy for someone to guess it. 'Sorry,' I reply, 'complicated family, you know.' The woman titters. 'It's Maris.' Maris was the name of our first and only pet, a hamster who had died from a shock-induced heart attack when one of Dad's friends had drunkenly slammed into his cage one evening. We had named him after a potato.

'Yep. Got it. I'll send you a new phone by courier. It'll be with you within the hour, Ms Patterson.'

Damn, some things in life were a lot easier if you were rich and influential. It had taken me three hours on the phone to even navigate to the right department to request a replacement when I'd lost mine at a conference last year. Then forty-eight hours before the new phone was delivered. Chris had gone ballistic when I'd rung him from the hotel's little desk phone. 'Is there someone there with you?' he had demanded when I tried to explain why I couldn't FaceTime. He had asked over and over. A conversation repeated in person when I arrived home the following afternoon.

But for Leah, life was easy. The nice lady even promised a replacement custom phone cover so it would be as good as new.

The phone now ordered, I make some coffee, swearing in exasperation at the fancy coffee machine, which seemed to require an engineering degree to operate. Eventually, I give up. I need to check in with Chris anyway – it'll be better for me to call him first than risk him FaceTiming me and seeing Leah's house in the background – and so I decide to find a coffee shop to call him from. Google Maps shows me there are four 'boutique coffee houses' in the vicinity and one chain place on the next street. I doubt Leah has ever set foot in a chain coffee shop, it doesn't exactly scream 'influencer', so it's unlikely anyone will recognise me— her, I mean. Just in case, I dig out a Sweaty Betty cap from her wardrobe.

Squashed into the corner, with a macchiato and pain au chocolat, I take out my own phone and take a few pictures. Not pretty, well-framed and overly filtered concoctions to post on Instagram, but simple and functional records of my purchases, little reminders in case I forget. My only concession is cutting off the address of the cafe when I take a photo of the receipt; even though I don't personally care which branch of Starbucks I'm in, I don't want Chris to spot it if he checks my photos. Once satisfied, I remove the cap and shake out my hair. I could be in any coffee shop, in any suburb.

Chris answers my FaceTime on the second ring.

'Nice of you to call,' he says gruffly.

'Work is slammed,' I reply, 'first break all day. We've got a new client and he wants me to look at ways to improve the productivity of his team. . .' I can see he's not actually listening; his eyes are focusing on something behind his phone screen. After all, he only wants to know what I'm *not* doing, that I'm alone and busy with work and not off having fun.

'I've got another call coming in,' he says. 'Ring me properly tomorrow night.' And then he's gone and I can breathe again.

Back at the house, I settle at Leah's desk and begin my painstaking research into her life. I start a list, written in tiny little letters in the middle of a notebook I sometimes use for work. I'll need to commit it all to memory and then destroy it, but for now the act of pen on paper is soothing. I already had a good handle on the persona, the smile she wore in public, the woman with the fake array of books behind her when she spoke to the press and the writers' magazines, convincing them she had more material to put out when I knew she was incapable of stringing more than a few sentences together. The first book had been the combined efforts of my English degree, a ghostwriter paid handsomely to keep schtum, and a hell of a lot of luck. But I need to know the private Leah, who she was when the door was closed and the camera was switched off. How much of the old Leah she had retained when no one was watching?

She has three email accounts: one for 'Leah Patterson' and used for what she called 'work', one for 'Leah P' for personal things, and the final one in the name 'Heather Taylor'. My breath catches in my throat. Heather Taylor is the name of Chris's PA. A friendly, middle-aged woman who spent over an hour at his office Christmas party last year telling me about her daughters' GCSE and A-level exam results. Leah must have borrowed the alias so I'd never suspect what was going on, even if I'd done a little snooping. Which I hadn't, but now I really wish I had. I open Heather Taylor's inbox and a little icon tells me there are over three hundred emails. They go back well over a year. My anger rises as I scroll down, backward through time, eyes scanning the first line of each one:

Happy Valentine's Day, baby!

Thinking of you today

Wishing you were here xx

Waiting to give you your Christmas treat!

There is a photo attached to this one and I click on it. I hold my breath, half expecting to see a picture of Leah in some state of undress, but instead I'm confronted with an image of a perfectly formed Finnish bundt cake, the same one his 'Mumu' used to make and which I've never been able to master, much to his obvious disappointment.

I scroll down further. The messages are banal, pedestrian even; emails about movies and music, random TikToks designed to make each other laugh. There's one of a dog looking horrified by a squirrel on the TV.

What a bastard! *I* sent him that and he forwarded it to his fucking mistress!

43

They were obviously having an affair. Not a little dalliance in a hotel, ill-advised and regretted in the morning, but a full-on, maybe-we're-in-love kind of affair. Back at the top, her most recent email shows pictures of the tickets for a concert she had intended to take him to. The concert is in two weeks. If I was still Leah by then, would I have to go? Take my cheating husband on a date and pose as his mistress? Would I have to make love to him, as her? I shudder at the thought and go to close the window. But then I spot it, a separate folder marked 'Private'. I don't want to click on it, but I can't help myself.

Inside are hundreds more emails, excruciating details of his more niche fetishes, the ones he has never divulged to me, his *wife*. Do I know this version of my husband at all? I blush at the thought of doing the things he wanted Leah to do to him.

Jesus – I swallow audibly at the final one on his list he had entitled 'my dirty little secrets'. I want to vomit. She had replied with a single line: *Might need a few Mai Tais for that ;-)*

Mai Tais? I can almost taste the burn of rum at the back of my throat and the cloying sweetness of the grenadine on my tongue. It was the second time we'd visited that hotel and I'd been so excited to go back after our anniversary trip. It had been a disaster. I can picture the earnest-looking waiter assuring me this was what I'd drunk last time as he placed the orangey-red cocktail in front of me with a flourish. Chris at my elbow telling me I'd loved the Mai Tais before and not to make a scene.

Had Leah and Chris been laughing at me behind my back? Giggling together about how I couldn't remember my previous visit to that place, taking the mickey as I worried I was losing my mind?

Or had she been part of it? Setting me up somehow?

Chapter Four

Leah has some kind of password manager thing set up on her laptop. It allows me to access every password just by using face ID. She is a fool – even I don't use this kind of thing, it's a security disaster – but I am thankful. Her bank accounts are a revelation. My sister is rich. Not just I-sold-an-exposé-and-bought-a-nice-house-and-can-live-fairly-comfortably rich. But proper-serious-piles-of-money rich. I already knew she'd paid cash for the house, and assumed similar for the cabin, but there are also two flats in Soho she rents for an eye-watering sum. I find a portfolio of shares carefully diversified to minimise risk exposure, plus a more volatile series of investments with small entrepreneur hubs that have enjoyed astronomical growth for the past two years. There are bonds and receipts for precious metals futures – there is a lot of gold with her name on it. And cash. Cash in savings accounts. Cash in current accounts. A hoard of foreign currencies sitting in accounts all over the place. I would estimate that her liquid assets are worth somewhere around five million pounds. Factor in her property and you could double that to get to her net worth.

She has been fiscally savvy and very lucky. She took the exposé money and used it to seed a series of other investments, really hammering that mantra of 'it takes money to make money'. Such a contrast to my own finances and the huge mortgage on the home Chris and I bought that makes me sweat just thinking about it. A millstone around the neck of our marriage. Would I jump if it weren't there to drag me down? I have ten thousand pounds in premium bonds, the sole trophy of my ten-year career and a rather damning indictment given that up until a few years ago I was working as a chartered accountant. Every year I would earn more, and every year I would fail to add more than a few hundred pounds to my meagre savings. Funny how your expenditure always grows to match your income and how you never feel any richer. The extra income spent on more expensive clothes needed to ensure you look the part and that in turn cost more to maintain; that need dry-cleaning or a special little comb for the bobbles. Or more money spent on food that is quicker and easier to cook, but that still must be balanced because you can't afford not to look the part, remember. And then the cost of haircuts, nail appointments. All of it, all the time. Chris is even worse; money runs through his fingers like water; as soon as he gets a bonus he's off buying stupid shit we don't need.

Although I'm kidding myself if I think the only reason I've stayed with Chris is because of money.

In addition to her investments working overtime, Leah herself is busy. The book still provides a trickle, although I don't know who is buying a five-year-old exposé. Surely it's yesterday's news by now. But she also earns a fortune from a company called Angels Inc. I look them up online. They describe themselves as the 'revolution in influencer management'. Based out of Los Angeles, they employ thousands of people worldwide to promote products, locations and experiences. You name it, and if someone can smile while pointing to it or holding it, they can make money.

Last month, they paid Leah tens of thousands of pounds. An itemised list with the Angels Inc. logo at the top reveals what she did for the money: four dinners in fancy restaurants, complete with tweeted commentary and a spread on Instagram; drinks in seven bars; dinner with the son of a certain royal family who has been rumoured to be involved with some shady dealings. That's interesting. I remember reading an article that alleged the family were up to their eyeballs in international bond debt and were apparently trying to bolster their legitimacy by pimping out their middle child and his best friend to well-loved socialites on the London circuit. It was a move that asked 'How could you possibly be anti the west if you party with them?' All in all Leah had worked – and I use the term extremely loosely – for about thirty hours in total. Perhaps pretending to be her was going to be easier than I had thought. Especially as she seemed to pay a small fortune to someone called Zach to manage her social media accounts, creating content on her behalf and responding to comments.

Unfortunately, the next morning my confidence is shattered by a WhatsApp from an 'Emma': *Just leaving for the cabin. Be there shortly.*

Who the fuck is Emma? And why is she visiting Leah's cabin? My fingers fumble on the touchpad as I rush to type: *No! Had to come back early. Totally forgot to tell you!*

She replies: *Thank God! I wasn't relishing the drive on those atrocious roads. Meet me at the usual place. Midday.*

It takes a full five minutes for my heart rate to slow back down to something approaching normal. I have two hours to figure out who this 'Emma' is, where's 'the usual place', and how I'm going to convince her that I'm really Leah.

The picture on her WhatsApp profile shows a woman about my age, blond and pretty in that slightly horsey way rich girls often are. I remember a series of emails in Leah's work inbox from a woman with a double-barrelled surname.

Yes. Emma Baptiste-Harbington. Leah's manager. The pair have been tagged repeatedly on Instagram at a stupidly over-priced-looking restaurant not far from the house. I pray this is the 'usual place'. It seems that Leah and Emma often sport a 'posh ladies who lunch' uniform of a retro tweed jacket, leather elbow patches perfectly matching to knee-high boots worn over skinny jeans.

Thank God for social media! At least now I know where to go and what to wear.

I want to find out more, to read through all their email ex-changes and messages, but I'm out of time. My palms are slick as I arrive at the restaurant and I wipe them frantically on my jeans before I push open the door, eyes scanning for Emma. She's not there, but my gaze lands on the expectant face of a dark-haired woman sitting alone. Her smile lights up her features and my heart drops to my stomach.

Fuck! Wrong Emma!

Time slows as I watch the woman's smile turn to confusion while I remain rooted to the spot. My brain is screaming at me to run but I can't move.

A blast of cold air from behind rouses me and I spin on my toes, directly into the lavender stench of a tall woman. The smell is so strong I positively recoil as she envelops me in the cloud of it, screeching 'dah-ling' in my ear.

'Now then, dah-ling, let us sit and talk.' Emma Baptiste-Harbington ushers me past the dark-haired woman, whose attention is now on her phone as she scrolls through Instagram, probably one of Leah's followers who will tell her friends about what an aloof bitch I was. Emma summons a waiter with a flick of her wrist. 'So, first things, first,' she says as she flips over the case of her tablet and jabs at the screen a few times. 'That dinner with Jabir was fabulous. Huge profile boost, good coverage. Just the right kind of thing for now. I'll arrange another evening with them. And well done for turning down his offer. That will definitely help your social capital.'

She sits back a little as a waiter appears with a plate of salad for each of us. 'I took the liberty of ordering when I booked the table,' she says, inspecting her knife for water-marks before waving it to the waiter for him to replace. 'Too much to do and never enough time. You know how it is, dah-ling.' I wonder just how hard this woman's job really is, see-ing as it appears to involve lunch and setting up dinner dates. 'Now. The next few weeks. . .' Her voice trails off and she stares expectantly at me.

Am I meant to say something? She breathes out heavily, a little huffing noise like a parent at the end of their tether. I sit up straighter, pulling my shoulders back, and slide my hands under my thighs so she can't see the tremble. She's looking at me, staring at my face. Can she see the lie?

'Do we have a problem?' she asks. *Do we?* 'Leah?' As she says the name, I feel myself relax. Whatever she thinks the 'problem' is, it isn't that I'm not Leah.

'Of course not,' I reply. 'Sorry, I didn't sleep very well.' I'm contrite and apologetic.

'Promise?'

'Promise.'

'OK then,' Emma says and with that, the matter is closed and she moves on. 'So, the next few weeks are going to be a bit of fun for you. Two new bar launches and this new concept place. They're doing pool, old-school, the hipsters want to rejuvenate it. . .'

On and on she goes as I pick at the salad in front of me. I make the right kind of noises, or at least I think I do, the odd 'ooh sounds fun,' and 'lovely idea,' and 'yes of course.' It's enough to keep her dominating the conversation and I start to feel some of the tension ebb away, my appetite returning as I nibble on a delicious and still-warm bread roll.

I realise she has stopped talking and is looking at me, her head cocked to one side. I reach for another bread roll from the basket in the middle of the table, wanting to fiddle with something and avoid the hardening of her stare.

'Look, Leah. . .' She trails off, but then the equine smile snaps back into place. 'How about we take things easy the next few weeks? Get Zach to use some of the content we've been saving for a rainy day?' I nod at her. That could be a lifesaver. 'Great! I'll need a few soundbites about this Wuhan virus thing, you know a "thoughts and prayers" job. But otherwise, take some time. No one will even realise.' Then suddenly she looks at her watch; it's one p.m. She has given me exactly an hour of her time. She begins to pack up her things. 'Important things to be doing, dah-ling!' she trills as she motions to the waiter for the bill. 'Perhaps next time you'll be feeling a little more yourself, hmm?' Then she turns and walks out of the restaurant, leaving me somehow both relieved and uncomfortable. I assume Leah is normally more talkative, more forceful. They probably usually 'bounce ideas off each other'.

I play the scene over and over, wondering what it is that Emma Baptiste-Harbington thinks is wrong with Leah, as I walk back to the house, my hands buried into the folds of Leah's heavy navy blue coat. It's gorgeous and lined with grey silk. It looks incredible, but the silk is so cold it feels damp against my skin, and I am freezing.

Later that afternoon, after I have warmed myself up with tea and a custard slice, procured from a bakery I passed coming back, I send a little note to Emma to apologise for being quiet. Even if I was normally like that, it couldn't hurt to be polite. Plus, I really need a heads-up on what she thinks is wrong.

Emma messages me back: *I'm not surprised you feel under the weather with how much wheat you ate.*

No pleasantries. No top and tail of nicety. Ten seconds later another message: *You should be more careful, Leah. Be better.*

Be better! Who the hell does that little jumped-up bitch think she is? Be better! And who gives a shit about my wheat consumption anyway?

But even as I think it, my eyes are drawn to the fancy magnetic board by Leah's desk, covered in rectangles of creamy card inviting her to all sorts of events. One of them has a gold border and bevelled edges. It cordially requests the pleasure of Leah's company at the 25th Annual Fundraising Dinner in Aid of the Coeliac Foundation. Handwritten at the bottom in beautiful cursive: *Perhaps you could say a few words about your own experiences?* Fuck! How did I miss that? Here's the thing: Leah was not coeliac. She was, however, an attention-seeker and it looked like she had jumped on the gluten-free bandwagon for exposure. Her fraud had almost ousted me.

Fucking Emma, calling me out. She was right, though. I did need to 'be better'. More meticulous, more careful, more like I am in my normal life. And I need to think of a proper plan.

I also need to call Chris and check in properly. I got away with the coffee shop call yesterday, but tonight I need to Face-Time him from my hotel at nine p.m. His way of making sure I am not with anyone I shouldn't be.

Luckily, my twin had expensive taste and an appetite for the finer things. I pile up pillows around the headboard of the spare room bed. Dig out a huge tray from the cupboard under the stairs and lay it up with a plain white plate, silverware, an apparently ironed napkin from the kitchen drawer. Leah must have a cleaner – no one in their right mind irons napkins themselves – and I must figure out when she's next going to turn up at the house. I am careful about how I stage the scene: a little smear of ketchup on the plate and a bread roll shredded into pieces. A half-drunk glass of wine to complete the look. I change into the fluffy white robe hanging in the guest wardrobe. Luckily, it's plain, not embroidered with a hotel's crest. Obviously not stolen then – I guess Leah had more class than that.

Balancing my laptop on a cushion, I make sure it really does look like I'm in a hotel, stuffed full of room-service burger, before dialling my husband. He is in our living room, his computer on the arm of the sofa. A sudden pang of homesickness strikes me. Not for him. For that sofa and the place where I actually feel like me.

'Hey, Meggie.' I can see that he isn't looking at his laptop; he's watching TV over the top. So much for spending an hour setting the scene. 'How's it going?'

'Good.'

'Cool.' His voice is distant. He's not listening to me either. 'So, I'm going to be away from Friday, probably till next Wednesday. We good?'

'Sure. You remember that client I mentioned yesterday?' I pause, I know he wasn't listening before. 'Anyway, I need to put in a huge amount of work to prep a series of workshops for him. It might give me an edge at promotion time if I can pull it off, but I need to work all weekend.'

'You staying in town?'

'Yes.' I hold my breath, fingers crossed behind my back that he'll buy it and accept the excuse for my absence this weekend.

'But you'll be home next Friday?' There's an edge there, a challenge in his tone.

'I'll be home.'

'Steak?' He says it like a question. We both know it's a demand.

'Yep.' The same as every second Friday. I wouldn't dare deviate from his routine.

'See you next Friday then. Love you,' he says.

'Love——' But he's already hung up before I can finish my lie.

Chris and I have been married for just over three years. We spend between four and five nights apart each week: one or both of us travelling for business, to attend a conference, to work at a client's other office. I do a fair bit of work with the Dubai branch of my consultancy and so do a lot of my work on a Sunday as it's their first working day of the week. So, Chris and I have a ritual where we always ensure we are at home in Guildford every other Friday evening. That is 'date night', a term I hate as it sounds so damn forced. Like, this is the night that we will 'have fun', 'be a couple' or, my most hated, 'reconnect in a physical way'. Scheduled sex is never satisfying sex. Not that we have scheduled any for a while now. Guess he was getting enough from Leah.

However, this level of freedom will come in very handy as I try to juggle Leah's life with my own. Just so long as I make it back next Friday.

You're probably wondering why I was so upset about the affair given the state of my marriage. I don't care that they were fucking. I care that they both gave so little of a shit they carried it on for so long. And I care that I'm far too afraid of what he would do if I tried to leave him. Despite everything he's done, I will still have to smile at him next Friday, pretend that everything is OK. It's exhausting and frustrating and sometimes I hate who he has turned me into. Especially now he has turned me into a murderer.

Seeing as I'm already in the bathrobe, I decide to have a bath. Leah has a tub that is big enough for two fully grown adults and it comes complete with jets and a range of settings. I am just about to get in when Leah's phone emits a beep: *Sea Lanes Hotel. A week on Monday. 5 p.m. I have a treat for you. Xx*

The message is from Chris.

Sea Lanes is a gorgeous little hotel in Dorset. Chris took me there for our anniversary last year and again about a month ago. I think he has taken her there before. Taken her there so she can sip Mai Tais in the bar.

I sink below the bubbles and the world around me disappears as I try to think of how to prevent Chris getting suspicious about it not being Leah he's interacting with. But as he begins to send me a fairly constant stream of increasingly explicit (and terribly written) texts, it becomes very clear that I don't have the stomach to pretend to be my husband's mistress. I always thought I was quite open-minded, quite experimental. I am in fact a naïve child made nauseous by the predilections of the man who shares my bed. I won't go into details but some of it is filthy and degrading. Some of it I don't even really understand and I'm not going to google those terms, no matter how intrigued I am.

If I don't show up at the hotel, he will know something is wrong. If I do show up, he will know it is really me by the disgust on my face I won't be able to conceal. I need to palm him off, somehow, without making him angry or suspicious.

His final message of the night: *Wear the blue underwear. The photo freaked her out. We could do so much more xx*

So there it is. The final confirmation. Chris *has* been fucking with me, I guess I should be angry, but actually I'm just relieved. I feel a bubble of laughter threatening to escape and sink back under the water so it erupts into a geyser. I'm just a toy to him. Was just a joke to her.

I think back to the emails I found, 'Heather Taylor' and Chris and their cosy exchanges about cake. It didn't start there, I realise; the 'Heather' emails only began *after* the affair started. So where did it all begin?

I drag myself out of the warmth of the bath and pad to the kitchen, rivulets of water running down my back. I need answers. But first, I need wine.

I had assumed all the text messages sent between Chris and Leah would have been lost when her phone clattered through the deck into the cold water of the lake. But I hadn't realised that she took a full backup of her phone memory. Extended storage on her laptop kept everything. Guess how long my husband had been fucking my twin? Almost two years! Two goddamn years. I hadn't even dreamed he was cheating on me. Bastard.

She'd told me she didn't know who he was before I introduced them. That was a crock of shit. They had been in communication since early in my and Chris's relationship, back before we got married. He had reached out to her, asking her to please consider coming to the wedding. She had refused but they had started to exchange messages. A few awkward back-and-forths at first, then one day she had 'accidentally' sent him something explicit. Followed immediately with an: *Oops, that wasn't meant for you* 😊. Jesus, was he stupid?! This was the oldest trick in the book, the accidental text to test the waters. What had he replied? *Shame. . .* A little word with enough weight to encourage her. Things had escalated pretty quickly. I'd been on a business trip when they had arranged to meet. *Be careful of Megan,* she had written, *she tends to see things that aren't really there.*

Don't I know it, my traitorous husband had replied.

I sit and stare at the pages of messages charting their affair, all the times they had met up when he'd told me he was away with work. All the times he had made excuses not to come to an event with me, or to visit my mum. There was the date of Hannah's birthday party when I'd had to go alone. The bastard had even been fucking my sister the weekend I had the flu and could barely crawl to the kitchen to heat up some soup. He had been so apologetic, so contrite when he found out how ill I'd been. God-damn it, he had almost cried with his guilt that he was working while I needed him.

I am so angry I don't know what to do with myself. I walk in tight circles around the living room, picking up trinkets of Leah's life and putting them down again. I want to break things, hurl that stupid glass bowl across the room to smash into a thousand pieces, scream at the top of my lungs, tear the curtains from their pole, destroy and rail and break.

Instead, I sit back down at the computer and type an email to Chris. Telling him all the ways I want to hurt him, all the things I want to call him, insult after insult pouring from my finger-tips on to the screen in front of me. I sign it off from Leah. Just as I'm about to hit send and worry about the consequences later, I notice there are four unread emails in her inbox.

As I open them one by one, it becomes clear that it wasn't only Chris who Leah was sleeping with. She was liaising with at least three other men, who all wrote desperately cloying messages of their declarations. There was also an email notifi-cation of a message via a dating app called eLove. From some guy called Tom. I open the app and navigate to his profile.

He looks like a model. Actually, scratch that, he looks like an actor. His face is not symmetrical enough to model, but so enigmatically handsome I can't drag my eyes away. Green eyes framed by long lashes, straight nose, defined cheekbones. A smattering of subtle freckles across his cheeks. Auburn hair, slightly curly, like a cockapoo. I want to run my fingers through it. His page says he is six foot two, although enough of my friends have warned me about height inflation to pique my scepticism. There are the usual photos used on these kinds of dating sites: walking in a wood with a nice filter to soften the edges a little, one with an older lady who was obviously his mum, another holding a small furry animal – in this case a roan-coloured collie puppy. Finally, there was one that looked more like a headshot, taken against a backdrop of high-rise office buildings, a typical corporate picture of the kind used for client-facing websites. In my own, with the Shard in the background, I wore an expensive black shift dress and make-up perfectly applied by a lady brought in to ensure everyone looked the part. The photos of Tom should be off-putting, they should make my skin crawl with the sameness, the cliché of them. But I am drawn to him, imagination firing over being the one behind the camera lens he is staring down.

Tom is forty-two, divorced, a senior investment manager at a large firm in the City – they have an office not far from mine. No kids, but a 'devoted uncle to three niblings', according to his profile. Good sense of humour. Such a redundant phrase to use though; it wasn't like you were going to put 'miserable bastard', was it?

Intrigued, I pull up Leah's profile. Unsurprisingly, she had used a photo of her in front of that bookcase, a few choice volumes turned to face out into the room, including her own million-copy-selling one. I scroll through the other pictures. Was there some kind of rulebook, a specific list mandated by these sites? One of Leah hiking; in the kind of shorts favoured by Lara Croft, with thick socks peeking out from chunky boots, she looked adventurous but sexy. Another of Leah holding a pint glass in a busy pub, apparently fascinated by some rugby match being shown. Yet another of her in a bikini, taken from behind as she looked out to sea, waves splashing around her ankles. Each picture chosen to show that she was one of 'those girls', the ones who were fun and outgoing and larger than life. Who were sexy and a little bit slutty, just enough that they'd let you do things but not anyone else.

Tom and Leah had been messaging back and forth for a while. The new message from him is short and polite, simply confirming the location and time of a dinner date on Saturday evening. He has not appended a picture of his penis and I am glad. The last two men Leah had received messages from on this site apparently had, the opening gambit of a man who has zero interest in dinner.

I should cancel. Send him an appropriately off-putting response. But there is something in his eyes. And I need to make sure things are as normal as possible. That no suspicions are raised.

Fuck you Chris, I think as I tap out a reply to Tom: *Great, see you there.*

He replies instantly: *Can't wait to finally meet you x*

Shit. Did I really just agree to go on a date?

Chapter Five

What do you wear to meet a man who thinks you are your sister? In the end I chose a simple black dress – rather on the demure side for Leah, with a skirt that falls in gentle folds to mid-calf and not too much cleavage on show – teamed with a pair of high black heels with an incredible peacock lining. I'd looked at the same pair with envy during a recent lunchtime shopping trip, before reluctantly accepting that three hundred and fifty pounds was too much for shoes. I don't think Leah has ever even worn them, nor half of the others in the huge walk-in closet adjoining the main bedroom.

I hesitate before I leave the sanctuary of Leah's house, running through my list of meticulous checks to ensure the back door is locked, the windows closed, hairdryer unplugged. A few months ago, I had left a candle burning in the bedroom and nearly set our house on fire. Chris had been livid. With the memory of his admonishment – which had quickly turned to sympathy when he saw the horror on my face – burning in my mind, I walk through the house once more checking for candles that may have spontaneously lit themselves. I could have sworn I'd blown out that one before, but the flash of terror in Chris's eyes had convinced me he wasn't acting and that time the fault really had been mine. Unless he was better at playing a role than I thought.

Finally ready to go, I think that it's not too late to back out, feign illness or something. But then the taxi driver beeps his horn twice in quick succession and I'm forced to run out before the neighbours start getting nosey.

All first dates are nerve-shredding, but tonight my fear is almost at fever point as a million 'what-ifs' roil through my brain. What if he realises I'm not Leah? What if someone else sees me? What if I say the wrong thing? What if, what if, what if! I realise I'm playing with my rings in the way my last boss used to reprimand me for, telling me it looked jittery—

What the actual fuck is wrong with me? I need to get a grip. This won't work if I swan around with a fucking band of platinum and the huge-ass diamond that Chris insisted on buying for me for our third wedding anniversary after he'd had a particularly large bonus. I'd loved the original engagement ring, with its subtle link of much smaller stones along the front. But Chris had insisted that people needed to see that we were doing well. 'I can't have my wife wearing little dinky things, can I? People will think I don't love you enough to show it.' It had made me uneasy though. Like he wanted a bigger statement of his ownership, something more noticeable, more obvious. *She is mine*, this damn thing screamed. Plus I'd been livid he hadn't used that bonus to pay down some of our mortgage. I slip both my engagement and wedding rings off and put them in my purse, zipping the inside pocket carefully. It would be just my luck right now to lose them.

Rings worn every day create a groove in the skin. Actually, not just the skin, it's the very flesh that wears away over time. I rub my finger vigorously. When I look up the taxi driver is grinning at me in the rear-view mirror. 'Big date, love?' How many times has he watched a man or woman trying to rub away the brand of their marriage in the back of his cab? Enough that he probably won't remember me. But I have to be more careful. I give him a tight smile in return that should shut down more questions without seeming rude. Anything to make me forgettable.

The restaurant is tucked away down a residential side road in Primrose Hill. It looks like nothing from the outside; you would scurry past to get to a more salubrious area. But it is renowned as one of the best places north of the river. I have never been here before, although I worked with a lady once who could not stop talking about it. Luckily, as part of my recommendations for their company restructure, her role was moved to Edinburgh and she followed. Last time I heard she was on the verge of making CEO and had bagged herself a very attractive toy boy, so I know she won't appear at the next table.

I have researched this restaurant obsessively, trawling through every photo on Leah's Instagram and laptop; reviewed the entirety of her Cloud storage, looked at every place she had checked into on social media over the past year or so. So many places and mostly only once or twice, a photo opportunity to be seen in the hottest place in town. Her social life looks exhausting and I am starting to question how long I'll be able to pull off the pretence, even with Emma's insistence that I 'take things easy'. Just long enough, I keep saying to myself. Just long enough to come up with a proper plan. A month. No more.

Leah had only been here once, and that had been months ago. But I have no way of knowing if someone will recognise her, if an acquaintance I don't know will run up and try to hug me. At the door, I am struck by a sudden rush of dread, a vision of my future in which I am ousted the very first time I set foot more than a mile away from her house. What would really happen to me? Would I be branded a murderer, called a sororicidal maniac, and spend the rest of my life rotting in prison? Or would Chris get to me first? I shake the images away and try to take a deep gulp of air. I push open the door. I can do this. I don't have a choice.

A man is sitting on a stool at the huge bar. It dominates one corner, the gleaming marble and chrome fittings bouncing light from a hundred small orbs hanging from the ceiling. The restaurant is a fantastical mix of modern furniture against a backdrop of exposed brick and the original low ceilings dating to when the building was a warehouse sitting on the water. It smells faintly of the spices that would have once been piled in this space, saffron and cinnamon and turmeric, blended with the scent of steak and garlic and rosemary. It is heady and intoxicating and I pause for a moment to take it all in.

His hair is the colour of burnished copper, deep and lustrous in the light. He is wearing a plain white shirt – the cotton is a thick, creamy type like expensive writing paper – open at the collar to show a hint of chest but not enough for me to tell if he waxes or not; the sleeves are rolled up his forearms in studied nonchalance. The shirt is tucked into dark blue jeans, slimfitting enough to show his frame but not so slim you worry about his testicles. I feel the flush on my face at the thought.

He smiles as he sees me, unwinding from the stool to stand with the air of someone confident in their own skin. Selfassured, comfortable, but not arrogant. I know instinctively he will have been the benefactor of a fiendishly expensive education and is most likely the eldest child in a very trad-itional family whose ancestors probably had a title they are still permitted to use, but do so only rarely. It would be vulgar to use it more often.

His smile broadens as I approach. 'Leah?' His voice hopeful.

I nod, not quite trusting myself to speak. Up close he is even better-looking than in his photos; the scent of fresh linen and a deep woody cologne emanates from him, making me almost giddy.

As he ushers me towards a table by the smaller window on the far side of the restaurant, a place where I could survey the room but no one would eavesdrop, I can feel the warmth of his hand guiding me behind my back without actually making contact. The perfect gentleman.

'Nervous?' he asks after we've sat down. His eyes are kind and the skin around them crinkles as he grins at me. 'I promise I won't bite,' he says, leaning towards me.

He's so earnest, so obviously trying to put me at ease, that I can't help but grin back. 'A little,' I reply.

'How about we have a drink and forget it's a first date?'

My heart drops a little and I realise I *want* this to be a date. He must see the disappointment on my face because he adds, 'Not that I don't want it to be a date. Just not an awkward first one.'

A waiter in a pristine uniform interrupts us with a tray of brilliant-red little cocktails and a small plate of delicate pas-try morsels. 'Negroni aperitivo and *stuzzichini*,' he says with a flourish in a strong Italian accent.

'*Perfetto, grazie*,' Tom replies and the waiter melts away. He picks up one of the glasses and raises it to me. 'A toast,' he says as I copy him. 'To a. . . what shall we call it? Third? Yes, third date.' He clinks his cocktail against mine, his eyes twinkling.

'To our third date,' I reply and take a sip, the bitterness of the Campari delicious on my tongue.

And just like that, the tension is broken and we start chatting as if we have known each other a while. I was right about the education: Harrow, he tells me sheepishly. And the title – minor baronet, although he has never used it himself. He is actually the baby of the family though. The adored little brother to three very bossy sisters who still treat him like he is a doll for them to dress up and play with.

'Honestly. We went to a wedding last year, huge thing of a family friend in their castle. They made me wear the full Highland get-up and paraded me round the reception party like they did when I was five years old in a sailor's outfit.' His eyes are bright as he talks about them, throwing his head back to laugh.

Conversation flows easily between us and I'm alarmed at how relaxed he makes me feel. Gone is the permanently jumpy Megan, with her lists and her obsessive photographing of every detail, always waiting to see how Chris will react to everything she says. In her place is someone confident, holding her own as conversation turns to politics and literature. I am amusing, interesting, almost beguiling.

I am also tipsy. I think I've had one too many glasses of wine – a deliciously extravagant Barolo to complement the toma-hawk steak we ate with rustic chips, roasted tomatoes, and grilled vegetables. We round off the meal with a glass of Fernet Branca. He asks if I would like to have another drink in a bar down the road. I nod, but my mind is desperately searching through the list of places around here that Leah had been to recently. Wine laps at the side of my brain.

The bar is small, all leather sofas and dark wood. Intimate and cosy, with only a few other patrons dotted around. We settle into an alcove and without asking me he orders two measures of Lagavulin. I am about to say that I don't drink whisky, until I remember Leah's goddam profile. Of course, Leah would *love* whisky. Every one of 'those girls' likes whisky. In the glow of the small lamp on the table, and with the heat of Tom pressed against me, the fire of it at the back of my throat is almost sensuous. Maybe I do like whisky after all, especially after Tom explains that a splash of water helps release the flavour. We have another. His hand brushes my shoulder. We have one more and his hand grazes my thigh. When he leans in to kiss me, his breath is warm and sweet. I close my eyes and kiss him back.

We share a taxi. Nice girls don't take men home the first night they meet, even if they have been pretending it's a third date. I keep telling myself that. But is Leah a nice girl? I doubt she cares what people think, or about propriety and properness. She never did in the past anyway. The air is heavy with anticipation, his woody cologne still strong, mingling with the heat coming from his hand on my leg. We both know where the evening could end, we buzz with the possibility of it all.

The taxi pulls up outside Leah's house.

But I am not Leah. Our doorstep goodnight kiss is almost chaste before I close the front door and sink to the floor with my back to the wall. I can see his shadow moving away and I fight with every ounce not to call him back.

I have never ever cheated on Chris. I am not the kind of girl to look at another man and think what if? To wonder how things might be with this one, instead of the man I promised to love for ever in front of his family and our friends.

I shouldn't have kissed Tom, I know that. Hell, I shouldn't have even gone on that date. I should have just cancelled and hoped that he would think no more about it and leave me alone. Then I should have shut down the dating sites that Leah used and made sure that I couldn't be in this position again. It's not like anyone would have cared if Leah wasn't seen on a date for a while. And then it hits me. What if Chris finds out about Tom? What if some fan I didn't even notice tagged Leah in a photo or something? What if he realises it's not her and figures out it was me kissing another man?

He won't, the rational headmistress voice in my head tells me. He will never know it was me.

The first year of our marriage was blissful. Until Kivi, and since then, Chris has been obsessing over my fidelity. Not that he lets his jealousy get in the way of my job and my requirement to travel; he is too dependent on my salary to pay the mortgage so he can spend his money on luxury tat. It started at some family thing with his mum's Finnish side. Vappu is a big national holiday in Finland, so on the first day of May we all gathered at a campsite in the New Forest to celebrate the end of the cold, dark winter and usher in the fabulous light of the summer. Kivi is his cousin, or second cousin, or some kind of cousin once removed – Leah and I had no other family growing up, Mum's an only child and Dad obviously hid our existence from his lot, and so I have never really got to grips with extended families and the like – anyway, Kivi is a relative of some type. Tall, blond, strong built, ski-jump nose, kind eyes. He was a constant focus of attention at the party. Chris hates that.

When other men are more attractive to women than he is. He cannot stand to be relegated to second – or heaven forbid third – place in the pecking order. And he was not best pleased when Kivi seemed to take a bit of a shine to me, all very innocently of course.

The campsite had been decorated in blues and whites like the Finnish flag, with a huge bonfire roaring in the centre of the clearing. To one side, a barbecue cooked venison sausages and burgers, sizzling under the expert eye of Kivi, who had been designated grill-master. Much to Chris's disgust.

'Rudolph or Prancer?' Kivi asked when I went to get myself a burger, bursting into laughter that quickly trailed off when he saw the look of horror on my face.

'*Voi paska!* I'm so sorry,' he said. 'They're just venison, I promise. You can't get reindeer that easily here.'

'You. . . you eat reindeer?'

'At home in Finland, yes of course. But these,' he motioned at the grill, 'I promise are just venison. No Rudolph at all.'

Later that evening he had come to find me to apologise again.

'It's OK,' I told him.

'I don't want you to think I'm a barbarian,' he replied, his eyes searching mine for forgiveness.

'Honestly, it's OK.'

We'd laughed and had a drink, and everything had been love- ly. Until I'd felt Chris's fingers around my wrist, and he wasn't being his usual gentle self.

'You filthy, disgusting slag,' he'd hissed into my ear, his grip tightening. 'Parading yourself around in front of my family. You're a fucking disgrace.' Then he had pulled me away from the crowd into the darkness of the woodland behind. Out of sight, he had slammed me against a tree trunk, my head bouncing off the wood, shock vibrating down my neck. 'What do you have to say for yourself?'

'I wasn't doing anything,' I told him. I was incredulous. How dare he talk to me like that! But my tone was a mistake.

He slapped me hard across the face. 'I saw you. You tart. Preening and giggling with that prick. Did you think I wouldn't notice?'

'I was just being friendly.'

'Friendly? Friendly? You were practically dry-humping him in front of my parents.'

'It wasn't like that.' He had started to really frighten me, his eyes on fire and a twist to his mouth like a furious sneer.

'No? Do you think I'm blind, hmm? Blind and stupid and happy to be a cuck?'

'Chris, I—'

'Don't you dare try and tell me that I'm wrong and you're just some innocent little thing. You're a whore, Megan. A nasty whore who can't keep her legs shut.' He was pressed up against me now, breath warm and rancid in my ear. How much had he drunk? He'd been knocking back the vodka, seeming on edge, the whole day. 'Just a slut who can't get enough.'

I was shaking by now, terrified by the change in him; normally he was so kind and gentle. I had no idea what this new version of my husband was capable of.

'I'm. . . I'm sorry, Chris,' I mumbled.

'So, you admit it?'

I didn't know how to respond. 'I wasn't trying to make you angry,' I said in the end.

'Well, you did.'

'I know.' My contrition seemed to placate him.

'You know what I would do if I ever found you cheating on me, don't you?' All trace of the anger gone. But what was left, soft and gentle, sent a chill deep into my bones. He moved a strand of hair away from my face and looked at me for a few moments. 'I would hurt you, Megan. Hurt you really bad. You understand?'

Tears streamed down my face as I nodded. He put one hand on my shoulder and pushed me down on to my knees, the ground beneath me damp and mossy. His other hand was undoing his fly. 'Show me it's only ever me you want, Meggie.'

Ten minutes later we were back at the party, having stumbled from the bushes to a cheer from a few of the younger cousins. Chris had responded by high-fiving a few and then slapping my bottom. 'Young love!' he exclaimed. 'Can't keep our hands off each other.' I spent the rest of the evening trying to avoid eye contact with Kivi and wondering why no one had noticed the red handprint on my cheek and the mess of my make-up from my tears. I guess sometimes it's easier just to pretend everything is OK and normal.

Did I think then that he was serious about hurting me? You didn't see the look in his eyes. That was the night I realised my wedding vows really had been the truth. Till death us do part was not a promise of everlasting love, but a threat. The only way he'd ever let me leave him was if I were dead.

I doubt he would be so possessive of Leah. She wouldn't have put up with that kind of shit from him.

As Megan, I would never have dreamed of it. But as Leah, maybe I could go on a second date. Kiss this gorgeous man without fear. See what it was like to live freely, just for a few hours at least.

Chapter Six

Last week, I managed to get away with not being physically in the office as Megan, fielding emails from Leah's living room and juggling my workload around as I tried to figure this whole mess out. But today is Monday and I have a meeting that I can't avoid, and so I need to spend the day at one of my clients' fancy office with its smoked-glass facade and glamorous receptionist just off Leadenhall Street.

My normal route to visit Green Units is a train to Waterloo and then 'The Drain' to City with all the other commuters coming in from Surrey and Hampshire. Instead, today I take the Northern line all the way to Monument, my heart in my mouth as I pray I don't bump into anyone I know. I have rehearsed my lie a hundred times: 'Oh, I was just staying with a friend up near Camden,' I would say if anyone asked why I was on this route.

Shit! I didn't bring an overnight bag with me, just my smart leather shoulder bag that just about fits my laptop and daily essentials. I squeeze it tighter to me, eyes raking the faces of my fellow passengers, scanning for any sign they know I'm not where I should be.

I keep my head down as I join the crowd of bodies pressing against each other as they attempt to exit the tube station. There are a few people wearing those white face masks; some more cases of that coronavirus had been reported in Italy over the weekend and obviously some people are being a little over-cautious. Although I envy their anonymity as I'm swept out into the street.

I take the most direct route to the Green Units office, even though it means grabbing coffee from Pret instead of the fancier place on Lime Street, desperate to disappear into the relative calm of the extortionately expensive space the company is still insisting on renting. I've been working with Green Units for a few months, trying to help them turn round their business after a particularly disastrous PR incident involving some kind of carbon credit scam. I won't bore you with the details, but trying to solve climate change with capitalism was never going to end well. The managing director is paranoid the company is about to fold. 'Our houses are on the line,' he told me in hushed tones a few weeks ago. 'The one in Devon and the one in the Languedoc. Can you even imagine?'

When I was thirteen, I remember plucking mould from the edge of the last slice of bread so my mum wouldn't cry. I struggle with sympathy for those who don't realise their privilege, especially this guy in the four-grand suit, his manicured fingers holding a Mont Blanc pen as he lamented having to make do with renting a holiday home instead of owning it. Oh, the humanity!

I have specialised my career into business turnarounds, offering hope to companies on the brink of failure by helping them with creative solutions for change. That is just a fancy way of saying that I run workshops where ideas get thrown about and I try to put some sense around them. I have none of the answers, although I'm exceptionally good at getting other people to come up with their own.

But today my thoughts are constantly slipping away from work, my mind bouncing between terror at being caught out and the image of her face just before I closed that freezer.

'What the fuck is wrong with you, Hardcastle?' Fi's eyes are flashing and her voice is like daggers.

Fi is one of those people you work with who becomes a friend, even though you probably wouldn't ever socialise if you met in different circumstances. She is tall and slim, brash and no-nonsense. She takes zero shit from anyone, and I hold her in equal parts of terror and respect. We often tag-team with clients; she will frighten them into submission so they realise just how serious their company's predicament is, then I will swoop in with my Post-it notes and icebreaking exercises.

We are in a meeting room, away from the eyes and ears of the remaining company staff who have tried to find every opportunity to talk to us in whispers about the potential viability of the company and their seemingly perilous prospects.

I know I'm not up to par – I mean who would be in my situation? – but I'm concerned that someone else has noticed. What if they can see the guilt on my face?

'You have to get a fucking grip. These guys are personal friends of Martin and his wife.'

Martin is our boss James's boss. A slightly overweight man who spends about three days a month in the office and the rest on the golf course, in a buggy rather than walking, from the look of him. For a man with no idea, he still likes to make all the decisions about assignments, promotions and, particularly, new hires. It is important – actually make that imperative – that we impress him.

'I just have a lot on.' My words sound defensive in my ears.

'Like the rest of us don't?' She jabs her pen at the space be-tween us.

'That's not what I——'

'Look. I like you, Megan. We make a good team. But I need you to bring your A game to this, OK? I need you on point, on side, and on-fucking-brand at the very least.' Her eyes are lingering on the blouse I am wearing under my suit jacket. 'I mean, when have we ever worn white lace under cream silk? Jesus.'

You can see a hint of my bra through the silk blouse. When I pulled it from the back of Leah's closet – the tags were still at-tached, so I knew she hadn't worn it before – I thought it looked suitably professional with a hint of femininity. It looked like something I would have bought, and I didn't have anything of my own at Leah's that was good enough for a 'Leadenhall day'.

'Whatever it is, Megan, you don't bring it to work with you.'

I'm hurt. She doesn't seem to care and immediately changes the subject to what we are going to do for Green Units. My cheeks burn at the thought that she will call a friend later and they will laugh about how I went to work with my underwear on show.

Companies who are about to go to the wall tend to work pretty long hours and so my weeks can often be exhausting. But Mr Seleucus Montgomery Patricio Titcomb – his real name, I have seen the Companies House registration – with his holiday home in the Languedoc believes in 'work/life balance' and sending the office home at fifteen minutes past four. With hours of evening stretching before me, I am thinking of taking a walk along the riverbank when Fi's shadow looms over my desk. 'You. Me. Wine.' It's a command, not a request.

I hurry to pack up my things and we find a bar about five minutes' walk away. We have barely sat down before she's shaking her hair from its tight bun and undoing three buttons on her blouse. 'Jesus, thank God today is over!' A glass of white wine materialises at her elbow and she drinks it eagerly. 'That guy is a pig. Did you hear him earlier? *But I thought all of your people were good at maths.*' She screeches a poor imitation of his accent. 'Jesus. "My people".' She mimes finger quotes around the statement. 'For fuck's sake, like there's some magical numbers gene embedded with a knowledge of how to use chopsticks.'

'You're shit with chopsticks.'

'Touché.' Fi's mum was adopted from Malaysia by a family whose own roots were in Nigeria. Fi's dad comes from a long line of Welsh sheep farmers. She makes a mean lamb suya with jollof rice that will blow your socks off.

'You didn't quite deserve what I said earlier.' This is the closest I will get to an apology from Fi.

'To be fair, you were right.'

'Of course. But I should have said it more softly. You OK?'

Funny how people ask that. Like it would ever be alright for you to scream, *no, no I'm not OK, I'm very far from OK and I feel like I'm drowning and I don't know how to stop it all.* Instead you must say, 'Of course. Just tired. You know.' So that way they can launch into a monologue about how tired *they* are and what exhausting things *they've* had to endure and how you would have no idea about their struggles – even if they tell you them constantly. In this case, it's the escape route I want. I don't want to talk about my feelings. I'm worried that the more I talk the more I'll give away. I let Fi go on about herself instead and I sip the cool, crisp Sauvignon Blanc as her words wash over me.

She breaks off in mid-sentence and jabs her head towards the door. 'Ooh. . . hottie alert.'

He has his back to me, but I recognise his hair immediately. I can't breathe. I watch in horror as he shrugs out of a formal wool coat, praying he doesn't turn round. I know I should move, but this bar isn't big enough for me to hide in. He leans over the bar, trying to get the bartender's attention, stamping his feet in an effort to warm his toes. He gets cold toes. He told me this the other night as we sipped our third whisky and shared embarrassing stories. He told me a girlfriend screamed in the night as her foot brushed his; thinking there was a corpse in the bed next to her.

I keep my eyes on him, and I can tell Fi is watching him too, her expression appraising, admiring him. Time slows to a crawl as he starts to turn round, coat now draped over his arm, his hand tucked into his pocket.

He sees me.

I see him recognise me.

I watch his face light up. Blood pounds in my ears.

'Leah?' He begins to walk towards me, and I try to keep my expression neutral. This is not the kind of place where Leah would drink, full of City guys and girls winding down after their day, people who have 'proper' jobs and think their work superior to other people's.

I cock my head to one side and narrow my eyes like I'm trying to place him. 'I'm sorry,' I say as he reaches me, 'I think you must have me confused with my sister.' Inside my head a voice is screaming. *Hi Tom. Coo-ey. Look here, Tom. This is me, the real me. Can you see me?*

'You're Megan?'

'Yes.' I sound uncertain.

'Wow. You really do look alike. That's uncanny.' There is an edge there. Like I've cheated him somehow. I mean, I obviously have cheated him, but that's not what I mean.

'You know my sister?' I see the flush bloom up his neck.

'Yep.' He grins like a boy. I like the way he grins.

'That's nice.' My tone is neutral. As if he's just another man my sister is into and means nothing to me at all. Not a jot. Even though my stomach is in knots at the thought of how his lips felt on mine.

For a few seconds he scans my face, and then he nods. 'Well, er, sorry for interrupting you.' And then he's walking backward away from me, his eyes on mine, waiting. . .

'Wow!' exclaims Fi. 'That was rude.'

'He just thought I was Leah.'

'Yeah, I wasn't meaning him. It was like he was a piece of shit on your shoe and you wanted to get rid of him as fast as possible before he stank up the air around us. And yeah, I know that you and your sister have that. . . thing. . . and you hate each other, yada yada yada. But he is *fine*.'

Yes, yes, he is. I want to say. *And he smells delicious and his kisses taste like. . .* 'Too posh and too pretty,' I reply instead. 'Not my cup of tea at all. And if he likes Leah, he can't be all that nice.'

Fi looks very pointedly at the huge diamond on my left hand. Fi got divorced a year ago and feels she has dibs on any man who crosses her path.

She sits up straight and downs the rest of the wine in front of her. 'I think you should go and apologise for being so rude. And then I think you should offer to buy him a drink and introduce us.'

'He's Leah's friend, Fi.'

'So?' She is not going to buy it. I can see it in the set of her shoulders, the way she is ever so slightly pressing her chest forward and the challenge in her eyes. 'Do it for me, Megs.' She pouts. 'Unless you want him for yourself – but that feels kind of greedy. . .' She trails off and her eyes once more are glued to the shining monstrosity on my finger.

So in the end I slide off my seat and head towards him. He whirls round as I tap his shoulder. 'Leah!' It is out of his mouth before he can stop himself. 'Sorry. It's just you are so alike. It's like you're the same person.' That look crosses his face again.

'I just wanted to apologise.' I tell him, trying to break eye contact. *Look away, look away,* my lizard brain is screaming, *you know better than to look directly at the sun.* 'If I was rude earlier.'

'It's OK. It must be weird to have people insist you're someone else all the time.'

'Can I buy you a drink? My friend would very much like an introduction.'

'I'm flattered, but I'll pass.' He grins and leans a little closer to me. 'I'm kind of into someone. Someone who looks very much like you.'

'Oh.'

'Oh, indeed.'

My face is burning, and I am trying to suppress a smile as I head back to Fi.

'And?' she asks.

'I think he's got a thing with my sister.'

'So? You hate her guts.'

'Come on. Let's go to another bar and find someone a bit more available for you to drool over.' I lead her out of the bar, passing Tom's table once more. He smiles at me and I feel like a giddy teenager again.

A few minutes later, I have Fi safely ensconced with a group of much younger guys, interns from an investment bank down the road who are probably fifteen years younger than she is. She's the centre of attention and loving it. My handbag vibrates. Leah's phone: *Just met your doppelganger, beautiful. Although she's not as lovely as you. Xx*

My fingers linger over the screen. Should I make a comment about 'her' twin? It feels weird to write about myself in the third person, but will he think it odd if I don't? I know I should just put the phone away and forget all about him. But I can't help myself: *Dinner Wednesday?* I reply, wondering if this time it won't only be steak on the menu.

I can't stop smiling as I get ready for dinner with Tom, trying on a whole pile of different outfits before settling on a semi-structured shift dress in a deep teal. It feels odd to riffle through Leah's underwear, but I do, and I find a whole drawer of lingerie with the tags on and pull out a coral-pink set. Perfect!

I catch a glimpse of myself in the mirror as I'm about to leave, and realise my mistake. I look like me. Like Megan. Bile rises to my throat. I need to focus! I can't let him question who I am, especially after he met Megan the other night.

Hurrying back into the bedroom, I wipe off my lipstick and smear a brighter shade over my lips; it's one of those plumping types that makes them sting and swell. I draw on more eyeliner and add another coat of mascara. My hair, that I have made all glossy and bouncy, I now scrape back into a high pony, a thick strand twisted round to cover the elastic. Checking my teeth for lipstick, I grin, wide-mouthed and teeth bared, at my reflection. At *Leah's* reflection. The person staring back at me is undoubtedly my twin.

Tom is waiting for me outside the restaurant, a small Paris-style place tucked down a side street, and I break into a smile at the sight of him. As I step out of the taxi, his own smile lights up his face, and then I'm enveloped in a hug, his arms wrapping tightly around me.

'You look incredible,' he whispers in my ear before dropping a kiss on my cheek, lips cool on my skin.

'We'd better get you inside,' I say, laughter in my voice, 'your nose is freezing!'

He takes my hand and leads me up a couple of steps to the door, which opens to reveal an intimate dining space in gorgeous deep burgundy tones with accents of gold to catch the glow of the lamplight. 'Monsieur Eagleton,' the maître d' says with a nod, '*et madame*. Welcome to Gauthier's.'

'You're a regular here?' I ask Tom, feeling a small spark of jealousy as I wonder if he brings a lot of dates here.

'I went to school with Sebastian Gauthier, his dad opened this place last year. Seb pulled some strings to get me a table; there's normally a month waiting list but I wanted to take you somewhere special.' There's a faint blush creeping up his neck.

'So you don't bring all the girls here?' I'm teasing. Or at least that's how I hope it sounds.

'Only you, Leah,' he says, before a waiter interrupts the moment to take our order, and our conversation moves on to a decision of steak or chicken.

Over our starter, talk drifts to past relationships. I'm fairly quiet, providing something approximating my own – as in

Megan's – truth, at least up to the part when I met Chris. A few flings that never amounted to much. One boyfriend who could have been something, but the relationship had hit a rather significant stumbling block when his ex wanted him back.

Tom tells me about his wife. His ex-wife. He is polite and respectful. 'Sometimes life throws so many rocks at you that even the strongest foundation can't survive.' A sad smile crosses his face. I don't ask, not wanting to pry, but he takes my silence as an invitation to continue. 'We hadn't even been married four months when Juliet's brother was killed in a car crash.' He takes a deep breath. 'Then three months later, my dad was diagnosed with an aggressive form of cancer, although he did eventually pull through.' He gently taps the wooden surface of the table three times in a superstitious gesture.

He takes a large sip of wine and it's clear there's more to his story. He doesn't meet my eyes, telling the glass of Beaujolais instead, 'We tried for a year to get pregnant, but when it finally happened, we miscarried at eight weeks. It put us off trying again for a while.' His eyes flick to mine. 'Then Juliet was made redundant and struggled to find another job.' There isn't much wine left his glass, but he swirls the remnants round the bottom. 'A whole lifetime of bad shit condensed into just three short years. We stayed together another three. The resentment grew. I think we both wanted out, but didn't know how to say it. Eventually it all boiled over and our final argument was like an inferno.' He puts down the glass and sits up a little straighter. 'She moved back up north, and I've been concentrating on my career.' His solemn expression cracks and his face transforms into that glorious smile, the corners of his eyes crinkling. 'Then a friend convinced me to at least try internet dating. I just didn't expect to meet someone on my first foray.'

Someone what? I want to ask. But it's there in his eyes. *Someone special*. I feel like I'm falling; falling with no fear of crashing to the earth, knowing he will swoop in to catch me at any second.

He asks me about Megan as the main course is served.

'We're not close.'

'I'm sorry.' He flashes me a small smile, concern on his face. 'It must be tough.'

'How do you mean?'

'Well, to grow up with someone who is so like you in so many ways. To invest all that time and effort and for the relationship to still not work.'

'She's my sister, not my spouse.' I hope I sound like I'm joking.

'Same thing in a way though.' He shrugs.

I guess he's right. Because even if you spend every hour of every day of your life with someone, you still don't really know them. And you certainly don't have to like them.

I could say the same thing about Chris.

Instead I mumble something that sounds like a vague agreement and turn the conversation towards more neutral ground: TV we like; favourite books; that incredible Sam Mendes film everyone is talking about, the one that appears to be a single continuous shot.

Dessert is a simple crème brûlée with a perfect crust of burnt sugar. 'The colour my hair goes in the winter,' he points at the sugar, 'it bleaches in the sun and darkens when the weather turns foul.'

Perhaps it is the wine – I probably should stop drinking so much until I have truly nailed this new 'Leah' character – but when he starts talking about his family again, I find myself telling him that Megan and I have drifted apart only since Megan's marriage.

'Megan's husband is a bit. . .' My hand gropes the air.

'Of a douche?'

'That's not quite—'

'A dick? An idiot? Controlling misogynist?'

I laugh with him, but I run each moniker against an image of my husband. His insistence that he have access to my online banking 'because women can be shit with money'. I'm a chartered accountant with five years of post-qualified experience. But obviously, I have a vagina and so therefore cannot be trusted not to buy too many shoes. To be fair, I do buy too many pairs of shoes. It seems to be a thing Leah and I have in common; I think back to her overflowing closet. Chris can be an idiot too. And a dick, especially when it comes to my mum. He is a douche too. But they aren't the words I'm really thinking of.

Sociopath.

Narcissist.

Monster.

'He just doesn't like her to spend too much time with me. I think he's worried that she'll see the way her life could have been and realise there is greener grass.'

'He's worried she'll leave him?'

'Maybe she would prefer to have dinner with a delicious man in a fancy restaurant with the promise of a night of passion?'

He raises an eyebrow at me. 'A promise?'

'OK, OK, a hope!'

He leans in, his words drowned out by the din of the other patrons around us, and whispers the things he wants to do to me that evening. I ache for his touch.

An hour later we are back at Leah's place.

The grass is definitely greener.

Later that night, we are sitting in bed eating toast and drinking tea.

'Guaranteed to stop a hangover,' he tells me.

It turns out that he doesn't shave his chest. But the hair is soft and fine, darker than that on his head, closer to the colour of burnt caramel. It curls across his lower stomach, tickling my lips as I gently kiss a trail downwards.

I want to correct him when he calls me Leah. I want to look into his eyes and hear my own name tumble from his lips. But I can't. I won't. No matter how hard I wish that I could.

He brushes my hair from my face, now freed from the ponytail. 'Your hair looks gorgeous loose,' he says as he tucks a strand behind my ear. A moment of confusion crosses his face. 'You're not like I thought you'd be.'

'I'm not?' I'm half teasing and half wondering if this is my first major fuck-up.

'I was worried you'd be one of *those* girls.'

'Which girls?' I sound innocent. But I know exactly what girls he means. Leah *is* one of those girls. Megan is not. I have failed. Shit!

'I guess we all have a public persona though.' He shrugs and runs his hand through his whisky curls. 'Wait till you see me as full business wanker in my three-piece suit spouting corporate spiel.' He thinks this is the real Leah. That the social media stuff is an act, part of her job. 'If you'd like to see me again, of course.' He drops his eyes and picks at the corner of the bedspread a little.

I answer by pulling him towards me, kissing him deeply and wrapping my legs round his waist.

'Do I take that as a yes?' His voice is soft. He rolls his weight on top of me and I feel his skin melt into mine.

I wake up with the sun shining through the window and a sudden moment of clarity.

The best way to get away with murder is for there to have never been one.

Corpus delicti. No body, no crime.

If everyone thought Leah was still alive, then I couldn't possibly have killed her. It is surprisingly simple. There are only two major issues: the body in the freezer at the cabin and the fact that eventually people will realise that I am not Leah. Yes, I could pretend for a few weeks, but eventually I would either fuck up, or my worlds would collide in some terrible moment. Or I'd just run out of hours in the day to be both. So, Leah will still need to disappear. But in a way that makes people think she is alive. She just needs to disappear from London and stop working with Angels Inc.

She could find God? I stifle a laugh, trying hard not to wake Tom. Or go to India to find herself? Could I make that stick? She did yoga occasionally; could she go on a retreat or something and have an epiphany about splashing her life all over social media? Or could she simply go on holiday and then disappear? Somewhere so far away that no one would ever look around here. I could fly to Thailand on her passport and then make my way back somehow via a different airport, and fly into the UK as myself.

Tom shifts beside me as I start to make a mental list of the things I will need to do to make this actually work. He is still half asleep as he curls himself around me. I am the perfect fit as his little spoon.

'Morning, beautiful,' he whispers in my ear and I press myself back into his embrace, list forgotten. I even manage to forget that tomorrow is Friday and I need to go home. To him.

Chapter Seven

The thought of seeing Chris makes my skin crawl. And how am I going to be natural around him? How will I hide my lies so he never suspects?

We live just outside the centre of Guildford, in an old Victorian house with tiled steps leading up to a blue front door. Half a million quid doesn't go very far round here, and we were lucky to have found it, putting in an offer after only a cursory look around; a place like this doesn't stay available for long, with its huge living room, original sash windows, and a decent-sized garden complete with decked patio area. We even have the second bedroom that Chris has commandeered as his home office and man cave. He spends an inordinate amount of time in there, looking at the huge screens installed over his desk. I still don't really understand his job, something about trend-spotting on a macroeconomic level. He thinks it would be beyond my comprehension and so offers me no further detail. I overheard him talking to a colleague once, about how he was a little surprised I had managed to qualify as an accountant, and wondering how I held down a lucrative job despite my intellectual shortcomings. When I was ten years old I joined Mensa. Not that he remembers.

I used to love our house, the patio adorned with potted plants and a green metal table and chairs like in a quaint French bistro, the perfect spot to drink wine in the evening and watch the floodlights come on in the grounds of the old castle. A castle I had never even realised existed – despite having lived in the area for years – until Chris took me there for a date. We ate a picnic and drank wine that came in squat plastic glasses with foil lids. It reminded me of the fluorescent drink cups Leah and I used to have on the beach when we were kids, bright green or luminous orange and so full of sugar it would take just seconds before the wasps were on us. The wine was warm and foul, but the castle was magical. We went there again on our first anniversary, this time with a better quality of 'beverage', and talked for hours and hours as the air turned frigid around us. On our second anniversary it was raining, but we still walked around the grounds. He apologised over and over about the weather, seeming so desperate for me to forgive him for the day being less than perfect. Such a perfectly choreographed remorse for something I could hardly blame on him. I didn't know at the time that it was the day after he first fucked my twin. Now the castle is tainted, and I will never be able to go there again.

The kitchen is tiny, all the appliances squished together and no room for anything. I have never been a great cook, so it didn't matter, when we first bought the house at least. But now, as I stand in my kitchen with arms outstretched so my fingertips graze the walls on either side, I am struck by envy. Leah's kitchen is huge and white and sparse. Not sparse in a bad way, but because there is so much cupboard space everything can be tucked away neatly out of sight. Not in my kitchen, where cookbooks jostle with skillets and the knives live on a metallic strip on the wall so they don't take up one of the drawers. Squeezed into the corner is a little table and two chairs. Was it only the weekend before last when Chris made me pancakes and we sat at that very table to eat them as I wondered if he was trying to poison me?

My best friend Hannah texts me. A slightly passive-aggressive message berating me for not responding to her text earlier in the week. It is not the first time I have left her hanging. I dig around in the fridge to find a half-drunk bottle of Sauvignon Blanc – probably the same one I was drinking the night before I. . . well, we all know what I did – and I slop some in a glass before I call her. Walking to the living room on speakerphone, I leaf through the handfuls of letters from the week: bill, bill, junk mail, bill, some newsletter from my accounting body, bill, junk mail, request for support from my alma mater. Nothing to write home about. I smile; that was what Tom said last night when I grilled him more about his job.

'Megaaaannnn! Hellooo!' Hannah's voice screeches from the phone. 'Earth to Megan.'

'Sorry, Hannah. I was miles away.' I snap my attention away from Tom.

'Err. . . you called me, sweetheart. Everything OK?' There is an edge of concern and a corner of barely concealed dread.

'Sure. Of course. Sorry, was flicking through the post. Just got home from a week up in town.' Hannah got very drunk last year and confessed that she worried about me. The way I seemed sometimes to space out, to forget things. That was when I'd started to document things better. Jesus, I'm going to need to be extra meticulous to pull this Leah thing off and convince Hannah that everything is OK. 'I need to ask you a favour.'

'Sure thing, Megs.'

'I'm trying to find someone who could rehome a cat. Do you think your mum would—'

'Yes. She's dying to get her hands on another waif and stray, driving my dad bananas! When from?'

'As soon as possible.'

'Let me text her now, stay on the phone.' I can hear Hannah humming in the background as she types the message. 'There, sent. You doing Friday date night?'

'Yep.'

'Harriers at six thirty?'

'Now you're talking.'

'Cool. Oh, Mum says just pop round with the puss any time.'

'Thanks, Hans.'

Just as Chris and I had established date night for Friday evenings to make sure we saw each other at least once every two weeks, so too had Hannah and I established meeting for an hour and a half first.

I am a few minutes late pushing open the door to the small pub we always meet in; I'd managed to bang my little toe on that stupid chest Chris insists on using as a coffee table just after I got off the phone. I don't think it's broken or anything, but it hurt like hell and left me hopping around the room cursing my husband's taste in interior design. The pub is warm, steam clouding the windows. She is sat in the tiny area between the door and the bar, two miniature armchairs squished into the space with a squat table holding a flickering votive like a sad little vigil. 'In memory of Dave.' Hannah motions to the candle. Dave was the most recent in a very long string of unsuitable boyfriends. They had been dating a few weeks.

'What did he do?' I wait for the ridiculous thing poor Dave had done to get the chop. The last one – Dan, I think – had farted on date four. Jacob had lasted two dates before he confessed to hating cats. Pete had asked her on date three to provide a certificate of her fertility, so he knew he wasn't 'wasting his time'. To be fair, I was glad she had got rid of him.

'Well. . .' She pushes a large glass of wine towards me and slugs down some of her own. She takes a deep breath, but then, rather than launching into her story, she cocks her head and frowns.

'What?' I ask with faux innocence. Can she see it on my face? What I have done? We've been friends for six years now. Could she tell?

'Megan. Louise. Hardcastle.' She enunciates every syllable carefully, dragging out my name. 'Well, well, well.'

'What?' My voice sounds too high in my ears, shrill; my palms are sweating.

'You don't have to tell me.' She leans in closer. 'But I promise not to tell another living soul.' She holds up her right hand in the Brownie salute, three fingers pointing upwards. Her eyes are large and round, expectant.

'What?' The whole 'my heart was in my mouth' is such a cliché. But at that moment, with my friend searching my face, silently begging me to dish the juicy gossip I was obviously hiding, I could feel my pulse in my tongue.

'OK, OK.' She puts both palms up and sits back. 'I won't pry. Just give me one blink for yes and two for no. That he's hot and funny and smart and makes you feel like a million dollars and is a gentleman, and all the other things you deserve?'

She is talking about Tom. It is not murder she sees etched into the lines of my face, but a post-coital glow. Shit, I hope Chris can't see it too. A cold shiver runs through me, but I try to push it away. I don't want to think what he'd do if he found out. Even if he did cheat first.

I blink once. Slowly, so she can be under no illusions. God, I want to tell her about him. But I can't. *You're a thirty-four-year-old married woman*, I tell myself. *Not a teenager gossiping in the lunch queue.*

She beams back and gives me a slow-motion wink before clinking her glass against mine. I realise that she mustn't think much of my husband.

Then her eyes darken and she looks around her furtively. 'Promise me you'll be careful, Megs.' She clutches my left hand and grips it tightly. 'Don't let him find out.' There is something in her voice that makes the hair on the back on my neck bristle. I can't quite think of the word for it.

I've never talked about him to Hannah properly, what he's really like. I don't know why not – she's my closest friend. It just never felt like the kind of thing you shared, like articulating the concern might make it all real somehow. But even though she doesn't know the truth, she's never been a cheerleader of Chris's. Which is pretty unusual, because generally the world loves him; he is lovely and charming and affable and self-deprecating. He will always make sure he maintains eye contact when he talks to you and is first to the bar for every round. He knows a little about everything, enough to engage you in conversation but not so much that he would show you up or make you feel small. I have always assumed it is just Hannah being Hannah. Never has a woman been so picky, so quick to discard a man because of a minor infraction. 'Why settle?' she will say with a shrug of her shoulders every time she finishes with one guy and moves on to the next.

There is some debate, among some of our colleagues and kind-of-friends, as to how I managed to bag a man like Chris. I had overheard a couple at our wedding reception:

'She's pretty, you know. But he's. . .' the woman had said. I think she worked with Chris.

'Even I probably would,' said her husband. 'I'm not sure why he settled.'

Chris is already at the table when I wobble into the restaurant keeping an unnatural focus on the space between us. He's tucked away towards the back, where the huge pizza oven dominates the open-plan kitchen and smartly dressed staff in crisp chef whites scurry behind a long gleaming steel workbench, churning out order after order of Italian favourites for the diners crammed into the cavernous space. The restaurant is heaving with Friday-night punters enjoying themselves: couples sharing spaghetti dishes, groups of friends, families with kids old enough for the later sitting. It is loud and raucous and God, it is boiling. I can feel a drop of sweat chasing down my chest as I make the marathon trek to the table.

'You're drunk.' His voice is light, a simple observation not a criticism, although I can see the spot on his cheek that suggests his jaw is tightly clenched.

'I had one glass.'

'I thought we were going to have a nice evening.' He offers me a sad smile. The perpetually understanding husband who just wants to play nicely and placate his disaster of a wife. I pick up the menu to avoid his plaintive stare. The words melt a little on the page. Perhaps I had two glasses with Hannah. Alright, it was two large glasses and a Scotch, but we're all friends here and no one should be counting. I put the menu down and smile at him.

'So. . . good week?' It sounds warm and friendly in my ears, not the voice of a woman who caught him cheating and dispatched his mistress, forthwith. Damn, I am drunk.

'Busy,' he replies and tries to flag down the harried-looking waitress as she rushes past. She gives him a signal that she'll be back in a minute and we wait for her in silence. He doesn't ask me about my week and I'm not inclined to proffer the information.

'A bottle of Cabernet Sauvignon and a large tap water,' he tells the waitress.

'Yes, red is fine,' I say curtly after she has gone.

He sighs and sits back in his chair a little. 'I didn't ask because I think you have probably already had more than enough. The water is for you. Then maybe we will see about the wine.'

Supercilious, self-righteous bastard. Although I should keep my wits about me. Getting pissed is probably not conducive to getting away with murder. 'I just need to eat,' I say in the end, not wanting an argument. 'I didn't have time for lunch.'

'You need to take care of yourself, Meggie,' he says with a semblance of concern. 'You need to be better.' Be better. He sounds like Leah's manager. He's watching me, waiting for my reply. I nod. 'Good girl,' he says, and orders a basket of bread and olives to tide us over until the main course arrives.

Even though I start salivating at the aroma of fresh warm dough with rosemary and garlic wafting towards me when the basket is delivered, I find myself holding back, before I remember that it is Leah who shies away from the gluten to maintain some story about her intolerance, not me. And so I dig in hungrily as Chris watches with a wry smile on his face.

We walk home from the restaurant; it's only a few minutes up the road. I stumble up the steps, keen to get out of the cold and into the warmth of the house. But once inside, Chris grabs me, pushing me back against the wall, lips mashing mine, tongue probing between my teeth like a fat slug. Suddenly he pulls back, eyes searching mine, breath against my face. I try to control the reflex to pull away from him and the garlic winey smell underpinned with a sense of something like food on the turn. He pushes himself off the wall and grins. 'Just gotta do a few work bits. Why don't you go and slip into something a little less comfortable, hmmm?' His hand is groping down my top and snaking into my bra. He pinches my nipple. 'Hmmm.' That waft again of rancidity as he exhales. 'You like that don't you?'

I have never cleaned my teeth so quickly, throwing off my dress and struggling into a pair of thick flannel pyjamas in an effort to get into bed before he comes in. Turning off the lamp, I slip Leah's phone from my bag.

My husband is in the living room texting lewd messages to my twin while he thinks I'm sitting in our bed waiting for him.

Look how hard I am for you, his message says, and he includes a picture of his erect penis. Classy.

I'll be thinking of you, it goes on.

I used to think this man was a catch. Jesus. All those months when we were first dating when I thought he was so sophisticated and suave, when I would ache for his touch. I can't believe how naïve I was.

Five minutes later, light from the hallway fills the darkness of the bedroom. I am curled into a tight foetal shape on the far side of the bed, a soft snore breaking forth every few breaths. 'You asleep, Meggie?' he asks and I feel his weight shift the bed and try not to shiver at the blast of cool air he lets in as he slips under the covers. He shuffles towards me and presses his hard-on into the small of my back. I snore again and try not to stiffen. 'Oh, come on, Meggie.' He presses into me a little more, grinding his hips a few times. 'Oh, fuck you then!' He throws off the covers and stomps to the en suite. He doesn't bother to close the door, so I drift off to sleep to the harmony of my husband masturbating into the toilet.

It is only when I wake up in the middle of the night that I remember the word I was trying to find to describe Hannah's reaction. Visceral. A fear that comes from a place beyond all reason and logic. A shiver runs down my spine. She sees him too.

Chapter Eight

I wake up to find the alarm clock is flashing 03:31. It was a present from Chris last year, when my paranoia over failing to set my alarm clock correctly had reached a fever pitch. It projects the time on to the wall in huge green numbers, with the time the alarm is set for underneath. This way I can lie in bed and be absolutely sure the alarm is set properly. It's been a godsend.

I slip out of bed and pad to the living room. I have hidden Leah's laptop in my work backpack. I bought a slip-on skin for it so you can't tell it's the fancy rose gold model; Chris will assume it's a work one. There are a few irate-sounding emails from Emma, asking why I was ignoring her instructions to jump on some new trend, why I hadn't provided Zach with some new pictures for him to post that evening:

Lots of talk tonight about getting beach body ready. Zach needs to post inspirational bikini pics.

Send the pictures. Build that following, Leah. Be better.

You know you pay me for this advice? Act on it.

So much for 'taking it easy'. And who the hell posts 'inspirational bikini pics' when everyone is still trying to hide their extra mince pie shame? I scroll through a few of Leah's friends' accounts.

Every single one of them, it transpires. The ubiquitous selfie in a luxury bathroom, the hint of a six-pack, no sign of mulled-wine bloat. *#beachbodyready*. *#hardworkpaysoff*. *#anythingispossible*. I want to laugh. Instead I flick back through Leah's feed. There are a lot of pictures of her in a bikini, or in her underwear. I feel ashamed. It's not my body in those images – hell, it might not even be Leah's, Photoshop is pretty easy to get the hang of these days – but it looks like me. I feel violated and experience a sudden burst of solidarity for the growing list of young actresses speaking up about the deep-fake porn being created of them. I hope to God Leah isn't famous enough, or considered pretty enough, for someone to make deep-fake porn of her. Of us.

Get a grip. Keep things separate. Isolated. In neat little boxes. That is the only way. The old woman's voice in my head, the one that now sounds like a Victorian governess, is right. I need to keep calm. To think of Leah as entirely separate. *Don't cross the streams.*

Chris got up early. A trip to visit one of his old university friends, he tells me. He will be out all day, stay overnight and be back tomorrow.

'Let's have a roast dinner tomorrow, Meggie,' he suggests as he kisses my cheek. 'And then I'll make up for what you missed last night.' He winks before he turns to walk down the steps of our house.

There isn't a cloud in the sky, so I pull on some warm gear, stuff a box of biscuits and a flask of coffee into my old backpack and go to the hills. I have no obvious affinity to Guildford. It wasn't where I grew up, or went to school, my university town is Brighton, my first proper boyfriend lived in Clapham along with all the other young graduates I knew. But I had decided years ago that I wanted to live in this small city, with its steep ancient high street and easy access to the trails of the North Downs. That is where I head now, knowing a few hours in the crisp sunshine of a bitter winter day will make everything clearer.

I walk for an hour, waiting for the epiphany to strike. But nothing comes except a jumble of images, real and imagined: Chris and Leah in flagrante delicto, Leah's face staring out from the freezer, Tom clinking his whisky glass against mine. Over these images plays a soundtrack, out of time so the sound and pictures don't line up: the thump of a wine bottle hitting bone, the plop of her phone sliding into the water, 'you like that, don't you?' said in my husband's voice, 'you're not like I thought you'd be,' said in Tom's.

I stop on the brow of a hill, looking down into the valley below, and drink my coffee as cold tendrils tease their way through the gaps in my scarf. With almost numb fingers I stuff everything back into my pack and set off once more, waiting for clarity. Still nothing.

How do you get away with murder? That needs to be the focus. Onwards I tramp. *You need to think about the body*, the voice in my head keeps saying. But no inspiration comes.

Just after eleven, Tom rings Leah's phone.

'Hey, beautiful,' he says, his voice warm. 'Having fun in deepest, darkest Sussex?'

I had told him I was going to visit a friend for the weekend. 'Yep. It's good to catch up. Remember old university times.' Fuck, fuck, fuck. Leah didn't go to university, didn't even do A levels. She made a big thing about it in the book and on social media. *#universityoflife* and all that.

'I thought you—' He cuts himself off and laughs in that gorgeous deep baritone. 'Another one of your professional quirks, I presume?'

'Something like that.' It couldn't really be so easy that he would just think Leah played a professional part, could it? But no, this only works if there is never any suspicion. From anyone. In Emma's words, I need to be better.

'I. . . er. . .' he begins. 'That is. . . errm. . . can I see you, on Monday, when you're back?'

I know I should turn him down, switch this whole thing off and get on with making Leah disappear, but I can picture him, his hand running through his hair, the boyish hope on his face. In my head, he's standing on a stone kitchen floor not wearing any socks, and I worry his feet must be freezing.

'I'd like that,' I tell him. 'Shall I cook?' But inside I'm screaming to myself. *What the fuck are you doing? On what planet does Leah cook?*

'I'd love that. Seven OK?'

'Perfect.'

'Have fun this weekend.' Then he is gone, and I am standing in the middle of a wood sporting a huge grin and hoping that he goes to warm his feet by a fire.

A few more days can't hurt, I tell myself. And then Leah can disappear.

Have I upset you? The message my cheating shit of a husband sends to his mistress. *You didn't reply last night. . .*

What *do* you reply when someone sends you a picture of their penis? Is there some kind of standard response, a common 'that's nice' message? I missed the etiquette on this stuff.

Hannah would know but I can't ask her, not without her thinking my mystery man is the one sending them. Somehow, I don't think it's Tom's style. Although, to be fair, I wouldn't have thought it was Chris's either.

In the end I decide to not mention it and hope it goes away: *Sorry! I was out with some girlfriends!*

It doesn't work and he sends another photo, followed by: *Guess where I want to put this, my dirty little princess.*

An involuntary sound emerges from the back of my throat, part gag and part laugh. Dirty little princess? Of all the terrible names he could think of.

Why don't you tell me? I send. There is one thing I know Chris is awful at, and that is talking dirty. He tried it once when we'd only been together a short time and it was excruciating. The phrasing of the first messages I looked at between him and Leah was all over the place, too. Thinking about him in a slightly mouldy hotel somewhere, waiting for his friends as he struggles to put into words the things he thinks his mistress wants him to say, makes me smile. Perhaps there is some fun I can have here.

And then I realise. There is a *lot* of fun I can have here. I can tear my lying cheating bastard of a husband down piece by piece until he's a weeping shell on the floor. He's always been so proud of how irresistible he is to women. 'Not that I'd ever cheat on you, sweetheart. But you know that the ladies will look. They can't help themselves.' How many times has he said some variation of that? Oh yes, my husband is a narcissist alright.

Perhaps I should even tell him I'm making amends with my sister, let him worry that we are rebuilding some of the bridges we burned before. Would we ever have done that? If

I hadn't. . . There was always a part of me that assumed we would reconcile, one day, when we were old and grey and all that shit from the past just didn't matter as much any more. Maybe then we would have come back together, been two little old biddies in a nursing home somewhere, finishing each other's sentences and eating jelly from little plastic pots. What would Chris do if he thought we were talking? Would he shit himself that she would tell me?

I almost run home from my walk, skipping into the off-licence to pick up a bottle of prosecco and a large bar of creamy chocolate. I am excited at the prospect of making my shitbag of a husband's life a misery. At least for a little while.

I sit cross-legged on the sofa in my favourite fleece pyjamas with Leah's laptop balanced on my knees, a stomach full of chocolate, swigging prosecco from the bottle. Oh, I almost forgot to tell you what he replied when I asked him to tell me where he wanted to put it. It took him over half an hour to come back with: *I want your lips on it.*

On it. Not *round* it. *On* it. Jeez. I replied: *Mmmmm. . . and then?*

For the past hour I have watched the three tiny dots that denote he's writing a reply flick on. Then off. Then on. Then off. Type. Delete. Type. Delete. I can picture him sweating, wiping his palms down his golfing trousers, or whatever activity they were doing that afternoon. Type. Delete. The best he could come up with after an hour: *I guess you'll find out next week.*

Might need to rearrange Monday. I take another swig as I hit send.

Work?

Something has come up.

That was a mistake. He sends me another picture of his dick. It is captioned: *It sure has!* This picture was obviously taken in the toilet of somewhere unsanitary. Do any girls ever find this sexy?

There's just something I need to do, I reply.

That's not me? I can hear the hard edge to his voice, the one he uses when he doesn't get his own way.

It's Megan. Advantage: me.

My Megan? Oh, so I'm *your* Megan now?

She's my sister, Chris.

You didn't mind before. It wasn't that Leah didn't mind that he was my husband, she *liked* that he was my husband. Chris obviously thinks he is just too irresistible. He doesn't realise she was using him too.

I think she wants to make friends. This will get him. Despite all his insistence to me that I should reach out to Leah, he doesn't really want me to. I know because every time I actually have hovered over her number, he will always find a way to talk me out of it and then by the next day my bravado is gone and I spend a few days berating myself for being a coward, before the cycle starts again. I realise he must think I never saw the picture of Leah on his phone. I bet he was disappointed that his plan hadn't worked. Now I really want him to think I'm contacting Leah to finally make amends. To hammer home the point, I pop on to her Facebook and update her status to: *Call from the blue #sisterlove.* Twenty-five people like it within seconds. I open my own Facebook and post the exact same message. No one likes it.

Immediately my own phone beeps: *Saw Facebook. You OK, Meggie?*

I answer: 😀 *Yep: will tell all tomorrow when you get home. Now go and have fun with the boys* 🍺

I can see him now, with his stupid friends, the jock ones who take their wedding rings off for their boys' nights. He used to promise me he wasn't like that. And I, like the good wife I was, would kiss him and tell him that of course I knew that, and I didn't mind if he went to a strip club. I have genuinely never minded if he went to a strip club; the girls aren't actually interested in the guys that come barging through the club doors. I do mind that he's been fucking Leah. And I mind a whole lot more that it's been going on so long, and that he messages her more than he messages me, and it was obviously not just a sex thing. Leah never wanted to just steal my stuff for a little while. She wanted to own it, control it, dominate it. Then she would make sure to destroy it so I could never have it again.

Chapter Nine

Chris finally makes it back from his weekend away at six on Sunday evening. The window for a roast dinner in the fabulous pub on the riverfront closed three hours ago and I'm pissed off at him. I had spent all morning picturing the look on his face when I told him that Leah had called me and we might meet up this week. That she had told me there was something I should know. How enigmatic, I would say to him, how intriguing. All the while watching him squirm and availing myself of slow-cooked lamb and home-made Yorkshire puddings.

In the end, I ate cheese from the back of the fridge melted on to freezer-burned toast and waited.

He is practically green when he stumbles through the door. Layering day drinking on to a hangover when you're almost forty is not a good idea. He falls over the little case I have already packed for my return to London and swears at me.

'Guess I'm not going to get to spend time with my wife, then,' he says as he rubs his bruised shin.

'I waited all day, Chris. You said you'd be back for lunch.'

'Do you always have to be such a nag?'

'I'm not nagging, Chris.' I sound tired and resigned. We don't often argue like this. Actually, we just don't often argue. But I had decided by about four that I just wanted to be back in London, have a bath in Leah's tub, and give myself some time to prepare for the week ahead. I need an excuse and him being a pig-headed shit is perfect. 'I'm just disappointed.'

'Just disappointed.' He mocks my tone. 'We agreed it was OK for me to go this weekend.'

'It was OK. Don't you dare make me out to be one of those wives. But you promised me lunch and I've sat here waiting.'

'There's that nagging again.'

'I'm not nagging, Chris.' I can see he is getting more and more wound up by the continued evenness of my voice. I am right and he knows it. He hates it.

'Why don't you just fuck off up to London,' he says. I smile inside.

Outside I glare at him. 'If that's what you want, Chris.'

Half an hour later I am on the train. I text my husband: *When you have sobered up and calmed down, call me.*

The best bit is that he will be contrition personified tomorrow when he replays our argument with a sober head, and I will be free from having to justify where I am for a few days, perhaps even the whole week. I smile as the possibilities stretch out in front of me.

My plan for Monday was to go to a fancy supermarket and find something to cook for Tom that evening, juggling a handful of work bits around my domestic goddess pretence. However, Mr Seleucus Montgomery Patricio Titcomb had other ideas, and I end up having to schlep to his office for what he described as an 'all hands powwow'. Normally I am the one who leads the workshops when a client finally realises just how bad things are. But Mr Titcomb is impervious to bad news and still thinks his company just needs a PR tart-up. He also thinks he can do my job better than I can, and so I am relegated to the corner while he spends four hours effectively recreating the same pattern of mistakes that led him to the brink of ruin in the first place.

It is gone six thirty when I finally make it back to Leah's, stinking of the City and desperate for at least a shower before Tom arrives. My hair is still wet and I've not had time to reapply my make-up when he rings the bell at exactly seven. Normally I'm a stickler for punctuality but tonight it would have been preferable for him to be late.

He has wine in his hand and an expectant look on his face, stepping into the house with his nose slightly raised to catch the edge of what I'm cooking.

'I have a confession,' I tell him. 'Things got away with me today and so I haven't had time to cook.'

He laughs and pulls out his phone. 'Takeaway?' He is already opening Just Eat.

We end up on the sofa, watching a movie and waiting for pizza to be delivered. It is perfect.

You know how in films the guy and the girl always fuck against a wall, her legs round his waist, his trousers simply unbuttoned in his haste to be inside her? I have never really understood the logistics of how this actually works in practice. The movie we are watching has that exact same scene and so I tell Tom. He grins. A huge charming grin. Stands up and reaches a hand out to me. Seconds later, my back is pressed against a wall, legs wrapped tightly round his waist and Jesus Christ he's inside me. 'It's all about confidence,' he says.

Later that night, we are eating pizza straight from the box on the living room floor. 'I need to tell you something,' he says between bites. 'I. . . well, I kind of googled you. I'm sorry.'

'Why are you sorry?' Pretty much everything *I* know about Leah has come from Google; it's actually kind of helpful to know we're sharing the same information source.

'It feels a bit stalker-ish. I just wanted to know more about you.'

'I wouldn't trust everything you read on the internet though.'

'Of course not. I mean, you're obviously not coeliac.' He raises an eyebrow at my slice of pizza. Jesus! Did everyone care about my wheat consumption? 'But I get it. Personal and professional lives.'

I don't want him to think I'm like that. That I would pretend to have something wrong with me for clicks and sympathy. But I can hardly tell him the truth.

I don't sleep that night; I can feel the heat of his body in the bed next to me, hear the soft snuffling noises he makes, which aren't quite a snore and are almost endearing. The edges of a plan flutter in the wind just out of my grasp. Is there another way this story could end?

After Tom leaves in the morning, I settle myself at Leah's desk to try to keep some kind of handle on her life. Thank God for Zach! After the tirade of emails from Emma about me failing to provide bikini pictures, he had managed to dig up an older one of Leah in her yoga gear, her body contorted into a shape I could never dream of pulling off. He posted it yesterday: *#yogaforlife* and *#yogaformindandbody* and *#summerfitspo* and about twenty-five other hashtags. It had well over a thousand likes and counting. Emma was pleased and I wondered if I should give Zach a raise for doing such an admirable job keeping on top of Leah's Instagram empire. Plus there were hundreds of comments and DMs from Leah's fans; can you imagine if I didn't have him to reply to them all?

But there is an email in Leah's inbox that has been sat for two hours, just winking at me as I try to ignore it:

Your turn to host, darling!

Apparently, my sister is in a book club. And it is my turn to host them this evening. The email is signed off with one irritating little line. *You know the drill xx*.

I do not know the drill. Fuck.

It takes me most of the afternoon to figure out the logistics and research my fellow book clubbers. Time that could have been much better spent on the proper plan out of all this mess. But anyway. Book club turns out to be an opportunity for a bunch of semi-famous authors to get together and take photos of themselves looking intellectual while drinking wine and gossiping. I wonder if they realise how little of her book my sister actually wrote herself? They meet once a month and so I'm able to study the pictures from their previous sessions, identifying each one and pulling up a few facts about their literary careers.

I have – well, Leah had – already selected the book. A well-received novel about the importance of forgiveness and one I have thankfully already read. At three thirty, an Ocado delivery turns up full of champagne, wine, and tequila, plus an assortment of fancy-looking nuts and nibbles to be tastefully dotted around the living room in posh bowls and which I doubt anyone will actually eat.

By five thirty everything is prepared and I'm furiously pacing the living room trying to remember key facts: who wrote what; the names of spouses, kids, and handbag-sized dogs; ages and life stories. This is my biggest challenge as Leah so far. Four other people in the house, who will have anecdotes and in-jokes and gossip. I can't do this. I have to cancel, feign illness, or a family emergency, or something. Anything. I can't let them in here.

But suddenly it's six p.m. and I'm too late to call them off as they arrive in a flurry of air kisses and a whirlwind of hair extensions. The biscuit scent of fake tans clings to one of them, Joey, who is wearing navel-skimming jeans and a cropped T-shirt to show off her abs. She looks like she has stepped out of a late nineties pop video; all that is missing is a twisted bun knot on either side of her head. She recently published a young adult novel written entirely in an epistolary style, as a stream of texts; she has sold well over a million copies apparently and there are rumours she's the favourite to win some prestigious literary award.

Kira is older than Joey, dressed in a pleated animal-print midi-skirt and leather jacket. Her recent book, aimed at the suburban mother, is a jolly jaunt into the world of stretch marks, breastfeeding and post-partum sex. In it she describes, in excruciating detail, how her husband finds the scent of her milk arousing, and how more than once he has masturbated as he watches her pump. And when I say excruciating detail, this particular scene covers five pages in an almost stroke-by-stroke account.

Amy is a pixie-haired socialite in a modern version of a twinset and Jodhpur-style trousers. In real life she talks with an irritating nasal voice, clipping her vowels aggressively. However, on the page she writes surprisingly gritty domestic thrillers with bold and intriguing female protagonists, one of which has just been optioned by Sky.

The last to arrive is a diminutive woman called Rachel, who, at fifty-five, is the oldest and, it becomes swiftly apparent from her demeanour, the matriarch of this funny group my sister is part of. Rachel had a breakdown when she hit fifty, threw in her marriage, her corporate job, the whole shebang, and took herself back to university to do an MA in Creative Writing. Her family laughed at her and told her she was ruining her life. Her book is currently number six on the *Sunday Times* best-seller list. She dedicated it to her Boston terrier.

Rachel kisses my cheek and then stands back to look at me. I've tried so hard to look like Leah does for these sessions: skinny jeans and a chunky jumper, hair in a messy bun, glasses on my nose that don't actually change my vision at all. She narrows her eyes and I feel dizzy, like I'm about to faint. This is it. The moment it all comes crashing down.

'You can tell me all the juicy details later,' she says with an exaggerated wink.

'Tell you what?' There's a roaring in my ears, like a wave about to break and drown me.

'All about whoever has given you such a glow, you lucky thing!' Her laugh is big and salacious.

Once everyone has settled in the living room, I bring in champagne and margaritas and take a seat. They are all watching me; I assume that as host I'm expected to lead the discussion. 'So,' I say, picking up a copy of the book from the coffee table. 'What did we all think?'

The others turn to look at each other, confusion on their faces. Have I got this all wrong? But they don't look suspicious. They look. . . well. . . disappointed.

'*You* read it?' The derision in Rachel's voice is clear.

'Err, yes.' Did Leah not usually even bother to read the book?

'Well, that's a first,' Kira says, like she doesn't think I'd be capable. I don't think I like Kira. Although I imagine she is probably Leah's favourite; she always did flock to the other bitchy girls.

'Oh, God! Does that mean we actually have to talk about it?' Amy downs the rest of her glass as she continues to throw me plaintive looks.

'So much for the drill, Leah,' says Rachel, shaking her head.

I realise my role within this group. I am the stupid one. The one the others laugh at. I wonder if Leah knew? So, I do what I have to. I burst into laughter. 'Oh. My. God! You should have seen your faces! Of course I didn't read the book! What do you take me for?'

I watch the others visibly relax.

'Thank God,' Joey says as she holds the book up and tries to find a way to get her selfie pout and the book jacket into the same photo without it looking like she has a double chin.

'Right then,' Rachel says as she digs around in the large handbag by her feet and pulls out an electronic vape contraption that looks like a battery pack for a small robot. 'I bought the super strong one.' She presses a button as she inhales deeply on the pipe end, closing her eyes as the vapour clouds around her head. 'Damn that's good. . .'

The vape contains a potent cannabis blend and within ten minutes the women are looking a lot more relaxed, lounging around the living room. There is obviously no intention to talk about the book at all. I pour more champagne for them. I have never been into drugs – I mean, of course I had the odd toke on a communal spliff at university, but that was the extent of it. I'd pretended to take half an ecstasy tablet in a nightclub toilet when I was eighteen, out on the town with a group of slightly older colleagues from the pub I worked in for the summer. Leah had come with us and had swallowed the tablet eagerly, swilled down by the brilliant blue of a bottle of WKD. I'd tried to smuggle her back into the house so our parents didn't see her. But we had been caught.

Dad had come back the February before our eighteenth birthday with his tail between his legs, begging Mum for forgiveness. For the first month he had been there all the time, leaving only to go to work and coming home straight after, spending the weekends taking Mum away on elaborate breaks to seaside towns hours from home. Then he had started to take on some 'extra work', work that involved him being away on his own at the weekends. Of course, Leah and I knew the truth. His first wife had kicked him out and so he had come to Mum. But then Kath had begun to thaw and let him home, so he tried once again to balance things. Mum was blind and let him stay, although his visits were increasingly erratic for almost six months before he finally went back to Kath full time.

Mum had blamed Leah and me for him leaving. Blamed the shame of his daughters going out and taking drugs and being disrespectful. We had been grounded for a month and I had missed my freshers' week at university.

Leah had always been more experimental, and I had always been the one to pick up the pieces of her life when the wheels finally came off. Although, that's a rubbish analogy, because actually she never did total her car, despite her insistence that it was OK to drive as long as she could count the drinks she'd had. I was the one who had the crash, rolled the car in a ditch and had to be cut out by the fire brigade. Somehow though, I had escaped with only a faint scar, like silver thread, running just under the hairline at the back of my neck, which you'd only know about if I pointed it out in bright sunlight. And I never talk about it; it always feels like that would be tempting fate. Especially as I told the police at the scene, and the doctors, that I was Leah. It was her car I was driving; I had her wallet in my bag so I could use her debit card to buy cigarettes, and the lie rolled off my tongue before I could stop myself. I had failed my driving test the week before, but Leah wanted fags and convinced me it'd all be OK.

Despite having to act as the stupid one of the group, I'm actually enjoying book club. I'm not really one for big girlie gatherings and prefer to be part of a smaller group, but these women are a lot of fun. They also don't seem to have noticed that I'm not taking my turn to puff on the vape, preferring instead to slowly succumb to the softening effect of a very expensive Sancerre. The wine is crisp and cool on my tongue with a hint of citrus and something almost akin to starfruit; it might have become my new favourite if it wasn't almost thirty quid a bottle. I'm only having two glasses though. I can't afford to let my guard down, even if these women don't seem particularly observant.

I have just refilled the little bowls of nuts and olives – the vape is obviously making everyone hungry – when Kira comes back from using the bathroom. She is holding something that glints in the light of the scattered candles.

'Something you need to tell us?' she asks me, holding out the object. It is my engagement ring, all two and a half carats of it. I'd put it in the drawer of the bedside table. *Hadn't I?* Time hangs suspended as I remember I left it in a little glass of gin in the en suite to clean it. Fuck! How the hell can I explain this?

'Ooh!' squeals Joey. 'Let me see!' She grabs it and holds it up to the light, turning it this way and that. 'So, who is he, Leah?'

Four pairs of eyes bore into me as they wait for my answer. I'm frozen to the spot, trying desperately to come up with something. Anything.

'It's just costume jewellery,' I blurt out. It's the best I can do.

Amy lunges for it. 'This is a real diamond, Leah.' How the hell does she know? 'Bigger than two carats but less than three.' She looks even closer. 'Good quality, not flawless but not too bad. I'd estimate somewhere around the twenty grand mark.' Chris spent fifteen on it, so she's not too far off. I had been so livid with him when he bought it.

'So, Missy.' Kira is standing over me. I definitely don't like her. 'Who is he and why are you holding out on us?'

'Oh. My. God,' Joey suddenly wails. 'I know!' I stare at her. She's nodding her head and scrolling furiously through her Instagram feed. 'Yep, yep, yep,' she says, still scrolling. What is she looking for? Eventually she stops and shows the picture on her phone to everyone except me. I wait to see my fate, trying to decipher the looks on the others' faces. Eventually, she shows me the phone. The picture is of Leah and Jabir, the disgraced prince, having cosy cocktails a few weeks ago.

Kira pales. 'Oh, Leah.' Her voice drips with pity and disappointment. 'You didn't.' Not a question. I don't think the implication is that Leah is engaged to this man, but that he buys certain women trinkets.

'*God no!*' I stand up and grab the ring, plunging it on to the fourth finger of my right hand. It is too small but I try to avoid wincing. 'Look, I bought it for myself, OK? A girl I was at school with got engaged, she's the last of my old friends who was single. I treated myself.'

'To a twenty-grand diamond?' There is an edge of resentment in Kira's voice. I'm assuming that writing about your husband's masturbatory habits doesn't pay as well as trashing your entire family does.

'Yes. Now can we move on, please?' The ring is cutting off my circulation but I will have to wait until they leave to remove it.

I had to use olive oil in the end to get it off. The only one Leah had was infused with basil. So now the ring is sitting in gin again to try to get rid of the smell.

***

On Wednesday, Tom invites me out for a drink. He's heading away for a few days and wants to see me first.

'Alright. . . I know this is going to sound crazy.' He grins at me, once we're sitting down with a glass of wine. 'But just hear me out, OK?'

I nod. His enthusiasm is infectious, my disquiet from an earlier argument with Chris all but forgotten.

'Come to Vegas with me.'

'Vegas? When?'

'Tonight. I'm giving a speech at a conference but aside from that I'd be free.'

'Tonight?' I can't go to Vegas. What would I tell Chris? But I think back to this afternoon, when I'd FaceTimed him from another anonymous coffee shop and he'd been in a foul mood. Swearing about someone he worked with and how 'the fucking imbecile had messed shit up' and he had to go away for a few days to fix it. He'd been expecting me to calm him down, layer on the platitudes and sympathy like I normally did, but I just didn't have the energy. He wouldn't even know I'd gone anywhere. And I'd be using Leah's passport, so no need to get mine from the safe back in Guildford.

To Tom I say, 'I can't go to Vegas tonight. I don't have any stuff with me.'

'Buy it out there. The shopping is fantastic. All you need is your passport.'

'What about a visa?'

'ESTA. Online application, instant acceptance. Unless you've committed a crime you should tell me about?'

Well, yes actually – I kind of killed someone. My mind fills with an image of her. Blood pooling on the deck. But I shake it away and force a smile instead. Do they have retinal scanners at the airport? Our faces are the same, but a retinal scan would tell us apart as if we were strangers. I can't risk it.

He is bouncing up and down in his seat like an excited child, willing me to say yes. 'Please, please, please. I'll teach you to play blackjack. . .'

'You'll teach me?' I raise an eyebrow. I helped finance my masters programme dealing cards in a seedy casino just off the

Brighton seafront. Although of course that was me, Megan and not me, Leah.

We get another drink while I think about it. In the end, the clincher is a message from Chris to Leah. I've been keeping him at arm's length but he's obviously had enough of Leah's rejections: *We need to talk. I'm coming over.*

No, you're not, I think. 'Let's do it!' I tell Tom, who jumps up and does a funny little dance in celebration. 'Now,' I add. He doesn't need persuading and soon we're in a taxi, speeding to Leah's house. I run inside to grab her passport, then throw myself back into the cab, giggling as we pull away just as Chris's car turns on to the street.

To Vegas! Because, even if there are retinal scans and fingerprint thingies, they will think it's an error on their side before they think I am a killer posing as my identical twin. Occam's Razor in action.

Chapter Ten

We breeze through Heathrow. It's quiet at this late hour, with no queues for security. No one looks twice at my passport and I feel myself beginning to relax. Even the sight of a whole group of other travellers in face masks trying to decipher some tiny poster about how the virus breakout in Italy has worsened doesn't really bother me. I stop to buy a book for the flight and my eye is drawn to the dark red and black cover of a novel called *It Wasn't Me*. 'Amy Monaghan at her chill-creating best', the jacket review promises. This is the novel Amy from my book club has just had optioned by Sky. It is about a woman trying to prove she's innocent of the murder she is accused of.

The cashier wishes us 'happy hols'. Tom leans in and whispers, 'God, I hate it when people say hols.'

I turn my head to kiss him full on the lips in agreement. 'Me too. Now, let's go get a cocktail.'

I have never been first class on a flight before. Business class, yes. I travel a bit for work and it is one of the small perks that tries to make up for the soul-destroying reality of getting off a plane and knowing you won't see any of the country you are visiting. That your meetings will be conducted in a sterile office block that could be anywhere, always in English, and they will serve you insipid tea because it is 'what Brits like'. It's not. I love chai, and that coffee in France you can stand a spoon in, and a fluffy frappe in Athens. But you can't say anything and instead must sip the dishwater like it's a delicacy while you thank them profusely for their misguided hospitality. Now I have experienced first class I will never want to sit in the cramped confines of economy again.

Half an hour into the flight and Tom puts down his book – some intellectual-looking literary thing that has won too many awards to count – turning himself to look at me across the vast distance between the seats. He leans over to say, 'I have to ask you a serious question.' His eyes are heavy with the enormity of what he is about to ask and I hold my breath as I wait for a life-changer. 'Do you want to do the whole mile-high club thing?' I had expected something profound and so I laugh at the unexpectedness of his question. He grins. 'Thank God! I was crossing my fingers that you didn't jump at the chance!'

'It's just that aeroplane toilets are so. . .' I grope for the word.

'Janky?' he suggests.

'Exactly.' We smile at each other.

'So now that's sorted, I'm going to have another drink.' Tom politely motions to the air steward and settles back into his seat to continue his book.

I peek at him, with his furrowed brow, and breathe a sigh of relief that he's not that kind of weirdo. Because Chris would always pester and try to cajole, but, especially in cattle class – with toilets so narrow anyone bigger than a size eight struggles to even turn round – it just wasn't my idea of fun. I'm not a prude, however many times Leah used to call me one when we were younger, or the few times Chris tried to push things and then got shitty about how I was frigid and harped on about my responsibility for his needs.

It turned out that Leah hadn't entered the US on her current passport and hadn't had an ESTA for a few years. We sail through border control at McCarran Airport. Well, not sail exactly; the crawling queue stretches for hours. Luckily, as first-class passengers, we don't have to wait as long as all that.

And at least the queue is a spectacle in and of itself. I can see a group of guys about my age, six of them dressed in jeans and T-shirts while the seventh is in a ballet tutu and a pair of fairy wings. They are hammered, almost incapable of standing. In front of them is another stag party. This time the stag has been dressed as a giant baby, complete with a nappy and an oversized dummy hanging round his neck. There is a stain down the nappy that I really hope is red wine. Further down the queue I spot a family: Mum, Dad and two teenage daughters, all wearing onesies in the design of the American flag. At least they will be warm when they step outside: March in Vegas is winter, and it is currently about ten degrees Celsius out there. The two guys in their Hawaiian shirts and flip-flops are going to be freezing, as are the two women I assume are their girlfriends with their overly made-up faces and tiny bodycon dresses.

We finally get to the front of the queue, to find that the man from border control is a bear with a long beard and a permanent smile on his face. It is a little disconcerting to have such an affable man ask you to place your right hand on the fingerprint scanner. Especially as you are holding your breath and praying that it doesn't flash up with some kind of error. Fingerprints are like retinal scans – unique, formed in the uterus by the developing baby touching its tiny closed universe.

But the bear is not paying much attention to the scanner. 'Business or pleasure?'

'Pleasure. Just a few days away.' I try to smile, fingers still pressed against the glass.

'Well, have fun. And good luck!'

And I'm through and nothing bad has happened and Tom grabs my hand and swings my arm as he skips – literally skips – down the corridor to claim his suitcase. 'I took the liberty of having the hotel concierge pick you up an outfit for this evening.' he says. 'Then you have tomorrow to shop while I deliver my very dull speech.'

'What's it on?'

He looks at me from under those long lashes. 'You'll be bored with just the title.' There is a hint of a smile at the corner of his mouth.

'Try me.'

'How the rise in micro-transaction forex trading has led to anomalous positions that may threaten unstable infant democracies, and what responsible nations can do to assist in smoothing short-term fluctuations.'

No wonder he thought Leah would be bored. But I'm an accountant with a side interest in politics and I want to know more. I'd love to watch him give his speech, but I know that even this moderated version of Leah I am with him wouldn't. So instead I giggle. 'And people pay you to talk about this stuff?'

'They pay me a lot.' He shrugs. I want to touch his face and tell him that I think he's brilliant, but I pull my hand back. If only I could introduce him properly to Fi. Not so that she could have him, but so she'd be impressed that a man like this is interested in me. Unlike when she met Chris and he tried to mansplain the US bond market to her, despite that having been the subject of her masters dissertation. Which she got from Yale. So, yeah, she definitely knew more than he did.

'Let's go find our hotel,' I say to Tom instead.

I've always had this picture in my mind of brilliant azure skies and the sun beating down on the bevy of half-dressed revellers spilling from the bars and casinos on to the Strip. But today the sky is a soft baby blue, the sun gently warming through the jumper I am wearing. Even the showgirls, parading up and down outside the big hotels, taking photos for tip money, are wearing tights under their skimpy thongs.

You see Las Vegas on TV and it looks like a gaudy nightmare of hotels crushed up against each other. The reality is so vastly different. We have a reservation in a restaurant two hotels up the Strip from where we are staying. We think we can walk it in about two minutes; after all, the sign is clearly visible – how far can it be?

We are still walking thirty minutes later, the sign growing in front of me only slowly as my feet weep for mercy. The sign, which I had assumed was, well sign-sized, is in fact about five storeys tall. The scale of the place blows me away. There are over four thousand rooms in our hotel, about the same as the population of a mid-sized village. Madness. True madness. But I love it.

The dinner we have is exquisite. Bacon-wrapped shrimp to start, really living up to the idea that everything tastes better when you add bacon. For the main course there is pepper-crusted New York strip. I am too full for dessert, but Tom orders warm chocolate cake with two spoons, which turns out to be the perfect end to a perfect evening. We wander very slowly back to our hotel, past the fountains and the dazzling lights shining in the desert. I feel almost disembodied, the jetlag, lack of sleep, huge meal, the wine, lights, and the warmth of Tom next to me combining to make my head spin.

On the casino floor of our hotel, Tom puts his arm round my waist to steady me. 'Bed?' he asks softly. I nod dumbly and let him lead me past the din of the slot machines and shouts and squeals from people playing table games. Vegas will still be here tomorrow, when I can actually appreciate it properly.

The next day I take myself for a walk through the swanky shopping centre in Caesars Palace. When I say shopping centre, that might bring to mind somewhere like Westfield. This is not like Westfield. It is like a small and very exclusive high street, shops on either side of a pedestrian thoroughfare, restaurants and cafes in the middle, interspersed with fountains and sculptures. I treat myself to some designer – 7 For All Mankind no less – jeans and pay an exorbitant sum for a cashmere sweater in the most beautiful hunter green. Walking past Agent Provocateur, I decide to get Tom a treat. One look at my colouring had the shop assistant turning to select an electric-blue set, but I swiftly shut her down. 'Burgundy,' I tell her. Tom's favourite colour. Soft silk and a touch of lace; demure, sophisticated and it makes me feel sexy as hell. Perfect.

You know the montage they always use in films? The one where the protagonist is doing one hundred things in quick succession, scene after scene flashing by, as he trains for a fight, or goes on a road trip, or falls in love? I have never thought real life was like that. Until this trip.

The next two days race by, leaving me an assault on the senses and a collection of memories I will treasure.

The cool night air blowing my hair as the taxi speeds down the Strip.

The scent of vanilla in the hotel reception.

The noise of a thousand slot machines ringing and hundreds of chattering men and women gambling.

Sugar-bombs of alcoholic slush drinks in huge novelty cups.

The collective gasp of the audience as the acrobat performs a death-defying aerial display.

The feel of the dice in my hand as I throw them for the first time, praying that they don't bounce out of the craps pit and into the casino.

The taste of rosemary and salt on my lips from the best fries I have ever had, followed by a pizza so loaded with toppings we had to use a knife and fork.

The communal exhalation of a heads-back 'Wow!' as everyone looks toward the light show on the canopy above them.

The view from the top of the replica Eiffel Tower, timed perfectly to coincide with the fountain show.

We wake up early on the morning of our last full day. Tom has a craving for fried chicken and waffles, a very un-British combination that had made no sense to me. Until I tried it and discovered that you could drown fried chicken in maple syrup and it would taste divine. As we are walking through the casino to the street, we pass a table of slightly drunk Irish guys obviously still up from the night before. They are playing a form of table poker against the dealer, whooping and hollering and generally acting like idiots.

Tom is drawn to random encounters, to sharing the experiences of others in a way that most people would feel uncomfortable doing. 'Shall we join in?' He raises an eyebrow.

'Poker?' There are a hundred varieties, all subtly different, a complete mishmash of rules and plays that I don't know every permutation of, despite my dealer background.

'We'll wing it,' Tom says.

In a casino the house always wins, every game designed for money to move one way, even if you don't realise it at the time. You can help yourself by at least knowing the rules of the game you are playing. To do anything else is to piss money up a wall.

Tom laughs at the serious look on my face. 'Oh, come on!' He grabs my hand to pull me towards them. 'It'll be fun!' Perhaps former accountants have a different idea of fun when it comes to putting your own money on a small circle of felt?

Tom and I slide on to the high stools and hand over our little stack of crisp notes to the dealer. We start small, a five-dollar bet here, another five dollars there. The odd dollar on the side bets. Despite it being nine in the morning and pre-breakfast, we have a glass of champagne. We play a bit more. The Irish are raucous. We have another glass of champagne. And then, as the cards start to swim, I suggest we call it a day and head for those waffles. We have fifty dollars left from our initial stake. With a shrug, Tom pops one of the green chips on to the ante marker. 'In for a penny,' he says under his breath, 'well. . . cent, I suppose.' A suited king and queen are dealt to him. With a shrug he pops the other green chip on the play marker. Fifty dollars waged on a single turn of the cards. Cards that are turned one by one: jack of hearts, ace of hearts, ten of hearts. A royal flush. Five hundred to one. Twenty-five thousand dollars!

After breakfast, with more champagne proving to be a delightful accompaniment to fried chicken, we weave our way through the throngs towards the Forum shops. The ceiling is painted to look like a real sky, the clouds moving against the blue. It's a pure illusion, but the effect is magical when you're sober and utterly enthralling if you've been chugging champagne for the past few hours. Tom is leading the way, the speed of his stride urgent, wanting to get to his destination.

'Ta-da!' he trills as we turn the corner. We are outside the exorbitantly expensive watch shop I had slowed down passing the other day. For over a decade, I had promised myself that one day I would buy a proper watch. Not a cheap one made in China, or even a high-fashion brand with a fancy face; no, a proper one, made by a real horologist in a small workshop somewhere. But I have never yet been able to justify the expense.

'I saw the way you looked as we walked past the other day.' Tom pulls me into an embrace, his breath on my neck. 'Like this was the best doughnut shop in the world and you were starving.' He pulls away to look me in the eye. 'Let me treat you, please?'

I look into those green eyes and shake my head. 'They are thousands of dollars, Tom.'

'Didn't I just win twenty-five grand?' He raises an eyebrow. 'Please?'

The funny thing is, I could get Leah's platinum card out right now and buy anything I wanted from Jaeger-LeCoultre. But it would mean nothing. I nod mutely and let Tom lead me inside. The boutique is small and exudes a kind of hushed luxury, like visiting a very intimate museum or the library of a well-respected university professor.

I choose a simple small timepiece with a classic face and a strap in the softest dark burgundy leather. It is the most beautiful thing

I have ever owned. Tom chooses a similarly classic style but with a stainless-steel bracelet and blue toning on the face. He hands over almost twenty thousand dollars in cash like it is nothing. The watches are so expensive that we have to complete registration documents for them. It is the first time I have signed Leah's name. Muscle memory kicks in; I used to sign all kinds of things for her when we were younger.

We spend the rest of the day exploring various attractions on the Strip, including taking a limo to the Las Vegas sign. The day ends with dinner at the top of the Strat, the entire Strip illuminated beneath us.

Back in the hotel, we order more champagne and make love wearing nothing but the watches.

Maybe I should whisper it. *I like Leah*. The Leah I am when I'm with him. She's fun and relaxed and evidently a bit witty, as she makes him laugh a lot. She's happy and it shows. I'm happy. Holy fuck.

Chapter Eleven

On the flight home I allow myself to dream a little. What if. . . What if Tom and I could have a future? What if it could be more than just a few snatched days in Vegas?

We are somewhere over the Atlantic when I sit bolt upright. Because what if? What if it was Megan who went away? Megan who decided that life was shit and she should start over somewhere else? Her husband was cheating on her. Her job was not quite what she had dreamed about when she was a little girl. She had a fair bit of debt. I don't actually have any debt, but it would be easy to rack some up. Megan could disappear somewhere, slip away from Chris's clutches in a way I had never before dreamed was possible.

I have thought of how to escape the confines of my marriage. Of course I have. You didn't think I wanted to stay married to him, did you? But I knew that he would never let me go. Not amicably, not in a way that let me keep anything I loved. He held me hostage in my own life. 'I would be lost without you,' he had told me once. 'Unanchored. Set adrift. And who knows what I would do then.' I knew he would hunt me down and hurt me. It was that simple. I had thought about running away, going somewhere far enough from him that he would never find me, leaving everything and everyone behind. The problem being that I couldn't abandon Mum. But if I became Leah, permanently became her, then I could visit as her. I could still have a mum, and she could still have a daughter.

Leah could leave the whole influencer bullshit behind, because I could live very well on the money she had already made, thank you very much, and I don't want to spend my life going to parties for likes and taking dodgy men to dodgy bars for money. It might have been a lot of money and I'm fairly sure Leah did not know who that man was, but I know and there is not enough money in the world to make me drink with a terrorist. Plus, she had turned him down. Emma thought it was good, that he'd want her more. But he had a reputation for just taking what he wanted if it wasn't offered, and I didn't want to be anywhere near that kind of shit.

Could I do it? Could I make Megan disappear and make it look convincing?

Heathrow is quieter than normal as we pass through. Queues thinner, a sense of something in the air. 'France went into full lockdown,' Tom tells me as we walk through Customs. 'People are getting jumpy, but I'm sure we don't really need to worry.'

I'll be honest, the virus isn't really on my radar. I've seen the news headlines of hospitals in Italy, but it isn't going to make it here. There'd been a super-spreader outbreak in Brighton last month; some poor guy who will probably carry that label for life had infected eight people after he returned from Thailand or Hong Kong or somewhere. But it had fizzled out. Apparently, there's been a strange run on the supermarkets and the shelves are empty of toilet rolls, hand sanitiser and pasta; but otherwise it's nothing. In December, Chris's mum, Valma, had ordered one hundred rolls of three-ply toilet paper for the bargain price of fifty pounds. At the time, I didn't have the heart to tell her that was actually more expensive than Tesco. But then one hundred nine-packs turned up on their driveway and I had to concede that it was a good price after all. Plus, we now have over a dozen stacked in the cupboard under the stairs. I must remember to bring a few up to London after the weekend.

But now I have to head back to Guildford and face my husband. Or at least start to work out how I can get away from him. What always felt like an impossibility now only just out of reach. But if I lean hard enough, just maybe my fingers can graze the very edge and I can pull it towards me inch by inch until I take flight. Imagine a life with Tom. Imagine a life without Chris.

I've noticed that whenever Chris and I are together, he spends a lot more time sending messages to Leah than when we are apart. It must turn him on to watch me and think about her. It makes my skin crawl. So far, I have been able to keep him at arm's length by deliberately making Leah's diary incompatible with his. I am biding my time before I break things off fully between them. It might be helpful, when Megan disappears, to have him feel he can confide in Leah. It might help me stay ahead of him if I know what he's thinking.

Back in Guildford, I message him – as Leah – and ask him if he could slip away that weekend, meet me at the cabin for a night of illicit fun. It's his mum's birthday this weekend and we are decamping to Tunbridge Wells to celebrate.

'Megan!' I'm sequestered in the bathroom, ostensibly dying my hair to cover the grey but really fielding his messages to Leah and my own to Tom.

'What?' I hate it when he interrupts me in the bathroom.

'No need to snap,' he calls back cheerily. 'Do you remember if Mum said she had anything planned for the Saturday?'

'Not sure. Why?' I know exactly why, of course. *I bought some new toys*, I text from Leah. I found a box of things under her bed and previous messages from the real her to Chris. I know he will like this.

'Just work. You know how it is, Meggie.'

I know exactly how it is. *I want you*, I text. 'Your mum is probably cooking,' I shout.

'Yeah. Probably.' He sounds defeated.

'Do you want me to ask her?' The good wife. *I want you to fuck me until I scream your name*, I text.

'Please,' he calls back. *Touch yourself*, he texts to Leah.

Not until you promise you'll come on Saturday, I reply.

Of course, on Saturday we are sitting at his parents' large wooden kitchen table, drinking wine as Val puts the finishing touches to the stew she has been slaving over all day. When I had called her, I'd told her that Chris was working too hard and needed a break, and would she please call him to insist we still came on the Saturday. So, here we are. Chris can never defy his mother. Even for all the filthy things Leah promised him. And the passive-aggressive message she sent this afternoon. Leah gets pretty grumpy when she doesn't get what she wants.

When he follows his dad outside to review the garden, I send him one more message as Leah: *I can't believe you didn't find some excuse and come anyway. Just think what we could be doing right now. I haven't seen you for ages and I ache for your touch. But I won't wait for ever.*

What did you expect this weekend? he messages back.

You, I reply.

Oh, come on Leah. That's not fair.

I turn off the phone and bury it in my bag. I know he'll be pissed off at her for interrupting his family time. Time with his wife is obviously irrelevant, but he'll be mad she messaged while he's with his parents.

'Are you OK, Megs?' Val asks, putting a large glass of red in front of me.

'Sure.' I smile and take a swig.

'You seem. . . I don't know, distant, I suppose.' Concern drips from her voice. Sometimes I can hardly believe that Chris was born from this lovely, bubbly, kind woman in front of me. How could someone so *nice* produce a son like that?

'Just tired.' That old chestnut. 'Work, you know.'

She stares at me for longer than would be customary and I take another gulp of wine to hide how uncomfortable she is making me. Eventually, she huffs out the breath she was holding. Her gaze is trained on the door to the garden, one of those old-fashioned ones where both halves move independently. 'Does he. . .' Her voice trails off. 'I mean. . .' She clears her throat. 'If. . .' She grabs my hand and the words come tumbling out. 'If he hurts you, I can help. Help you get free.' Then her hands are once more on her side of the table and she is smiling as she stands.

'You must be freezing!' The men are back. She throws me a horrified glance over her shoulder. I'm assuming that

Mr Hardcastle isn't always the teddy bear you would think either.

Later that night, I manage to get Val alone once again for a few moments. 'It's all fine,' I tell her, squeezing her hand gently. 'Nothing I can't handle anyway.' She smiles and nods but there is a tear in her eye. When Megan leaves him, she won't be surprised. I kind of wish I could take her with me.

The next day we meet Chris's sister Fran and her family at the pub for lunch. She and her husband Marcus have two little boys, George and Arlo, who are polite and well mannered. At least until they have chocolate cake and ice cream; there is then a half-hour window when they go batshit crazy, but they soon calm down after being released into the beer garden to run a few laps.

Fran is like a miniature version of her mum, except for one notable difference. She thinks the sun shines from her big brother's backside. 'You'll make such a fabulous father,' she coos at him as he plays with his nephews. 'I can't wait to be an auntie,' she goes on, 'and these boys need some cousins to play with.' Then she turns to me to add, 'Better not leave it too long though, eh? Not if you're going to have three.'

'Three?' I ask.

'At least. That's what you always said, Chrissy, isn't it?' She is the only person in the world who gets away with calling him that.

'Leave them alone.' Val tries to come to my rescue.

'But, Mum, you have to admit that Megan is getting on a bit if she's going to have more than two. I just don't want Chrissy's time to run out as a result.'

Fran never really warmed to me. I don't think I was ever good enough for her darling Chrissy. She was never outwardly hostile; her comments taken in context could be deemed innocuous. Except when she'd got pissed at my hen do. 'I never thought he'd marry someone like you,' she had slurred into her fourth strawberry daiquiri. 'You're so. . . so. . .blah.' She had waved her hand in my face to illustrate her point. 'Like you're a sepia photo of just. . . nothing interesting.'

If she thought he had married down, I thought she had married up. Marcus is a true gentleman and the real reason behind the boys' good manners. Without his steadying influence in her life, I dread to think what kind of a wreck she would have turned out to be.

After lunch we say our goodbyes and drive back to Guildford so I can start packing for the week ahead. I've told Chris I need to travel tonight to get a head start on a new project.

'Where to this time?' He is sitting on the end of the bed watching me.

'Milton Keynes.' I make a face.

'Video call me when you get there?' he says. 'I want to see the lovely hotel they have you staying in!'

It used to be a joke, back at the beginning. Which of us was staying at the worse place that week. We used to have a competition where we would find the most offensive item in our respective rooms and place it on the bedside table while we video called. But tonight, I was hoping to go straight to Leah's and have a lovely long bath before prepping for the presentation I have to give tomorrow. I'm not actually working in Milton

Keynes; my new client is very conveniently based just alongside the London Business School by Regent's Park. I could walk it in under half an hour from Leah's house.

Instead, I spend my evening schlepping up the M1 and finding a Holiday Inn. I pay for three nights as Megan Hardcastle, just in case Chris decides to call the hotel feigning some emergency. In the room, I video call him and walk through the room and its amenities.

It is gone midnight before I make it to Leah's.

The next day Chris rings my mobile just after six. 'Did you watch?' No pleasantries to open the conversation.

I don't reply. I am too busy trying to juggle two lives and driving unnecessarily to fucking Milton Keynes to have time for TV, for God's sake.

'The prime minister. Did you watch the press conference?'

'No.' What have I missed?

'He's telling everyone to avoid unnecessary travel, not go to the pub and work from home.'

'Why?'

'Are you stupid? This virus thing.'

'Oh, that. I'm too busy right now. Look, I'll be home on Friday, OK?' This week was kind of crucial to my Free Megan campaign.

That's what I'd started to call it in my head: Free Megan. The idea that Megan was trapped and needed someone to emancipate her. I had always told myself that I was strong, that I was a survivor and that whatever happened I would be OK. Now I think of myself in the third person like someone I need to rescue.

I have decided that Megan is going to run away. Leave enough clues that people know I have gone, but not enough that they know where to look for me. It is vital there is no suggestion of foul play, no inkling that Chris has done something awful. But at the same time, I don't want Chris to go looking and realise there is no one to find.

I use my work laptop for most of the planning, knowing that it will create a digital footprint just in case there ever is an investigation. There is a mammoth spreadsheet containing a list of the forty-five things I need to do before I go. I have searched flights to far-flung places like Malaysia and Thailand. Travel restrictions are being put on some places and so I'm making sure to keep an eye on the situation. I'll have to jump soon. I order a few things to be delivered to the hotel in Milton Keynes: language-learning books; guidebooks; a universal adaptor thing that could convert any plug on the planet to English. A girl couldn't be without her hair straighteners after all. The high-quality backpack that cost two hundred and fifty pounds, with the tagline 'the world's most practical backpack' which I figure someone hyper-organised like me would order, is delivered to my London office.

If you were to pack your life into a single bag and walk away, what would you take? There is another spreadsheet that contains an extraordinarily detailed list, including the dimensions and weight of each item. I am constantly adjusting and updating it, saving it often. Making the maximum number of imprints on to the work server, just in case. I mean, obviously I'm not ever going to actually pack this bag, but I am a planner, and everyone knows this. I'm a little notorious for lists. I even have one of those productivity diaries, where I write down everything I want to do each day, ticking things off as I go along. Creating an everlasting journal of the micro-achievements of each and every day. People may laugh but I get a hell of a lot done. Or at least that's what I tell people; it sounds a lot better than admitting I write everything down because I don't trust my own memories. I have to approach Free Megan with the same tenacity that would be expected of me.

In addition to the stuff on my laptop, I keep a separate list. In a scrappy little notebook. No digital footprint of the truth of what I was doing, the t's to cross and i's to dot to be sure I lay a trail that is convincing without ever alerting anyone to foul play.

I am careful and meticulous. There is too much at stake now.

I begin to consolidate my money, cashing in my premium bonds and selling the handful of shares that I own. Chris and I have a joint account, which might prove tricky. We had opened it the day after we came back from our honeymoon. Drunk on love, high on a post-coital buzz, sleep-deprived and jetlagged, we had walked hand in hand to the bank at the top of the high street and proudly showed our marriage certificate to the uninterested woman sitting in front of us. Every month I would transfer seventy-five per cent of my salary to this account and ten per cent to our joint savings, and use the remaining fifteen per cent to pay a contribution towards Mum's care. Strictly speaking it's a state facility, but I top up the basic level of care provision, ensuring Mum gets slightly better food, someone to sit with her a few hours a day, someone who gives a small shit if she has been bathed in the past week.

Mum's care was another of the things Leah and I had argued about. I wanted the best for her, for her to be comfortable, peaceful, even pampered a little. Leah said it was a big old waste of money, that Mum had no idea who she was, who we were, where she was. Even though Leah made all that money from selling *our* story, she still wouldn't pay.

'Why bother?' She had shrugged her shoulders as she said it, barely glancing up from her phone. 'What's the point if she doesn't even realise?'

But what if she did? And even if she didn't, I wasn't going to let her sit in her own mess, eating the same old gruel day in and day out as she withered away to nothing. She is still my mum.

Chris had agreed with me, at first at least. Told me that of course he didn't mind if some of my salary went to help her. Note how I say my salary. When he wanted nice things, it was our money. When it was for Mum, it was mine.

Two years ago, I was offered a promotion with my company. We don't really have job titles per se, at least not ones that show our seniority. I am simply a 'consultant'. But we have a complicated banding system that is used internally to show hierarchy, and which determines the salary and perks we can enjoy. I didn't bother to tell Chris that I had leapfrogged two tiers and was now technically the second most senior person within my division. Nor did I tell him that my salary had jumped by over forty grand a year since then. That extra money I syphoned off into a separate savings account. The bonus I'd had last year I had squirrelled away too. The fund was there just in case. Just in case the Patterson curse does catch me. Perhaps there would be some comfort for me if I, too, ended up at the Jonas Institute.

I write a cheque to the manager of the Institute, instructing him to take it as an upfront payment for Mum's extras for the next two years. I will mail it from Heathrow as Megan's parting gift before she flew away. At least Mum won't suffer when her daughter vanishes into thin air.

There is a huge stumbling block to my plan, one that I have racked my brain to find a solution for. What do I do about the body?

Ideally, I want it – her – to disappear and never be found.

Could I use acid? I worked with a company once that stored chemicals in these huge great tanks in a scummy industrial area. There was a story doing the rounds about this company at the time, and I was never sure if it was an old wives' tale or actually true. Apparently, this guy who worked there had found out his wife was having an affair and had killed the boyfriend. To hide the body he stuffed it into one of these tanks, which held hydrochloric acid, figuring the body would dissolve over time. Then he got made redundant. Five years later, the tank was emptied for decommissioning. Inside was the perfectly preserved body of a man, looking pretty much as he did on the day he had died. The idiot had stuffed the guy into the wrong tank and put him in a preservative instead.

Given that I have no idea about chemicals, and even the experts are capable of fucking it up, I don't think acid is the answer.

Could I burn her? You see it all the time in films and things – just slip the body into an incinerator. Like it's that easy. Like everyone has access to an incinerator.

Could I bury her? In some deep dark woods somewhere where no one will find her? I'm sure I read something once about people adding lye to a shallow grave to help destroy the body.

What about water? Weigh her body down and push it off a bridge to sink into oblivion. But what bridge? And what deep body of oblivious water when we live in Guildford?

This is all too ghastly to comprehend. I am trying not to see my sister's face as I contemplate doing something so heinous.

I am drinking gin. Neat. Not even bothering with ice. It is probably a bad idea just before bedtime.

A thousand hands claw at me. Hands with a deathly pallor and the remnants of a French manicure; the nails chipped, skin jagged around the cuticle and a line of mud clearly visible. My eyes fly open but still I'm fighting in the pitch black that blankets me, hands clawing at my body, my neck. Just as I manage to break free, I realise I'm in Leah's bed, her sheets twisted around me. Before I went to sleep I'd decided I would bury her, somewhere far away from anywhere. But I can't do that now. Those hands in my nightmare were hers. We have always both hated nail varnish in gaudy colours; I read a magazine article about the royal family when we were twelve – they are not allowed to wear coloured polish, apparently. This always stuck with both of us.

For now, I'm planning to bring the body to Leah's house in London. I'll get the freezer – no need to even look inside – and put it in the garage where I can keep an eye on it. No one is going to suspect that Megan has been murdered, and so no one will come looking for a body. And as long as no one finds the body, everything is OK. It'll do. For a while at least. I'll need to hire a van. But first I'll need to find a hire company who won't ask too many questions.

***

'Please make sure you're staying safe, Meggie,' Chris tells me the day before I head home to tie up some more loose ends.

'Of course.' I dismiss his concerns and continue to stare at the handwritten list in my lap. Almost there. Just a few more days.

'This is serious, Meggie.'

I wish now that I'd listened to him. Heard the panic in his voice and taken him seriously for the first time in months. I wish I'd used that weekend enacting the final parts of the plan, instead of having dinner with Hannah – a final goodbye, even though she had no idea that's what it was – and starting to sort through the few things I would take with me when Megan walked out the door for the last time.

It is the late afternoon of the twenty-third of March.

Lockdown.

Stay at home. Save lives.

Red and yellow chevrons mocking me. There is no way to get to Leah's cabin. No way to hire a van and move the body to a safer place. No way to get away. I am trapped. Megan is trapped.

What the fuck do I do now?

Chapter Twelve

There is a silent scream in the back of my skull. It is getting worse, the pressure building and building. I think I will explode.

We cannot leave the house, except for essentials, for at least the next three weeks.

'It'll be longer,' Chris says in a smug 'I know better than them' voice.

I used to love that tone, thought it was fantastic to be with someone so clever and self-assured.

'How long?'

He shrugs. 'Six weeks at least. Probably more like three months. Depends on how much people actually listen and obey the rules.'

'Does this not bother you?'

'It should hardly be a surprise, Meggie.' If he wore glasses, he would be peering at me over their rims right now. 'I've been saying this was on the cards for weeks.'

Has he? I fall silent as I comb back through the last month. Have I been so busy with Tom and trying to figure out the escape, the body, juggle my own job, everything piling on top of me and that one thing I should have listened to just falling on deaf ears?

'At Mum and Dad's,' he says. 'Don't you remember?' He tips his head to one side a little. 'We had a conversation about how it might be the last time we saw them for a while?'

I'm silent as I play the memories through, searching for that conversation, which rings no bells.

'Oh, Meggie. Please tell me it's not happening again.' Concern drips from his voice like poison.

I have been so careful recently. Hypervigilant, making notes of everything. Every conversation that I had as Megan, every text, every email, every purchase, every outfit, is recorded on my phone. Every little thing that happened as Leah on hers. Everything that seems to have a place in both lives is in a small notebook, buried in the midst of boring minutes from boring meetings so no one would ever realise.

'I'm fine,' I say. 'It's just this whole lockdown thing, that's all.'

'It'll be fine, Meggie. We just stay here, work from home, get through it. Thank God we like each other's company, hey?'

I smile outwardly while my skin crawls.

'Imagine if you hated your spouse?' he carries on, warming to his subject. 'Imagine if you were planning on running away with your lover and then,' he claps his hands together and the noise startles me, 'BAM! Just like that you can't escape.' He is watching me carefully as he talks. I try to breathe normally. There is no way he could know; I have been so careful. 'Imagine if you were scared of what your other half could do, while the rest of the world ignored your plight in favour of their own problems.' He's goading me, but I'm not sure why. Unless he's trying to mess with me for his own sick fun.

'Imagine,' I say softly. I'm not going to play his games. There's a flash of disappointment across his face, so fast I wonder if I saw it at all.

'Now,' Chris's voice is back to normal, 'let's have some wine.' He gets up to pad to the kitchen. 'It's going to be fine, Meggie,

I promise. Just a bit of time watching Netflix, and drinking wine, and catching up on those books we keep promising we'll read. All over in a couple of months and then everything can go back to normal.'

I tell Chris I'm going to have a bath. I don't normally take baths here; the tub is too narrow and the bathroom so small claustrophobia sets in after a few minutes. But I've grown rather fond of a soak since I've been enjoying Leah's luxurious house, and anything is better than sitting downstairs with Chris.

Tom has left me five messages:

17:35 *Are you watching the press conference? xx*
17:45 *Damn, this looks bad xx*
18:00 *You OK, Leah? Call me xx*
19:00 *Are you still with your friend? Please call me so I know you're safe? xx*
19:25 *Where are you? xx*

I had told him I was going to visit a friend in the New Forest that weekend. A fellow writer who had a lovely little retreat where we could both work on our manuscripts in peace and quiet.

'You're writing another book?' he had asked with bright eyes. 'Tell me.'

'It'll be a surprise,' I had said, kissing him on the nose. 'A novel this time.'

'I can't wait to read it.'

Maybe one day, when this was all over, I *would* write that novel. I'd been thinking of the story for a long time. Nothing about twins or cheating husbands. Although there was a body in a freezer. A chill runs through me at the thought. Perhaps my book idea had provided me with some inspiration? Some part of my subconscious directing me back at the cabin. I swallow down the bile that threatens to come up and write back to Tom, the sound of water filling the bath beside me: *Signal appalling, struggling to even send texts! Still at my friend's and trying to figure out a plan. Thinking about staying here for a bit, working on the book with the peace and quiet. Will call you tomorrow when I can go for a walk and find proper signal. Love you xx*

Those last two words are out of my fingers and sent into the ether before I even think. I've not said it before. But it seems so right. And so very wrong: *Thank God you're OK! Agree that you are safer there anyway, London is looking a mess of cases. I love you too xx*

I smile at his reply. But inside I'm wondering how I'm going to pull off weeks or even months of staying here with Chris, while keeping Tom and whatever it is between us alive.

***

On the first full day after lockdown starts, Chris and I mark out our home-working territory. By which I mean that he retreats to his den in the spare bedroom and leaves me with the options of the sofa or the tiny table in the corner of the kitchen. My boss wants to have a meeting on Zoom first thing, and so I make some coffee – very easy given my proximity to the kettle – and set up on the kitchen table, with a cushion from the living room to try to make the hard wooden chair bearable.

James is in a sombre mood. Pretty much all of our clients have pulled their contracts; there'll be very little work for a while. 'Sorry guys. Strange times,' he says into his webcam with a grimace.

Strange times indeed.

There's a bit of chat between the team, but it's all quite depressing. Someone shares a video compilation called 'Funniest Fails of 2020 SO FAR!!' and we all smile dutifully, but no one's heart is in it.

'Terrible time to hate your spouse,' John says. 'Can you imagine if you'd been living a double life?' There is laughter across the displays as I sit frozen in place, a buzzing noise building in my ears as I wait for my carefully constructed lies to collapse around me.

'Oh, my, God,' splutters Nora from her immaculate kitchen in the pretty village of Cheam. 'Can you imagine if you had a whole other family!'

Thank God! It isn't *my* double life he's talking about. I stay still and wait though. Wait for the penny to drop with one of them that yes, yes I could imagine. Everyone knows the story of me and Leah and Mum and Dad, even if they haven't read the book.

It is Fi who eventually realises. 'Shit! Sorry, Megs.' As she says it, the others all stop laughing.

'Yeah, sorry,' John mumbles.

I plaster a smile on to my face. 'No worries, guys. Damn though. What would you do?' I learned quickly after the book came out that people love to gossip, to live vicariously, to imagine that they would behave better in certain situations than the protagonists in the stories we all tell. But now this isn't just a deflection method; I need their ideas. Because I need to find a way to convince Tom that I am simply staying with a friend.

It's not just Tom I need to convince either. Leah lived so openly, splashed so much of her life on to the internet, that she will be missed. And pretty quickly. With no 'Megan' work to be getting on with, I scroll through the Instagram accounts of Leah's peers, trying to figure out what they are planning on doing now everyone in the country is locked in their homes. It's been less than twenty-four hours and already Kira from book club has pivoted from posting aspirational content to pretending to be an ordinary person, and has started what promises to be a 'series of fascinating insights and humorous anecdotes of lockdown reality #WTF #homeschool #thisistorture #wereallscummymummies-now'. Eurgh: *we're all scummy mummies now* is enough to make me want to stick pins in my eyes.

Luckily, after I've spent over an hour swimming in the cesspool of other people's self-indulgence, Emma Baptiste-Harbington saves the day with a simple email:

> *You'll notice I locked all of your SM.* (I hadn't) *Zach and I will ensure your online presence is coordinated carefully to avoid a backlash like Carmella Bianchi's. Just sit tight and try to gain a few pounds. There will be a huge opportunity for post-lockdown diet and exercise transformations for us to tap into.*

I google Carmella Bianchi. A few weeks ago she was the darling of Italian Instagram with over two million followers hanging off her every exquisite post, the aesthetic curated to personify casual continental elegance. Two days ago she posted a seemingly innocuous picture of her doing sunset yoga on the wrought-iron balcony of her effortlessly stylish apartment *#mentalhealth #allinthistogether #italyunited*. Overnight *#italyunited* began to trend and was leapt on by a group of far-right nationalists. What had been an off-the-cuff hashtag created for clicks and likes became a symbol of hatred and the slogan for anti-lockdowners raging against the curtailing of their freedoms. Carmella lost over a million followers in a day. It was a disaster. But still, Carmella's downfall means I don't have to juggle Leah's social media without arousing suspicion and I'm grateful.

Late that afternoon, Chris, like the good community-spirited person he wants the world to think he is, goes to check in with one of the neighbours. Yasmin's husband has a whole load of health problems and so they've been told not to leave the house, not even to pick up his medication from the pharmacy. When he gets home, I ask if he had thought to pick up any essentials for us. Obviously he hadn't.

It gives me the perfect excuse to slip out of the house, ostensibly to see if there is milk and bread at the local shop – there isn't, nor is there any at the petrol station – but really I just wanted to call Tom.

'How's my favourite author?' Tom says as he answers the phone on the second ring.

'Feeling a little weird.'

'I'm not surprised. But you're much better off there. London is going crazy with cases and reports that things are getting bad, like Italy.'

'Are the streets quiet?' Although we live just outside the main bustle of Guildford, our local streets are normally busy with people going about their everyday lives, kids whizzing past on bikes, students stumbling home at all hours. But now it's deathly quiet. I imagine London feels like a ghost town.

'You know that film with the aliens, where he wakes up after the apocalypse and everyone is dead, but he didn't know it was happening?'

'Err. . . No.' What is he talking about?

'That one where he was in hospital when the aliens destroyed everything, and then he wakes up and everyone is dead, and it's just him left alone in London.'

'Do you mean *28 Days Later*?'

'Yep, that's the one.'

'It's about zombies, not aliens.'

'Ahh. . .' he says, and I can picture him running his hand through his hair as the penny drops. I realise I'm smiling at the very thought of him. 'That would explain why my colleagues thought I was mad earlier. Oh well,' he goes on without a shred of embarrassment, 'it's like that. But real.'

'Creepy,' I say, simultaneously disappointed to miss seeing the capital so void of crowds and glad to be away from the pandemic's centre.

'That's precisely the word I was thinking. Although, you know the boarding school I told you about, opposite my place?'

This was once a small teaching hospital but is now the home of an elite ballet school that takes only a handful of kids each year. Fi once dated a guy whose daughter was a student. She was terrified of the sombre, earnest girl with her hair scraped back into a tight bun. 'Yep.'

'The students are still there for now, and they keep writing messages on Post-it notes and sticking them to the windows. I thought they were all so serious, but some of the messages are pretty funny.'

'I wish I was there with you,' I say suddenly, trying to keep the longing from my voice.

'Me too, Leah,' he replies. 'But I'd rather you stay safe in the New Forest.'

'It won't be for long.'

'You have wine?'

'Of course.' I laugh.

'That's the important thing.'

'I hate the patchy signal though,' I say.

'I'll email you. It'll be romantic, like old-fashioned love letters between two lovers whose families are keeping them far apart. A modern-day Romeo and Juliet.' I don't have the heart to remind him they both ended up dead.

'I just don't know how often we'll get to talk.' I doubt I'll be able to escape from the house that regularly without raising too much suspicion in Chris.

'We'll make it work.' I can hear the smile in his voice. 'A few weeks apart isn't going to matter in the long run. I love you, Leah.'

I know he said it in his text, but to hear the words 'I love you' out loud, in that gorgeous baritone of his, makes my heart almost burst.

'I love you too,' I say back. I don't think I've ever meant it like this before.

We hang up and I head back to the house. I wish he could call me by my real name. Will I ever get used to being her? Or will there always be that flicker in my chest, that stab of guilt and fear when I hear her name on his lips?

***

I have been trying to get through to Mum's home for two days now. Every time I ring, I get a recorded voice telling me they are very busy but that the home remains in safe hands and staff will be in touch with all the families of residents over the coming days. 'Don't call us, we'll call you.' It isn't fucking good enough.

I am pacing the kitchen in tiny circles, my phone overheating by my ear. This is now the tenth time I have listened to the message. In frustration I finally put the phone down and pour myself a large glass of wine. It's only four o'clock, but it's not like I have any work to do, and there *is* a global pandemic raging outside. I sip the cold wine greedily, enjoying the little head-rush it gives me. Hannah sends me a picture of an elephant with a little squiggle over his face: *If you can guess the animal, I'll open some wine.*

Not just me then who is blurring the lines between what is acceptable and what is not with regard to day drinking. Hannah has decided to spend lockdown with her mum and all those cats. She sends another picture, this one of her sitting on the sofa with a large glass of wine in one hand and a ball of grey fur curled in her lap: *Lockdown buddies* 🖤

It looks like Hannah and Earl are becoming fast friends.

My phone ringing on the kitchen surface brings me back to reality. Finally, the home is calling me back.

'Mrs Hardcastle?' It's Tina, the friendly nurse who always has plenty of time for my mum, who makes sure she has a shower, that her hair is brushed and her nails trimmed.

My heart is hammering in my chest when I hear it is her and not the brusque receptionist I was expecting. 'Is. . . is—'

'Everything is fine,' Tina says. 'Your mum is fine. Please don't worry.'

'When I couldn't get through, I thought. . .' I trail off. I'm not sure what I had thought, to be honest.

'We're sorry for the worry. We just needed to make sure our protocol was in place. We have decided to fully lock down the home. All staff are moving in, no contact with the outside at all for the duration of the lockdown. No visitors, no nothing.'

'Oh.' I'm struggling to process what that actually means.

'You won't be able to visit, I'm afraid. But I'm sure you'll understand.'

'But you'll be there?' I ask, thinking that at least Mum will have one friendly face.

'Yes, we're putting up tents in the back garden. It'll be a bit of an adventure for all of us.'

'A tent?' Tina is fifty-eight and I'm not sure she has much camping experience.

'Needs must. So, don't worry about your mum, I'll call every few days to check in.'

The relief floods over me. At least I know that Mum is safe and being well looked after.

The next day, the sun is shining and I have no work to take my mind off everything, so I take a coffee out into the slightly scraggy garden. In the far corner is what the estate agent called in the sale particulars the 'summer house', a pentagon-shaped wooden structure with peeling paintwork and only one remaining window. The other is covered in plastic and cardboard.

I have an idea. I could return the shed to its former glory as a proper summer house. A space for me to get further away from Chris. Where he wouldn't overhear my conversations with Tom. I head back into the house and pop some shoes on, grabbing the keys from the hook in the kitchen.

Inside the shed is the usual pile of crap. But in the far corner is a large chest freezer. There's a tarpaulin covering most of it, except for a gap at the bottom where the vents are. I had begged Chris to get one just before Christmas, but he had refused. I'd even suggested it could live in the shed if he was worried about space inside the house. He had looked at me aghast, like I had said I wanted to kick a puppy. But damn, it would have been so useful; there are talks of mass food shortages and he who has milk and bread in the freezer would be feeling like a king right about now.

For a moment, I wonder if he has bought it as a gift and tucked it away in the shed ready to unveil it to me with a flourish.

But I can hear it humming. It is on.

How long has it been here? Did I know what would be inside before I lifted the lid?

I stumble outside. I gave up smoking years ago. But sometimes I like to have just a little one, and so there is an emergency packet hidden inside the barbecue at the corner of the decking. Today, right now, I need one. I take a deep drag, my mind racing. Chris finds me a few minutes later sucking nicotine and tar and all the other shit hungrily into my lungs.

'Smoking again?' There is pity in his eyes.

'Stress.'

I try to keep my voice even. I try not to look at him directly.

'And you think this is a good way to deal with it?' His voice is soft and gentle.

No, I don't. My first thought was to drink an entire bottle of vodka but that wasn't really an option. I need to be on point. I need to be more alert than ever.

The game is just beginning.

And it is advantage Chris.

Because inside that freezer is the body of my dead sister.

I need to find a way to stop myself from picturing her face. Left there, in that freezer. She looks so different, so far removed from both the young girl who would dress up in Mum's finery to put on little fashion shows for the neighbours and the woman who took photos of herself to post all over Instagram. Now, even though it's almost like my own face staring back at me, the face is pale, cold, and I barely recognise her.

I race to the downstairs bathroom and heave into the toilet.

Desperate to keep my mind and fingers busy, I end up spending the afternoon going through all the stocks of food we have in the house. It turns out we have very little. A single bag of pasta, a couple of jars of sauce, a very well-stocked spice rack with nothing to spice. For an hour, I try in vain to get a supermarket delivery slot, panic rising as I join a queue of twenty thousand others doing the same. The news was full of reports of empty shelves and fights breaking out among perfectly normal-looking suburban housewives. The whole world is descending into chaos. But all I can think about is her. Her blank face, like a lifeless doll. Her blank face that should not be here in my summer house.

In the end I order us pizza and we sit in the living room with our banquet spread out on the rug in front of us. I need to keep Chris close. How long has he known the truth of what I did? How long has he had to plan what he will do next? I have to watch him closely, figure out if he knows that I know. I have to assume he does. So, what now?

'Have you spoken to your parents?' I ask him as I pick pepperoni off a slice of Meat Feast.

'They think it's all a big storm in a teacup.' He shrugs. 'I hope they're right.'

'But they're taking things seriously, aren't they?' For all that I had married a psychopath, I was genuinely fond of his parents. Well, his mum at least.

'Sure. Lisa will make sure they don't need to go out.'

Lisa has been his sister's best friend since they were toddlers. She lives three doors down from his parents with her husband, two children, three dogs and a cat called Mittens. Boring and predictable is how Chris describes her. I always think of her as safe. The one you would want around when the world is coming to an end.

Part Two
Chris

Chapter Thirteen

I never thought Megan would actually kill her. Damn, that girl was hiding some deep-seated anger she'd never shared with me. If only she'd brought that passion to the bedroom every once in a while. Maybe then I wouldn't have had to make my own fun, wouldn't have felt the need to toy with her so much. Poor little Megan, with her messed-up family and her constant terror that her mind was starting to get away from her like a slippery fish. It was all just so easy.

I've debated whether I should tell my story. You could argue that I'm something of an accomplice, an enabler of Megan's deception, what with keeping the body in my shed and all. I don't know the punishment for 'perverting the course of justice', but it's probably obscenely harsh relative to being the one actually lumping someone round the head with a wine bottle and then stuffing their body into a chest freezer. But this whole thing is just too good not to share. So, I'll take my chances.

Besides, Tom, that ginger-haired twat who thought he could fuck my wife, will be the one who swings for this eventually.

Are you sitting comfortably? Have you got a nice cup of tea next to you, or possibly a glass of wine? Well, then let me begin. Right back at where this all started.

I knew exactly who Megan was that first day I introduced myself on the train to Guildford. Having already read her social media profiles – Facebook, Insta and LinkedIn – I knew she'd just taken a job with a large consultancy and was trying graspingly hard to wash away the shame of the exposé her sister had written. All it took was a gin and tonic (and a slightly warm one in a tin at that – she never did have any class) and a little flattery. 'You're nothing like her,' I had told her.

She'd laughed and showed me a photo of the two of them taken a few years before. 'Really?' She raised an eyebrow.

I leant forward, eyes sincere, voice low and even. 'You might *look* the same, but she's a brassy, money-grabbing, attention-seeking whore.' Her eyes widened at the word, like an innocent child hearing it for the first time and finding it rather enthrallingly scandalous. She even giggled a little. 'But you're intelligent and sophisticated and have class,' I went on. She blushed and smiled at me, not getting the irony of my class comment as she accepted another tin of gin and tonic.

Of course, it was Leah I was really interested in. Well, her money anyway. More than enough to warrant a longer con than normal. I would mend their broken relationship, bring them together to be best friends and ensure Megan (who would, of course, have married me by then) was the beneficiary of Leah's will. Then I would kill Leah and, once her money was safely in our marital account, Megan would appear to finally give in to the distress of her sister's death and in a fit of pain and misery would kill herself. Or at least that is what I'd make it look like. I would be the pining husband. The distraught but wealthy widower, offered slots on every primetime show in the country – because of course it would be a public travesty for both twins to die so close to each other. Onwards and upwards I would go.

But Jesus! Megan could hold a grudge. To be fair, there were things Leah had done that even I thought a little beyond the pale. That thing with her first boyfriend. . . ouch! But if I'd thought Megan was stubborn, then Leah was worse. And she hated Megan, beyond even the most extreme sibling rivalry. I never did find out why.

The problem was that I needed to find a way to get what I deserved, what I was born for. Two hundred years ago, a wealthy old great-great-grandfather had bequeathed his huge fortune down the generations. Every Hardcastle would benefit from his largesse to the tune of the princely sum of twenty thousand pounds, paid on their fortieth birthday on the proviso that they were married. In 1810 that was a ridiculous amount, equivalent to about one and a half million today. But with every generation the gift got smaller in real terms and twenty grand would buy you less and less. It was only just enough in 1995 for my dyke aunt to bother with her sham marriage to that weird skinny dude with the stringy hair. Now I could just about afford a holiday and a new freezer, if I was lucky.

The whole thing with Leah wasn't planned; I hadn't thought she'd be interested in me, to be honest. But she couldn't resist messing around with Megan's life and I was more than happy to go along for the ride. And *what* a ride! Leah looked so much like Megan it was uncanny, but she wanted things my wife never wanted, begged me to do things Megan would baulk at. Like bend her over, inch those little blue panties down and fuck her deep in the arse.

But nothing lasts for ever. Leah was bored with hearing me talk about Megan's mounting paranoia and, like a cat wanting to play with a defenceless mouse, wanted to see for herself.

'Why should you get to have all the fun?' she'd asked, pushing out her bottom lip like a petulant teenager. So Leah had helped me plan for Megan to find the photo on my phone. Had giggled as I ordered a load of things that matched the bright blue of the underwear to dot around the house. When I'd described the sheer panic in Megan's pretty, dumb eyes as she knelt by her own underwear drawer, searching for the set she was terrified she had forgotten buying, Leah had practically clapped with joy.

We knew Megan would follow Leah to the cabin to find answers. Leah couldn't have advertised her whereabouts any more clearly; she wanted to rub it in her sister's face that she had won. That she had the money, and the fame, and had even managed to snare Megan's husband. I thought there would be a showdown, something I could use to form the basis of a new plan to get my hands on her fortune; I was excited to watch what would happen. I didn't expect to arrive just in time to watch my wife drag her sister's prone body across the deck and try to lift her into the chest freezer to cuddle up with bags of bait ready for the next fisherman to visit. At that moment, I'd been intrigued to see what she'd do next. I have to give her some credit; if I'd just been some chump of a husband without the sense to keep proper tabs on my wife, I might even have believed the lies she told. As Megan. And as Leah. Some seriously messed-up shit I married into.

Running a long con, one that may span years, takes a fair amount of effort. It's too easy to get bored, get complacent. And so I made sure I had a side project in the form of the great Patterson curse. There is no *actual* curse. No genetic link to

the 'problems' her mum faces. I've checked with a few professionals, played the concerned husband card, and found that
people are surprisingly verbose and loose lipped. I must admit,
though, that when you look at the shit-show of her life, the
mum's that is, you can understand why someone might seek
refuge behind a veneer of mental illness, to give their stupidity and
complete lack of self-awareness, their *gullibility*, some kind of
reason beyond their control. The dad was a con man, a complete bastard who should never have had one family, let alone
two. But you still have to admire him a bit; to have one woman
worship you is a compliment, to have two – and the mum was
a stunner back in the day – is downright intoxicating.

Perhaps when I get my hands on all that cash, I'll set myself
up with a couple of pieces. Nice, young, pliable things. The
idea of sailing the world with a harem of beautiful girls in bi-
kinis certainly has a nice appeal to it.

It actually started quite innocently, just two days after John
Lewis delivered the gifts from our wedding list. Our house has
old-fashioned hardwood floors, the original ones from when it
was first built, all worn with age and pockmarked with dimples
smoothed over time. My previous flat had underfloor heating
and I'll be honest that I was a bit grumpy about how cold the
floor was on my bare feet. So, in the spirit of compromise that
precedes all weddings, we added a thick rug to the gift list. It
was the colour of sand and in wonderful contrast to the single
teal signature wall I had painted.

'That light colour is a disaster waiting to happen,' Megan had
said, a supercilious edge to her voice that was rather unattractive.

'Oh, don't be neurotic.' I'd dismissed her concerns with a
wave of my hand.

To be fair, I shouldn't have been eating a Thai red curry balanced on my lap on the sofa. The stain was huge and pink, and even after I scrubbed and scrubbed it, it just looked at me. Staring its recriminating stare. *I told you so*, the mark whispered to me in Megan's self-righteous tones.

When Megan got home that night, she walked into the living room and stopped, eyes flicking around the space. 'What have you done in here?'

'What?' I kept my tone casual.

'It's all different.' She said it as a statement, but there was a question in her voice.

'Different?' I stood up to pour her a drink. 'You alright, sweetheart?'

'You've moved things.'

'I put out the vase and a few bits on the mantelpiece,' I said, motioning in the direction of the new candles we had been given by a friend of Megan's from university. 'Those candles smell divine, by the way.'

'The furniture?' That was a question, and her voice was louder. I waited for the bollocking, but there was no anger, just sad confusion. And fear. I could smell it coming off her. That was the moment I realised just how terrified she was of ending up like her mum and just how much she believed it was only a matter of time before the madness came for her. If it wasn't already here.

I handed her a glass of wine and guided her to the sofa, now further forward in the space, with the chest we stored blankets in pulled into the middle of the room as a coffee table. Directly over the pink stain. Her fingers turned white as she gripped the glass, and I kissed her gently on her shoulder. 'You've just had a long day, sweetheart. Too much stress trying to catch up on work after the honeymoon.' My voice was soothing, and I could feel her relaxing against me. 'Let's just chill, eh? Maybe have an early night.'

***

We'd been married about six months when I went on a work retreat to Canterbury. One of the newest recruits had just completed her masters in psychology and was all academic brilliance, button-up cardie and fuck-all life experience. On the last evening, she sucked me off in the corner of a rather grubby nightclub, the knees of her jeans soaking through with beer and alcopops. In celebration of the event, I bought a small statue of the cathedral made from bronze-coloured metal from the souvenir shop and popped it on to the shelf in the corner of the living room. Megan didn't notice for two weeks, but I felt a little frisson every time I glanced towards it.

'What's with the cathedral thingy?' She had held it between her finger and thumb, turning it over in the light.

'From that trip we took.' I had squinted at her. 'You know?'

'What trip?'

'When was it, three months ago, something like that.' I shrugged. 'We went on that horrendous walking tour and then I nearly fell in when we went punting.' I mime the action as I creep towards her.

'I. . . I. . . don't remember.'

'Of course you do. We drove down there. You said you'd never been, and I told you that was ridiculous and so we jumped in the car.'

Megan shook her head and looked at me, her head tilted a little. When we had first met, I'd found the action endearing, like a confused spaniel; now I just think she looks like an imbecile.

'We went to that fancy place for afternoon tea and then we were going to visit the Roman Museum but that pigeon had its accident on your hair and so we went and got drunk instead.' I watched tears welling in her eyes that she was desperate to blink away. She didn't want me to worry. Didn't want me to think, so soon after the wedding, that she might be damaged, might not be perfect. It was kind of sweet in a way.

***

For a month last year I did nothing but turn her alarm clock off at night. So simple, but so effective. I don't sleep much and so I would normally be awake when she was fast asleep. It was as easy as flicking a switch. The first morning she berated herself, cursing as she rushed around to get ready for work and not miss the train. The next morning she cursed herself more harshly. I was the perfect gentleman who offered to drive her to the station so she wouldn't have to walk and could use the extra few minutes to run through the shower. The next night I heard her in the bedroom, repeating over and over to herself that she had put the alarm on before she turned out the lights.

In week two of this little assault, I let the alarm go off on Monday and Tuesday. Lulled her into a false sense of security. She had a big presentation on Wednesday, some kind of pitch to a new client that she'd been stressing over for the whole weekend. I wanted to go the whole hog, but in the end her job is rather lucrative, and life would be more difficult for everyone if she got fired. So I did the gentlemanly thing once more and set my alarm.

'I know how important today is to you,' I'd said as I held her in my arms and rocked her gently. She was so fucking grateful it almost broke my heart.

Another week went past and the alarm failed to go off almost every night. Eventually, and it look longer than I thought it would, to be honest, she had broken down and begged for my help. As I had stroked her hair and wiped her tears, I'd promised her we'd come up with a plan. My poor broken wife, her pretty green eyes red-ringed, dainty nose running, shivering in my arms. Just thinking about that night still sends a shiver up my spine and makes the hairs on my arms start to rise.

Before you brand me as some kind of sexually deviant monster, it does not turn me on to see her like that. At least not in in a way that I would normally consider arousal. It's the thrill of what I could do that I enjoy, the planning and scheming. It is pure. Cleansing.

What was I hoping to achieve? I'm not really sure, to be honest. But there were worse ways to spend the day. In the end though, I paid a fortune for a fancy alarm clock that projects the time on to the wall so she can check the alarm is set from under the duvet, and moved on to finding other ways to mess with her.

***

We've now been in lockdown for three weeks. Megan's work basically stopped – I guess no one wants those stupid workshops she runs right now – and so she's been pacing the house and trying to keep busy with banal shit. But I'm getting bored now, and I want to get the game started. Lockdown has made things so much easier for me.

We're sitting on the sofa, watching the daily news update about the virus, both with a gin and tonic in hand. Just like she has every evening, Megan makes some thinly veiled joke about how we are turning into my parents. Instead of my usual guarded laugh, I take her hand. 'Except my mother never killed anyone, did she?' My words are quiet and it takes her a second to realise what I've said. I squeeze her hand, grinding flesh and bones together. She turns to look at me and I smile the gentle but vulpine smile that I know makes her nervous. 'You've been a very naughty girl, haven't you, Meggie?' I grind her hand harder in mine.

My darling wife now realises I know she has killed her sister. I have been waiting for this moment since lockdown began, biding my time while I worked out just what to do next.

'Megan.' I'm sitting so close I can feel her body radiating heat. She gets warm when she's angry. I'll have to be gentle this evening, I suppose. Make sure I don't push her too far, too quickly. I need her compliant 'So, what is it that you think I want?'

'I. . . I. . . don't know. . .' There are a couple of tears reflecting in her eyes, so I hand her a tissue. But she doesn't use it. She merely begins to shred it into tiny pieces. I follow the journey of one small piece as it stirs from the pile of its brethren and floats to the floor I have only just hoovered. I clamp down my anger. Now is not the time.

'Well, let's be honest, Meggie, shall we?' I take her hands and gently pull the remaining bits of tissue from her grasp.

'You know what you did was very wrong, don't you? And I think the police would be interested in hearing exactly what happened that evening. How you finally lost control and killed her. We all know how much you hated her, Meggie. All our friends, our good honest friends, will feel that they must step forward and attest that you and Leah had a fractured relationship. Don't you think that Hannah would feel compelled to tell the truth? I'm sure if she is put on the stand, we'd watch her pile all your dirty secrets on top of each other like the upstanding citizen she is. So much motive there for you to hurt Leah. Plus, of course, your fingerprints are all over that body. You know yours and Leah's don't match, don't you?' Condescension drips from my voice. 'I have the body, Meggie. I moved it from the cabin. There's more than enough evidence to convict you. No chance of parole. How long is a life sentence these days?'

Although I haven't moved away, I can no longer feel her heat radiating as her anger is replaced with terror. I smile at her. 'So, what are we going to do about this whole fine mess, hmm?' I rub her hand in the way I have seen the care assistant minister to her mum. It makes my skin crawl and I pray that I will never end up in a place like that. 'I could stay quiet. . .' She whips her head round to look at me, disbelief swimming in her eyes. 'I could. . .' Rub, rub, rub. 'But why would I?'

'What do you want?' Her voice is small and childlike.

'Now that is an interesting question.' She is searching my face for a clue to where I am going. 'You're scared of me, aren't you, Meggie? I think that even before you knew that I knew you were a murderess you were scared of me. . . What did you think I'd do to you? Oh, don't answer.' I put my finger to her lips. 'How much is it worth? My silence?' I cock my head to one side as I look at her.

'You want. . . money?' She makes it sound dirty. Base.

'What else would I want, Meggie?'

'But. . . I thought. . .' Now here's the rub of it all. She actually thought this was about her! All those years she has thought it was about her. It's almost pathetic.

I sigh and pull away from her a little. 'You thought it was about you, didn't you?' I stroke her cheek. 'You thought that I wouldn't ever let you go because. . .' I smile sweetly and it spins her confusion against the harshness of my words. She looks away from me.

'I don't have any money, Chris. Our accounts are joint, you have access to everything already.'

'Oh, Meggie. I know you don't have anything. But Leah does.'

'You want Leah's money?'

'Not *all* of it. But a chunk. I think I deserve it, don't you?'

'But. . . I don't have access.'

'Nice try, Meggie.' Her eyes widen at the change in my voice. 'I've been watching you.' They widen further. I smile, but my hand has moved to her upper arm and I am gripping her harder and harder as the seconds tick past. 'You *are* going to get it for me. You understand that don't you? Because if you don't, you will spend the rest of your life in prison for murder.' My other hand is gripping her other arm now, pinning her down beside me on the sofa.

'You're hurting me,' she whispers.

'Good,' I whisper back and kiss her hard on the lips.

Chapter Fourteen

I don't sleep much and it's a blessing. People always bang on about how the human body needs seven to eight hours and that sleep is the most important thing in the world. Maybe for those people: the weak-minded, unable to cope with their reality, incapable of processing things with their conscious mind so they must rely on their subconscious to sort it all out for them. Just think where we would be as a species if people slept a bit less and thought a bit more. I read a fascinating book once on the habits of the brilliant, showing their routines by the hour. They all had one thing in common: not bothering with the things that most people rely on, the props they create for themselves. Sleep, fancy food, alcohol, love. None of it matters, none of it is important.

Not sleeping also gives you a lot of time to read. To listen. To watch. I've always been so fascinated by the way the mask slips when people think no one is looking. The way people turn into someone else as soon as they close their door on the world outside.

Leah wore so many faces it was impossible to know which of them was the real her. She fascinated me. I had hopes for her, a desire to crack through that hard outer shell to get to the soft squishy bits in the middle. I wanted to peel the layers away. But then Megan went and ruined it all, ripping Leah away from me before I was finished. Megan is boring in comparison to her sister. Megan has a 'home persona' and a 'work persona'; she thinks they are different, that her work colleagues would be ever so shocked by how different she is at home. Professional, smart and reliable versus fun-loving, spontaneous millennial; that's what she thinks. In truth, they overlap by at least ninety-eight per cent. My wife is dull and predictable, the kind of person who will mould themselves to those around her. She thinks that makes her enigmatic, that she is ephemeral, a changeling who flits around depending on the group she is with. But it does not make her funny, or charming, or kind, or any one of the other seemingly positive characteristics she labels herself with. It just makes her a weak fool whose only personality trait is that she will be whoever she thinks you want her to be. It's not even limited to people she knows well; she'll do it for shopkeepers, waiters, even the person sitting next to her on a flight.

Leah and I used to laugh about Megan and her pliability. Leah would tell me stories of the kind of trouble Megan got into when they were kids because she was always so quick to accommodate any request.

'I bet she was popular at school,' I had said.

'You'd think. But that was the one thing she always refused.' Leah had shrugged her shoulders. 'You know how frigid she is.' We were lying on Leah's bed, the sweaty sheets a tangled mess against the footboard. Her hand was stroking sweeping arcs across my stomach and chest, moving steadily downwards. 'Do you like it when we talk about her?' She shifted so her breath was warm against my shoulder, her hand moving lower. 'I think you do.' It was obvious that she was turning me on. 'I think it makes you feel powerful that you can have both of us. And you get a kick out of knowing how much this would hurt her if she found out.' Her fingertips brushed against me and my breath caught in the back of my throat. And then she grabbed my hand and guided it between her legs. 'It turns me on too,' she whispered.

I'm not sure whose idea it was to take messing with Megan up a notch. I'm sure Leah would have said it was hers; she did like to be in control, to take the credit even if it wasn't entirely due. She spent her whole childhood taking the credit for all the good things Megan did, and passing over the blame for her own indiscretions. I don't think she knew how else to be. She lived her life as if there were no bad consequences, no morals to bind her to a course of action, no sense that some things should be sacred. 'Take, take, take' was her motto. Appended with 'and if you can't take it, prise it from the cold dead fingers of the one who won't let you have it'. It made her a greedy, shameless lover and I couldn't get enough of her.

She had also been greedy in her desire to get a rise out of Megan and I had been forced to reel her back in a bit.

'Subtlety is the name of the game,' I had to tell her when she wanted to take things a little too far. Her beautiful face had dropped, the lips turning into a pout. At that moment I'd seen a flash of a woman who one day I would have to deal with more forcefully; but she had been future Chris's problem.

***

In early November, I took Leah to a hotel in Dorset, the big manor house where Megan and I had spent our third anniversary. The man on the check-in desk welcomed us back.

'Mr and Mrs Hardcastle. Such a pleasure to have you back with us again so soon.'

Leah raised an eyebrow as the man directed us to the suite.

'Trust me, you'll like this,' I whispered in her ear as we took the rickety lift towards the top of the house.

The suite was huge, a super-king four-poster bed in the centre of the room, flanked by oversized bedside tables hewn from the same dark mahogany. Through a set of glass doors was a plush living area, a dark blue velvet sofa that could seat at least five adults and a curved bar in the corner with rows of spirits glittering along the back wall. Even more impressive was the marble bathroom with twin basins and a jacuzzi bath big enough for even Snoop Dogg to entertain in.

'Swanky,' Leah said, bouncing on the edge of the giant bed and looking around. I'd known this wouldn't impress her too much; she was a lot richer than I was, after all. 'So, what is it I'm meant to like?'

'Megan and I stayed here for our last anniversary. And in just a few weeks we're coming back again, some rewards scheme so it's practically free.' I grinned. 'Just think how confused she'll be when the staff mention things she doesn't remember doing, meals she ate, the drink she always ordered.'

I watched the realisation slowly dawning on Leah's face. 'You are a very naughty man,' she said. I could tell she was impressed. 'So, does she still hate rum?'

'Can't stand the stuff.'

'Well, let's head downstairs for a little cocktail then, shall we?'

We sat at the ornate bar, Leah toying with the barman, who looked like he'd only turned eighteen about a month ago. 'I just hope he doesn't get fired before you bring her back here,' she said to me under her breath. She could be incorrigible and

I watched with a sense of pride as she got the barman to make her a Mai Tai, keeping up a constant stream of chat with him about how she didn't normally drink at three in the afternoon, but she was on holiday and so it didn't count. The choice of cocktail was inspired; rum is a no-no for Megan, and she would never normally order something that came with a cocktail cherry.

Later that evening we went to the restaurant for dinner.

'What would she order?' Leah asked.

'Probably mussels to start and then steak for main.'

The waiter asked if Leah would like the steak done medium-well like last time. She smiled sweetly and placed her hand on his arm. 'Last time, I ordered it rare. You just had it cooked medium-well.' The waiter had blushed and apologised. Her steak was still bleeding when it was brought to the table. 'Perfect,' she told him. She left a huge tip at the end of the meal.

The whole thing worked a treat. When I took Megan to the hotel a few weeks later, the staff treated her like an old friend. A Mai Tai was presented with a flourish as we headed to the bar that afternoon. Blood from her steak was seeping into her dauphinoise potatoes as it was served.

That first night, back upstairs in our room, Megan was angry.

'Are they messing with me? I don't drink rum,' she said, 'you know that.'

'That's what I told you last time we were here. You ordered the Mai Tai because you'd seen the name in a book you were reading or something. I warned you it was rum. You said you wanted one anyway.' I'd shrugged then, like the hard done-by spouse I was. 'Then you tasted it and said it was divine. You kept ordering them all night.'

'But the steak?'

'Meggie, sweetie. The waiter is a kid, he probably doesn't remember what he ate for his own breakfast, never mind how you like your steak cooked. These posh hotels want you to think they understand service, but do they really?' I had wrapped my arms round her in an expression of solidarity. 'And you could have sent it back.'

Of course, she had eaten it, her face twisting in disgust as she chewed the raw meat. She would never send a meal back; she didn't like to get the staff into trouble.

The next morning, a copy of *The Times* was slid under the door. Megan reads the *Guardian*. Of course she does. A carafe of strong French coffee was delivered to the suite, 'like last time.' Last time, Megan had lain in bed while I went for a swim, reading the paper and sipping her way through a huge pot of Darjeeling tea. She had been particularly taken by the tea cosy they had sent up to keep it warm. This time I didn't go for a swim; instead I watched her scroll through her photos from the last visit. She had taken a picture of said tea cosy. I had deleted it a few days ago. I enjoyed the moment of panic as it crossed her face.

The final piece of my plan was the knock on the door from the laundry service. 'You left this last time you were here with us, Mrs Hardcastle. I had it laundered.' A small box was handed over. Inside was a rather plain black silk negligee. Megan is not one for fancy colours, or too much frilliness. It looked exactly like the kind of thing she might have picked for a naughty weekend away. On Megan's phone was a picture of the same item. I had messed around with her system settings so it looked like it was date-stamped three days before we had come the last time. Date-stamped four days later was a photo of her wearing it, a selfie taken in the marble bathroom of our suite, an awkward over-the-shoulder photo taken to make sure it looked OK from all angles. It wasn't really Megan, but I'd softened the edges of the photo just in case she looked too closely. Leah had left the negligee thrown across the seat of the dressing table when we checked out.

'What's up, beautiful?' I had asked Megan. 'Aren't you pleased they found it? It looks expensive.' It was expensive, for something so skimpy anyway.

'I. . .' she had started, confusion reigning on her face. I could see the struggle.

'You could pop it on again?' I went to stand in front of her. 'It was fun last time, you looked so sexy in my lap on the sofa.' I watched the look flit across her face again. I had taken her hand and put it on my crotch so she could feel how turned on I was by the memory.

I had taken the negligee back to Leah a few nights later, keen to continue the game a little longer. But Leah had dismissed the garment and told me she had something much more fun.

God, I miss that woman. For all I had my eyes on her money, and I knew things would end eventually, I do wish we'd had more time.

I have made a list of all of Leah's assets that are held in accessible deposits. I am not going to be greedy; I don't want everything. Just enough that these past few years living with Megan were worth my time. Plus, I will have to divorce her and that will go on my record. Finding other gullible women will become slightly more difficult, an ex-wife always gets their backs up. I'll have to field questions about Megan for ever, about what she was like and why we broke up and if she's likely to try to stalk me, or if she has issues with jealousy. It's going to be tiresome, so I intend to be appropriately compensated.

There is a savings account and two current accounts with a high street bank, their combined balances total just over one hundred thousand pounds. We are in the kitchen, Leah's laptop open on the small table, Megan sitting in front of it. I stand behind her, my hands heavy on her shoulders. 'Buy bitcoin,' I instruct her.

'Bitcoin?'

I know she is familiar with cryptocurrencies; she was an accountant for God's sake and these things are hardly new. I stare at her until she shrugs. 'Fine. What's the account?'

I read it out to her. No way I'm going to leave that information just lying around on a sheet of paper. Although within ten minutes all those funds will have been moved over a dozen times, bouncing around a range of accounts I have set up in preparation over the years. Untraceable. Except by me.

Then it's on to the main account. The big one. Pullman is a serious bank with a head office in the centre of the City. They serve only high-net-worth clients. Leah has an account with over three million pounds sitting in it.

'You can't buy three million in bitcoin,' Megan tells me. 'You'll flag on every terrorist monitor.'

I doubt it, but I pause for half a second. 'Just do it.' With my hands still on her shoulders, I can feel her pulse in her neck and it is fluttering like a hummingbird. Perhaps she should see someone about that elevated heart rate. I'm not sure it's normal.

The interface for Pullman is understated, in muted tones of dark grey and royal blue against a cream background. It evokes a sense of posh writing paper, the stuff that feels creamy beneath your fingertips. It takes a few moments for Megan to locate the online sign-in icon.

Leah has a programme that stores her passwords for everything, and even the codes for this account are on there. I still can't fathom how these girls made it to adulthood sometimes. I mean, who even does that?

'Oh shit!' Megan says as the Pullman site asks her to input her keyword. A word that is not in the password-breaker app.

'You don't know it?' My fingers briefly tighten and she flinches.

'Of course not. How the hell would I know it?'

'Can't you guess?'

She brings up the password software and scans the list of other keywords that Leah regularly used. Then she laughs, a deep throaty laugh that catches me off guard in its sheer unadulterated sensuousness. It is not a sound I have heard from my wife before.

'Sorry.' She clears her throat.

'What is it?' I'm irritated she's not sharing the joke.

'When we were kids, we had a whole imaginary family thought out. Uncles and aunts and cousins and even a baby brother. We had this fantasy that one day we would meet them all and live happily ever after, and then we would meet twin brothers and marry one each and then have an even bigger family,' she explains. 'All the names she uses are those family members, except there is one she hasn't used. My twin was Oberon. Hers was Tarquin.' She types the seven characters into the little box and hits enter, her breath catching in her throat as she waits to see if she's right.

Keyword accepted. The words flash on the screen and she releases the end of the breath.

Initiating facial capture.

'You'd better move out of view of the camera,' she tells me and I oblige as the little red dot above the screen flashes on.

When she motions that the face scan is complete, I step back behind her.

Please move closer to the camera to commence retinal scan, the instructions blink rhythmically.

Megan turns to me, fear in her eyes. 'Retinal scan?'

'Problem?' But I already know. They share the same everything; even I could barely tell them apart. But their retinas were as different as yours and mine. 'Can you override it?'

She taps at the screen and scrolls to the bottom. 'No.'

My fingers dig into her collarbone. *Think man, think!* What the fuck am I going to do now? I need that money. I feel her trying to pull away from my grip, but I dig tighter.

I will get what I deserve. But now I need a new plan.

Chapter Fifteen

The day after lockdown started, Megan had begun smoking again. Or I should say openly smoking. She'd always enjoyed a clandestine cigarette, huddled out on our patio like I wouldn't realise. There must be some gene for it because Leah also used to sneak outside, sucking angrily on her cancer sticks when she thought I was asleep and tangled in her sheets.

I hate smoking, especially the smell of stale tobacco on the fingertips. My father smoked when we were kids and Mum would nag him constantly about how disgraceful it was and how it wasn't really the kind of thing people *like us* did. My mother is a snob, but a provincial one. My great-grandparents had taken their familial sum in 1925 when it had purchasing power similar to over one point two million today. They had used it to buy a rather grand house on the outskirts of Worthing and to seed an export business sending dry-cleaning chemicals to the United States. During the war they had taken a ton of government contracts and then reneged on them all, eventually losing everything when my great-grandfather was imprisoned for fraud and embezzlement.

My grandparents' sum was worth the equivalent of about half a million when they took it in 1955. They were sensible; they invested in a modest village house and the education of their son at a well-respected private school. That was where my father met my mother; she was at the local Catholic girls' school, one of the many young ladies who hung around Eden-bridge in the hope of marrying up.

His own familial worth was the equivalent of sixty grand in 1985 when my father hit forty. Luckily my grandparents passed away a year later and so he inherited the house.

I think my mother had greater dreams when she was younger, had thought she was marrying into old money that would give her a level of status and security. She still acted like the minor royalty of their village, mind, and headed up both the WI and the local church choir, ensuring that things were run just how she thought they should be. My mother was born to have staff at her whim, but she made do with the local villagers instead.

My full name is Christopher Aimo Jeremiah Hardcastle. Growing up my father called me Kit. My mother, who is half-Finnish, snuck Aimo into my name – it means 'generous amount'. A dig, I presume, at the familial sum on which she was expected to raise me. I have used it for certain parts of my work in the past, telling horny old women that it's not money that the generous amount refers to. Amidst the blushes and the giggles none of them ever seemed to think that, given it is a name my mother bestowed on me, it's a bit creepy. Unless that is part of their Jocasta fantasy – most of them were at least thirty years my senior, after all. I miss those days sometimes. Carefree, lazy days with the occasional evening entertaining, for two hours at most. But it's a young man's game and I had to move on.

I earn my living now working for a very small, very exclusive and very private company. We specialise in understanding trends and picking out patterns in a sea of certain meaninglessness. If that sounds vague, it's because the job is elusive and constantly changing. I'd been wondering what I was going to do with my life as I hit the big 3-0 and the old ladies began to call slightly less frequently. As I surfed the web one day a little pop-up had appeared, an advert for some IQ testing site. I was bored and so I took the sample test. Five minutes later I got an email asking me to complete some psychoanalytical profiles and offering me five hundred quid for a few hours of my time.

The company trades mainly in favours, making sure that certain people know certain things before others realise, and with a sideline in making sure to buy or short the right currencies and the right shares. We predicted Brexit and Trump and the billions lost the day that Kardashian sister said Instagram was dead. In December, my small team started to discuss the virus in Wuhan. We waited until late January and then we began to move. I recommended a position in distilleries, online supermarkets and a distributor of mid-price garden apparatus like plastic-framed swimming pools and inflatable hot tubs. By the end of March, the distilleries were making hand sanitisers, online supermarkets' websites crashed because traffic was up two thousand per cent, and orders for garden pools had trebled. But more importantly, I knew exactly when the country would go into lockdown, and exactly what kinds of chaos and confusion this would cause.

Intelligence and preparation are a powerful combination.

Knowing lockdown was coming, I had ordered a replica of Leah's phone. I knew Megan would try to keep her relationship with Tom alive while we were trapped at home, but I couldn't be having that. Leah's iPhone looked like an exclusive model, but it was actually just an ordinary iPhone with a fancy case. Swapping it out without Megan realising was easy.

My mum has an aunt who still lives in Finland, and I would spend quite a bit of time there when I was a boy. She would call me Pikku Prinssi, 'Little Prince', and she doted on me like all great-aunts should. When we went into lockdown, she sent me a case of Koskenkorva Salmiakki. It's a salty liquorice-flavoured Finnish liqueur and is the perfect antidote to the smell and taste of liquid Nytol. I don't drug Megan every night, just when I need a break from watching over her. She believes the stress of the pandemic is exhausting her.

Megan thinks she is emailing Tom, but since I switched Leah's phone last week it has been me she's sending lengthy love letters to. I'd debated hacking into his actual email, but in the end I just set up a free email account in his name. She didn't notice. It's quite fun, pretending to be him. I drop in little snippets from the times the two of them spent together, when Megan didn't realise I was watching and listening, making notes of the smallest detail to recycle later. It's so very easy to take control of someone's smart TV, stream the feed from the inbuilt webcam directly to your own computer without anyone knowing. Plus, the CCTV cameras I'd installed in that fancy Belsize Park house let me see what is happening in all the other rooms.

Intelligence and preparation plus attention to detail are even more powerful.

Obviously, Tom still needs to receive emails he thinks are from Leah. This was a bit more tricky to set up, but I made it work in the end. I need to be able to control their interactions, make sure that neither party does anything that might compromise my efforts. For a while I was sweetness and light, but there has been a subtle undertone that Tom is blind to in his infatuation. Now it's time for old Tommy boy and the games to start. I've been waiting for this.

I send Tom a message: *I don't think we should see each other any more.*

He replies quickly: *We haven't seen each other in weeks!*

That's not what I mean, Tom. I just think it might be for the best.

Tom replies with a flurry of messages of love and support. 'Leah' asks him to stop harassing her. *I need some space to think.* He continues to message. He's starting to beg. 'Leah' responds: *Leave me alone. You're frightening me. Do I have to call the police?*

Then finally: *Tom. I'm really getting scared now.*

I back up the texts with emails. One particularly long and rambling one where I miss the odd keystroke and fail to make sense. It ends with: *Are you not going to take no for an answer?*

This evening, after the national news bulletin, I switch channels. I've been looking forward to this moment.

'Local news?' Megan raises an eyebrow at me. 'We really are turning into your parents.' She giggles as if it's funny. How has she not realised what is coming? I do sometimes wonder if she isn't a bit simple. Perfectly capable of holding down a job and brushing her teeth, of course, but not exactly ever going to get into Mensa.

'Watch.' I enjoy the way the laugh dies on her lips. It took a bit of effort on my part to change which region of local news we could watch. I had to spoof the TV's location in the end and it was fiddly as hell. I'm not going to let her foolishness spoil this for me.

'Welcome to BBC London.' The crisp accent of the newsreader in her prim little cardigan.

'Aren't we South East?' Megan asks.

'Just fucking watch.' She will not ruin this.

'Breaking news this evening is the disappearance of a local celebrity, writer and influencer Leah Patterson, who lives in the Belsize Park area of north London.'

Megan turns to look at me.

The newsreader continues: 'she was reported missing yesterday by a concerned friend who has asked to remain anonymous at this stage. We are appealing for anyone with knowledge of her recent movements to contact the information hotline number at the bottom of your screens.'

'Who reported her missing?' Megan's voice is tiny like a child's.

'Who?' I smile lazily and shift closer to her on the sofa. 'Me, of course.' I laugh and reach out to stroke her hair as she recoils from me. 'If I can't get her money alive, then I'll have to get it dead.'

'But. . . but. . .'

'But what? Use your fucking words, Megan. You're not five!'

'But. . .'

'I'm not going to tell them it was you, am I? For fuck's sake.' I tap her temple with my index finger. 'Think, Megan. You're the beneficiary of her will. You can't be a murder suspect, can you?'

'I. . . err. . .' It's almost painful to watch the cogs trying to turn.

'Let me lay this out for you, shall I?' She nods dumbly. 'You cannot access Leah's money because apparently she didn't trust you and so used high-level biometrics that you couldn't break—'

'It's fairly standard when you're a twin.'

'What. Have. I. Said. About. Interrupting. Me?' The words are almost a growl. 'Now,' I'm back to nice Chris again, 'as I was saying. Because your sister thought you were a lying bitch – her words, for the record, not mine – she made sure you couldn't actually take her money. But that is a bit of a problem, isn't it? So, I have made a Plan B.' I smile and stroke her arm. 'Leah is missing. In a few days some evidence will materialise that suggests foul play. Don't worry, I can't have you tied to her murder, can I? I doubt you'd be able to inherit everything if you were convicted of her homicide, I think there are probably some rules around that. But anyway, there will be an investigation, but the case will remain forever unsolved. You will inherit everything. And then you'll give it to me. Simple.'

'But. . .that could take years. . .'

'It could.'

'But, what i—'

'You say you won't? Then, Megan – and this would be far too easy, you understand – then I will kill you and it will be labelled a suicide and your estate will pass to your loving widower.'

'But you can't kill me until the will—'

'You're going to run away, are you?' I can feel my anger rising. 'Remember that until the point that money is in my account, I can have you arrested for her murder and produce enough evidence so that any jury in the country would convict you.'

I don't want to have to use force. But I will threaten her with it if I have to. 'Or I can just hold you here, lock you in the attic with the spiders if necessary, drug you up to the eyeballs.'

I grab her face between both my hands, digging my fingers into her skin until she looks me in the eye.

'I am getting that money, Megan. You *are* going to help me. Whether you like it or not.'

Chapter Sixteen

Megan rings the hotline ten minutes later as I sit next to her, my hand resting on her thigh.

'I'm her sister,' she tells the rather brusque-sounding woman on the other end, who finally puts her through to one of the police officers looking into the disappearance. Megan agrees that we will drive to the station to see what assistance we can provide.

It would normally take about three hours to drive from Guildford to Belsize Park, but with zero traffic on the roads due to lockdown, the trip takes less than an hour and a half. In the car, I drill Megan on exactly how this is going to go down.

'You'd better make sure that you've got those acting skills on point,' I tell her.

She is the one driving; I'm not a big fan of driving in the dark, plus she knows that area of north London better than me. 'Leah was the actress, not me,' she says, eyes on the road, hands a perfect two and ten like it's her driving test.

I'm surprised, to be honest. Megan always struck me as the one who would have been into amateur dramatics, and music camp, and all the other things that the nerdy kids did at school so the popular kids would have something specific to bully them about. I would have thought Leah would have been out with all the boys.

'She never told you that, huh?' Megan asks. 'Not her scene, that what you're thinking?'

'She doesn't strike me as the drama type, that's all. I would have thought she'd be. . .'

'She liked to have people to boss around. The boys in the club would do anything for her. Like they were her very own entourage.'

Megan's voice is tinged with the jealousy that rears its head whenever there is talk of boys and their teenage years. I know that Leah shagging her first boyfriend was a bit below the belt, but Megan was hardly whiter than white in all of that. Leah had confided in her twin, told her about the boy in the year above who Leah was into. Who Leah had lost her own virginity to. Megan had gone blabbing to their mum, their mum who by that time had found Jesus and was balancing on a soapbox of abstinence. She had gone batshit and marched into school, still dressed in her pyjamas, and dragged Leah out of class by her hair, screaming that she needed to learn a lesson and wouldn't be leaving the house until she apologised to God for allowing a boy to defile her. Of course, her mum had thoroughly failed to make Leah apologetic, and she had refused to stay locked up in the house. I do sometimes wonder if some of the more kinky things Leah had been into were really just to get back at her mum, like she could imagine the horror on the woman's face if she knew what her darling angel was up to, and that was part of the appeal.

Megan and I haven't really talked about my affair. I mean, it's not like she has a leg to stand on. She murdered her sister. That is a tricky place from which to claim the high ground.

'You need to talk about her in the present tense, Megan.' Better for me to keep my own high ground and cut off any conversation that might circle to my infidelity.

'I'm not stupid, Chris.'

I want to laugh. *We wouldn't be in this mess if you weren't.* I don't say it out loud. Especially as it's not really true. She did save me a job that I had originally planned. I'm not sure I ever really wanted to dirty my hands with Leah's murder. I just hope Megan behaves now. Does what she's told. Staging her suicide sounds messy. Vomit with an overdose, all that blood if she slits her wrists in the bath.

'What are you thinking?' Megan asks.

'Hmm?' I snap back to the here and now, the deserted streets slipping past the windows. She's confident driving here, after the month she lived here pretending to be Leah.

'I asked what you were thinking,' she repeats, breaking her focus on the road to look at me.

'Just thinking of all the ways I could kill you and make it look like you committed suicide, Meggie.'

Her knuckles turn white as she grips the steering wheel harder.

'So. Let's just not fuck up tonight, eh?'

With her body in profile, I watch as she swallows. Her neck gleams milky white in the streetlights. I'm captivated by a vision of my hands round that pretty throat, her eyes bulging as I increase the pressure and she kicks and squirms beneath me. Perhaps I need to stage her murder instead. A violent affair perpetrated by a psychopath. I would need a better patsy.

'We're here,' she says, pulling into the cramped car park of the police station. She takes a few attempts to reverse into the only space, her hands beginning to shake. I jump out to help guide her, like any thoughtful and considerate husband would do. Her eyes flare as she looks over the steering wheel at me. For a brief second, I know exactly what she's thinking. She's running the calculations in her mind of what would happen if she just gunned the accelerator right now. Ploughed me down and drove off somewhere, free from all of this. Except there's a roadblock a mile away doing checks on why people were travelling given the current COVID restrictions. And a CCTV camera pointed directly at the car. Instead, she lets me guide her into the space and out she hops.

I take her hand as we walk towards the bright lights of the station foyer. 'Game face, Meggie. You've *just* found out your sister is missing, remember.'

But when I look at my wife, there are tears on her cheeks, her mascara is a mess and she's clinging to my arm as if to stop herself drowning. Damn. Leah might have been the actress, but Megan really can play the part too when she puts her mind to it.

Megan continues her performance inside the station. I'm actually impressed. 'We're here about Leah Patterson,' she tells the bored man on reception, her voice cracking. She holds up a bag of things she has brought that she thought might help the investigation. Pictures, details of Leah's social media accounts, a list of friends' names.

A dumpy, uniformed woman appears. 'Let's go and find an interview room to talk,' she says to Megan.

'Can I sit in with her, offer moral support, Officer?' I ask her. To my ears my tone sounds obsequious, but the woman positively beams at me.

'Of course,' she says. 'I wish my partner was such a sweetheart.' There's a longing there. 'And please call me Milly.'

Megan is still clutching at me as we are ushered into an interview room. I hand her some tissues as we sit down, and rub her shoulders; the jealous gaze of Officer Milly burns my flesh. Plain little Officer Milly who just wants to meet a nice boy and settle down into matrimonial bliss. Silly little Officer Milly who sees so much shit in her day job but still thinks it could never happen to her.

At first Megan looks terrified that something awful has happened, but when the police reveal it is just a missing person report, Megan begins to relax a little. 'I thought you were going to tell me that Leah had died,' she says softly. Officer Milly apologises for the misunderstanding and the two women chat for a while about mundane crap I have no time for.

'So, you and Leah aren't close?' Officer Milly asks as she deposits yet more tea in front of Megan.

'No, not really,' Megan replies with a wan smile. 'Families can be kind of difficult.'

'Tell me about it,' Officer Milly confides. 'I have a brother. . .' She rolls her eyes and Megan offers up a false polite laugh. 'Sorry.' She clears her throat. 'So, when did you last see her?'

'Probably six months ago or so. Before Christmas.' The lie is so smooth, she almost convinces me too.

'Did you know her friends?'

'Some. But only those from the olden days, you know, school and where we grew up.'

'Which was where?'

'Wiltshire. Salisbury – well just outside, really. My father was in the army, he was stationed there. Or at least that was what we thought, anyway.'

The real Patterson curse is not one of memory loss and paranoia and make-believe. It is actually a curious desire to spill the deepest secrets of one's life to every stranger in the street. Megan told me once she does it to pre-empt the fact that they will have read the book, or seen the film adaptation, or the million and one other ways that Leah had monetised their misery. But I actually think she was always like this. Leah was similar. Zero filter, with anyone, least of all with those she met only fleetingly, like barmen and air stewards. I had been to the bathroom in a restaurant once and came back to find Leah telling the wide-eyed waitress a story about a wealthy sheikh who liked to serve his guests their dinner laid out on the bodies of someone their guest had preselected from a catalogue. It was not clear from the story if Leah was a diner or the serving platter, and she revelled in the ambiguity.

'Do you think any of them, those friends from your youth, would want to hurt Leah?' Officer Milly asks this carefully and I watch Megan's reaction closely.

'You—' Her voice catches and her eyes dart to mine for support. Support that I provide with an outstretched hand and concerned expression. 'Do you think someone *hurt* her? I thought we were just trying to find her?'

'Well, we can't rule anything out right now.'

'But. . . but. . . I thought she was just missing, you know, like she's gone away and not told anyone. Like she did when we were kids.'

'She has a history of running away?'

Megan nods. 'That was what she did whenever things got a bit difficult. She'd always turn up though. A few hours later when we were really little, then she'd be gone a bit longer the older we got. I used to pretend to be her so she wouldn't get into trouble. I'd keep running up and down the stairs changing between my clothes and hers so my parents would think we were both at home. I managed to convince them for a whole weekend once, although it had been a bit touch and go at dinner.'

I throw warning daggers at Megan. That story – and a story is what it is, a complete crock of shite – is not on-script. I will make the bitch pay for that later.

'So, you think she'll turn up?' asks Officer Milly.

'She probably just ran off somewhere, had an argument with her boyfriend or something and wanted some space. Did you look at her social media?'

'It doesn't look like she's been posting for a while. A lot of influencer types have gone dark, apparently. It's nothing we worry about.' Officer Milly sounds like she spends a *lot* of time wishing her life was as glamorous as some other people's.

'No, I suppose not,' Megan replies.

'Do you know who she was seeing?'

'I think he was married,' Megan replies. I dig my nails into the flesh of her hand – where is she going with this? – but her smile doesn't crack one bit.

'What makes you say that?'

'She liked to take what wasn't hers. And if he wasn't married, she'd have wanted people to see him, would have splashed his picture all over social media.'

'But she was definitely seeing someone?'

'She was *always* seeing someone,' Megan replies.

The interview wraps up and Officer Milly promises to be in touch if they find anything or hear anything. She thanks Megan for her help.

In the car I am silent until we are home and through the front door. As soon as it clicks shut behind us, I whirl round to face her.

'You will regret that.'

'What?'

What? What? She has the fucking audacity to stand there and ask me what? 'You know, Megan. Don't play cute with me.' I have never hit a woman in anger – well except when she shamed me by flirting with Kivi in front of my family – it is not how I like to handle myself. But a punishment is justified if the crime is particularly heinous, and she needs to understand that she cannot act like that without consequence. Our hallway runs adjacent to our neighbours' front room, where they seem to spend their entire lives sat in front of mind-numbing TV. So, I grab her upper arm and drag her into the kitchen, throwing her on to her knees on the tiled floor.

'What the fuck, Chris. . .' Her voice peters out as she tries to stand up but stops when she sees me.

I have slipped my belt from the loops of my jeans and I'm folding it in half and then in half again.

'You have to learn, Meggie,' I say, cocking my head to one side, a compassionate smile on my lips. 'You have to learn who is in charge here, and what I will and will not tolerate.' I tap the belt gently against the palm of my hand and relish the soft crack of leather on skin. 'Now, take off your jeans.'

'No!' My wife, although in a heap on the floor, is defiant.

I laugh. 'No?' I squat on my haunches to bring my face level with hers. 'OK. I'll give you a choice then. Take your jeans off, and I will take this belt to your bare arse so you won't want to sit for a week. Or keep them on.' I hold the belt in my left hand above my head and drop the buckle end so it falls to the floor. 'Keep them on and I will take this metal end to that pretty face of yours. Your choice.' I push myself back to standing and wait for her answer.

She raises her chin and stares at me as she struggles out of the jeans, which have become a little too tight during lock-down. Something else I will have to deal with, I suppose. I can't have my wife not looking after herself.

'That was the right choice, Meggie.' I smile beatifically at her and fold the belt again so the metal end is in my palm. 'This is for your own good, remember. I don't get any pleasure from this at all.'

I take her phones away. The one she uses to ring her mum and text that bimbo Hannah and the other vacuous bitches she chats to. And the one she thinks I have no idea about that she was still using to talk to Tom. Or who she *thinks* is Tom. Obviously, that whole charade has to stop.

She is now totally alone. I don't think she had really realised that before. I think she'd had this idea that something would happen, and all this would go away. Even with the police interview I think she still thought it would be OK. But it's starting to sink in. I can feel her fear now. It's palpable in the air around her. The brave face she's been wearing has slipped.

She is starting to unwind in front of me. The old Megan, when she'd been scared of losing her mind and begging me to come to her rescue, was alluring, this greasy-haired mess sitting on the sofa all day eating biscuits is not. It has been three days since we went to the police. She is still obviously uncomfortable sitting down for too long, but I am trying to ignore her pathetic whimpers when she shifts her weight too quickly.

'You'll feel better if you shower,' I tell her. She pulls another digestive from the pack and nibbles the edges as she ignores me. 'C'mon Meggie. This is madness.' It was a punishment that she had well and truly deserved, and this was wearing thin now. To me, unfounded violence speaks of an inability to think coherently, to strategise. I preferred neat words to get people to do what I want, rather than messy fists. But there is a part of me that wants to drag her by the hair and bodily throw her in the shower. 'Megan!' The same tone I had used with the dog we had when I was a boy. 'Get. In. The. Shower.'

As she washes, I pick her out an outfit. A beautiful floaty summer dress with a fitted bodice and a full skirt. She had bought it years ago for a friend's wedding, and my heart had burst with pride at how gorgeous she looked. She went without a bra; the plunging back belying the demure silhouette. I remember the way she had sucked in a breath when my fingertips grazed the base of her spine over a dinner of dry chicken in a congealing mushroom sauce, and she'd moved from my touch, leaning in to whisper, 'Not here, you'll make me horny.' Of course I'd carried on, watching her face intently as she crossed her arms over her chest to cover her nipples, a blush staining her cheeks. She had nibbled her bottom lip and looked back at me from under her eyelashes.

When she comes out of the en suite, her gaze falls to the outfit lying ready on the bed.

'No,' she whispers, eyes flashing to mine.

'No?' I stand up and take a step towards her. 'No, to the dress?'

'No to. . .' Her voice trails off as she half motions to the scrap of lace on top of the dress. The bright blue panties Leah wears in the photo.

'These?' I pick them up, the fabric cool to my touch. I can feel myself already hardening at the thought of the last time they had been worn.

'I won't wear them.' She raises her chin slightly, the shower having evidently washed off some of the placid and meek persona she's been cocooning herself in out of misguided self-preservation.

'Oh, Meggie.' I sigh and hold them out to her. 'Yes, you will. And you will put on that dress as well. You will mix me a drink and then cook me dinner. We will laugh and make conversation like a proper couple.'

'No.' But her voice is uncertain again, the meek coming back.

I smile my vulpine smile at the little lamb in front of me. 'Yes, Meggie, you will.' I throw the scrap of lace towards her, laughing as she catches it, and saunter from the room. 'And put some fucking make-up on, Jesus Christ!' I shout over my shoulder.

Twenty minutes later she finally emerges from the bedroom, the dress swirling softly around her knees, wet hair braided down her back, eyes rimmed in kohl.

'Much better,' I say as I appraise her. 'But no lipstick? You know I like it when you wear it.' I watch her nod slowly and return to the bedroom, coming back a minute later with her full lips lacquered in a brilliant red the colour of overripe tomatoes.

'Perfect.' I smile and motion to the drinks cabinet. 'I'll take an old fashioned, please darling.'

I sit in the biggest of the armchairs and sip my drink, listening to her clattering round the kitchen beginning dinner. Megan is no chef, a disappointing fact I'd only discovered after investing six months in this whole endeavour, by which time it was too late to change my mind. The sound of swearing drifts into the living room, so I heave myself out of the chair and pad to the kitchen to find out what kind of a mess she's made now.

She has burned the sauce on to the bottom of the pan. She can't even make pasta without fucking it up. I sigh heavily from the doorway, enjoying the way her shoulders droop when she realises I've seen her fail. 'Oh dear me.' I cross the kitchen in three long strides until I am directly behind her, easing the handle of the pan from between her fingers and placing it down on one of the spare rings of the hob. My other arm snakes round her waist and I draw her close to me. I can feel her tension, the way she tries to pull away from me.

I have never taken my wife against her will. Not properly anyway. But she has never pulled away from me like this. Anger wells inside me and I want to hurt her, to make her actually feel something for once. My voice is low, breath tickling her ear as I whisper, 'Are you trying to make me angry?' She tries to pull away from me again and before I can stop myself, my hand is wrapping round her braid and I'm pulling her hair so hard her neck is exposed to the ceiling. A tiny whimper escapes her lips, and my heart beats faster. I slam my hips against her, pressing her bodily against the lip of the countertop. The silverware in the drawer beneath us rattles and I slam her again. Part of me wishes to open the drawer a little and see what potential weapon my hand comes to rest on. The other part holds back; I can't mark her, not yet at least. Instead, the hand that isn't wrapped round her braid creeps down, following the curve of her hip and upper thigh. She squirms against my touch and I let a bubble of a giggle loose. Under the hem of her skirt my fingers spider, slowly scrambling up the inside of her thigh. She is holding her breath, stiff and unyielding. I release my hold on her braid to wipe a tear from her cheek.

I won't do it, however much I want to. That is the line I have drawn for myself, and I refuse to cross it. Instead, I leave her sobbing in the kitchen and go to my office. On one screen I watch her via a CCTV camera I've hidden among the jars of spices she never bothers to use. On the other screen I pull up the feed from another camera, a piece of spyware installed on to a smart TV so I can keep an eye on someone as he paces his living room.

Tom is worried. And so he fucking should be.

Chapter Seventeen

I had promised Megan she would never be tied to the murder, and I am going to keep my word. But there is one rather significant problem. You cannot just declare someone dead if they are merely missing. Not for an exceptionally long time. At least seven years, and it can be even longer if the deceased has a large estate to be discharged. There is no way I'm waiting that long for what I am due. I've already waited long enough.

Luckily for me, I've been laying the groundwork for a while. After all, Leah always had to die. The patsy had been chosen months ago, someone just hanging out in the wings, ready to step forward if needed. Everyone knows it's always the husband or the boyfriend.

The affable ginger twat was someone who Leah would definitely have been attracted to. She'd always had this idea about dating higher, above her own class. I think that somewhere inside her had been this fairy-tale idea of the poor girl with the villainous family being rescued by the dashing Prince Charming. She didn't need his money, but she hankered for the respectability a bit of a title would lend her. The legitimisation of her own wealth, which had been bought off the back of a scandal and the double-crossing of her own sister. Plus there was that strange agency she worked for who had transferred a few very large payments in the days after she was spotted out with the son of a man with interesting affiliations. I wondered what he had really paid her for. If it was just her time, or if she had bolstered her income serving up a few 'extras'. Not that I could judge her too harshly; it's not like I've never charged for my time.

I had also been confident that Tom would fall for Leah. I doubt any man could really resist her. The twins have this classic 'girl next door' thing going on: long dark-brown hair, all bouncy glossy waves; green eyes; red lips without the need for much make-up; narrow waists and broad hips. 'Good, childbearing hips,' my grandmother had told me at my wedding as she motioned towards my blushing bride. And a more than decent pair of breasts. Funny though, Megan was always self-conscious about her appearance, preferring to hide her curves away with bulky jumpers in winter and midi-skirts in the summer. In contrast, Leah would squeeze herself into skin-tight dresses that stopped just below the crease of her bum. And she had a penchant for dressing up.

'What's your guilty fetish?' she had asked me one night. 'Who would you like me to be?'

'Yourself,' I told her, and she laughed in my face. 'OK,' I acquiesced and thought for a few moments. 'It's kind of weird. But I've always wanted to do it with a barrister. The whole gown and wig thing.'

The next evening, I arrived at her house and she told me to close my eyes as she led me through to the living room. When she told me to open them, she was standing in the full regalia: black gown drawn close around her, wig balanced on her hair, which was otherwise flowing down her back, and I could just spot a peek of a stiletto heel under the robe. 'Sit,' she demanded as she slowly opened the robe to reveal her underwear beneath, that electric-blue set I liked so much. Swishing the robe to one side, she straddled me, wig slightly askew.

But anyway, it wasn't Leah who Tom fell for in the end. I was a bit surprised by how much he appeared to like the version of Leah that Megan created. Somewhere in the middle of the two of them, but definitely without the immediate appeal that came naturally to Leah. Even when Megan dressed in Leah's clothes, I always felt there was something missing.

I had watched the taxi pull up to Leah's house after their second date. Those doorbell camera things are extremely useful, you know. If you know the details you can just log right in from anywhere and keep an eye on your street. Anyway, I watched as my wife, all dolled up in someone else's clothes, turned back from the third step and went back to the taxi to drag that ginger prick up to the house. She kissed him square on the mouth about three inches from the little camera. Imagine what that looks like when you're alone in your marital home, and all you can see on the big screen TV is a close-up of the woman who vowed to love you for ever kissing some guy. I wasn't going to let either of them get away with that shit.

You know Megan made me wait? Before she let me into her bed. Not just the standard three dates that 'nice girls' like to convince themselves is an appropriate amount of time after which he won't think you're a slut. Not even the increasingly fashionable five dates. She made me wait for almost two months! I'd been let in the house for a coffee, an actual coffee not a code, and we'd kissed and stuff. It was ages before she asked me, all wide-eyed, if I would like to stay the night. But the ginger prick she let into her bed – well Leah's bed, to be precise – after just two dates. I watched him swinging her round and fucking her against the wall in Leah's living room. I was furious.

Who the fuck did he think he is?

She is *my* wife.

I'd had the doorbell camera installed for Leah a few months ago. Had told her I just wanted to make sure she was safe, and she should always make sure she knew who was at the door before she opened it. Of course, I made sure I could access the feed, so that I knew who was coming and going from the house. She didn't know about the other spycams I'd secreted around the house: a tiny camera hidden within the spine of a book I knew she'd never even glance at, another embedded in what looked like a little diamond decorating a candle on a shelf. I also popped a little bit of spyware on to her laptop while I was at it. My home office has two computer screens and so I can get up her screen on one to see what she's looking at and pop the webcam feed on the other so I can watch her.

It turned out to be even more useful, the spyware, after the 'incident'. I learned a lot that first night Megan rummaged through Leah's files. Things flying up on the screen that I hadn't seen Leah really care about, like the value of her stock portfolio or the itemised receipt for the work she did for Angels Inc. There is also a camera in her bedroom and one in the spare room. Just in case. I'm not a peeping tom.

Although I hope the police will think that ginger twat is. Especially when I send him a random email later to trigger a little piece of code I have written. Code that will leave a lovely trail, exposing his obsessive watching and recording of Leah months before he actually met her.

Did I mention I was a bit good with computers?

I have a friend who has always been a whizz with these kinds of things. We'd had a good thing going when I was in my twenties and used to escort. Horny old rich women are stupid. They would pay me an absolute fortune to cum on their tits, while my mate slipped into their hotel suite – it was always a suite, normally paid for by some dolt of a husband – and hacked their phones. We would then syphon money from their accounts, use their credit cards and the like. After a while, he taught me how to do it myself, to cut down the risk of him being caught in the suite. It snowballed from there. We made a killing, until he met some girl and decided he should get a proper job. He still helps me out occasionally, though, if things get a bit too tricky. For old time's sake. Before we both had wives.

It's been four days since the first call for information on the disappearance of Leah Patterson was televised. I have been looking forward to this evening all day, willing the hours I had to spend on my day job to pass quickly. Although, I did notice that the sanitiser company I had bought shares in – only a small number, what I could afford with the remnants of our joint savings account – had jumped up in value by over one hundred and fifty per cent. After that I got a bit sidetracked looking at the bitcoin Megan was able to transfer. It has increased by a few per cent in just a week, the hundred thousand pounds making me four grand in just days. I'll have to diversify it soon, too risky to leave it all in bitcoin. But just think what I can do when I get the rest of the money from Leah. Holy fucking shit!

The daily press conference has finished and the evening yawns in front of us. Megan can feel there's something different about this evening; there's something special in the air. She is tense on the sofa next to me, like a spring coiled tightly and about to make a leap for it. I let the vulpine smile slip from my face and replace it with a clown's grin.

'What do you think, Meggie?' I watch the confusion cloud her pretty face as she struggles to understand where this is going. 'Why don't you go and get me another gin and tonic, hmmm? And then you can sit here nicely and watch me have a little fun.'

Megan nods mutely and goes to top up my drink. I notice she is still walking a little stiffly, each step a bit tentative, the pain of the punishment lingering.

When she returns, I pat the sofa cushion next to me, instructing her to sit. I enjoy the way she cowers when I put my arm round her and pull her closer. Pulling out a cheap untraceable mobile – one of the many I have secreted away for times like this – I call the number of the police tip line. 'I have information regarding the disappearance of Leah Patterson,' I tell the operator. 'I was walking my dogs a week ago, just outside of East Grinstead. I walked through a little car park, it's fairly remote with just a single trail running through it. I don't think it's used very often. Anyway, there was a car parked and I could hear that the people inside were have a blazing argument. A proper screaming match. I figured I'd keep my distance, but then the passenger door opened and this woman got out. A man immediately got out the driver side and went running to her. It looked like he was trying to stop her running off, almost dragging her back to the car. She slapped him across the face, it made a ringing sound that got my dogs' backs right up, but I don't think he was hurt. But then he threatened her. Told her if she didn't – and I quote here so apologies for the language – that if she "*didn't get back in the fucking car and shut her fucking mouth, he would fucking kill her*.' I wondered at the time if I should have done something. But then I saw the picture of that missing woman on TV and realised. It was her. The woman in the car park.'

'Do you know who the man was?' the operator asks me.

'He was tall. Over six feet. Slim build. But it was his hair I noticed. Bright orange it was. Distinctive. Plummy accent too. I think I heard her call him Tim, or Tom. . . yes, definitely Tom.'

'Anything else you can tell us?'

'That's it. I just thought I should tell someone. I couldn't live with myself if I said nothing, and then it turned out that something bad had happened to her.'

'Thank you, sir. Can we contact you again regarding this?'

'Well, I'd rather you didn't. You know. . . what with the restrictions and all, and I may have been a little further from home than I should have been. You know how it is, the wife jabbering in my ear all day and the kids running round like heathens! I took the dogs out for a good few hours.'

'I understand, sir. But it would be helpful for us to have your name and contact details in case we need you to make an identification.' She sounded nice. Young and cheery. Probably hadn't been working a police tip line for long; I could only imagine the kind of psychopaths who might call those lines.

'I'll call back if I think of anything more. . .'

I put the phone down and grin at my wife.

'Oh dear! Do you think I was a little obvious with my description?'

I watch her swallow as she remains staring straight ahead, eyes focused deliberately on the TV in front of her to avoid mine. She has always worn her thoughts for public consumption; so easy to tell what she is thinking about. What she is worrying about.

'How long before they act on the tip, do you think?' I ask. I want her to face me, but she doesn't give in. 'I think it'll take a while; I doubt they'll go to talk to him tonight. Tomorrow, possibly.' I sigh, world-weary loud. I stretch my arms over my head and yawn loudly, bringing one arm round her shoulders like a sixteen-year-old at the cinema. 'Now then, Meggie. How about you tell me about him, eh?' I stroke her cheek with the back of my hand. 'Tell me about how you thought you could get away with cheating on me?'

'You cheated on me first.' Now she faces me, eyes blazing anger.

'That's different, Meggie. You know that. And I was thinking of *you* the whole time.'

'Bullshit.'

I put my hands up. 'Cross my heart and hope to die. It was only ever you, Meggie. If you'd just been a little more accommodating' – I tilt my head a little – 'If you'd just been a little sweeter to me, I wouldn't have had to, would I, eh? But now we are all in all kinds of trouble, aren't we? A big old mess that *I'm* trying to clear up for us, before we drown. Isn't it lucky you have me to make everything OK again?'

We sit side by side on the sofa for the rest of the evening, except for the few minutes she takes to fetch me drinks or snacks. I make her pee with the door open so I can keep an eye on her. I can't risk her calling the police to redact my story or make up a load of lies to save *him*.

Just after eleven, an alarm on my phone beeps. The doorbell camera, the one that Tom won in a competition he didn't remember entering a few months ago, has been activated. I take my wife by the hand and lead her to my study. I sit her down in the large chair in front of the twin monitors.

'Watch, Meggie,' I whisper in her ear as I stand behind her, the glow from the screen lighting the room with a greenish tint from the night-vision cameras I am streaming. There are two policemen standing on Tom's doorstep, just waiting to have a conversation with the tall red-haired man. All thanks to a very polite, but a little nervous, dog walker who gave a tip-off about him a few hours ago.

With my hands on Megan's shoulders I can feel the twitch of her muscles, the tension building in her as the policemen wait for Tom to open the door.

'I wonder what he's doing in there?' I say as I lean forward and, in a few clicks, fill the other screen with an image of Tom's living room, the spyware in his huge TV activating without any sign. 'Let's have some sound, shall we?' I press a few keys and his plummy voice comes blaring out of my speakers.

'We need to ask you a few questions, sir,' one of the officers tells him.

'Is this about Leah?' Tom's voice is frantic, his hand swishing through that stupid hair.

'Yes, sir.' The officer is brusque, his tone perfunctory.

'Have you found her?'

'No. But we have reason to believe that you and Ms Patterson had an altercation recently. Something that you failed to tell the officer you spoke to.'

'Altercation?'

'A witness has come forward.' I note that he doesn't mention it was just an anonymous tip-off and that they have no idea who I really am.

'Witness?' Tom looks around himself in confusion.

'Yes.'

'When did they say they saw this?'

'Last Thursday.'

'I was working last Thursday. Here all day, on and off conference calls.' Actually, Tom had a three-hour break in the afternoon when he had cooked himself pasta and read a book on his patio, plenty of time that he won't be able to prove he wasn't out threatening his girlfriend. I could prove it, with my collection of recordings. Not that I will.

'Can you prove that, sir?'

Tom crosses the room and opens his laptop. I click a couple of buttons to shift the view from his smart TV to the laptop camera, his face now filling my screen as he peers at his.

'He should moisturise more,' I say to Megan. 'Those wrinkles will only get worse.' Another click and I mirror his laptop screen on to mine.

Tom pulls up his calendar from last Thursday and shows the officers the list of meetings. He also pulls up the history of his company online chat to prove he was working most of the day.

'What about the afternoon?' the officer asks him.

'Lunch, bit of reading. You know, nothing special.'

'Can anyone vouch for where you were?'

'I didn't see anyone. We're in lockdown.'

'Sure.'

The other officer leans in to peer at Tom's screen, his face now filling the entire frame. 'What is this?' He is pointing at something. I know it will be at the folder marked 'Camera Feed.' 'If you've got CCTV on this place, we'll just watch the footage to clear everything up.'

He double-clicks the folder.

I wish I could see Tom's face, not the policeman's. On to the laptop screen tumble hundreds of video clips. All from Leah's apartment. Videos of her changing, of her and Tom together, of her jiggling her breasts in the mirror as she turns this way and that to get a better view of her nakedness.

'What the. . .' exclaims Tom. 'These aren't my videos.'

'This is Leah?'

'It looks like it.'

'Well, Mr Eagleton. You will agree that your laptop doesn't really exonerate you, does it? I suggest we continue this conversation at the station.'

I laugh in Megan's face. Mascara carves a groove down her face. 'Is little Megan upset that her lovely boyfriend is a stalker freak?' I ask as I wipe a tear from her cheek. 'Do you think he enjoyed watching *you* jiggling your bits like that? Oh don't worry, sweetheart, he's never seen those videos before now.' I break into a wide smile. 'But I do think he might be just a little bit fucked. Especially when they find all the other treats I've left.'

A few months ago Tom had thought he'd been a victim of credit card fraud, because someone had been making some suspicious purchases on his account. To be honest, I'd assumed he wouldn't notice; rich bastards don't often notice a few extra hundred quid missing here or there, they just think they bought an extra round in a bar or something. I've met enough men like him to think that.

Turns out that he's a ridiculously fastidious chequebook balancer, like my mother used to be.

She would sit at the kitchen table every month and go through every single transaction to make sure the bank hadn't made a mistake. I know we weren't as well off as she'd hoped we would be, but we weren't so poor that we had to look out for every pound. And guess how many mistakes she found in the eighteen years I lived at home and had to watch this monthly charade? Yep: you've guessed it. Not a single one. Not ever. But still we would have to go through it, and as soon as I was old enough to count without using my fingers she would force me to help, the heady scent of ginger from traditional *piparkakut* in the air as we pored over the numbers. Although, to her credit, I am probably a lot more careful with my own finances as a result. So perhaps she was right all along.

But anyway, turns out that Tom is cut from the same cloth. So, he found the suspicious transactions and dutifully reported them to his bank. It will perhaps give him the plausible deniability he needs when the police find the cameras in Leah's apartment that I bought with his money. Although perhaps it just shows what a long and intricate game he's been playing.

'You're framing Tom,' Megan whispers, her eyes wide as if she's in shock.

Interesting. Does she actually care about this guy?

'They'll never make the charges stick. Not without proof she has been harmed. Corpus delicti, Megan. If there is no crime, there is no perpetrator. *We* have the body, remember. They'll let Tom go soon enough. At worst they'll think he's a peeping tom. Hint's in the name, huh! Although, I *could* make the police think there was some foul play. If you step out of line.'

'He's your insurance policy.' Her voice is flat. I think the penny has finally dropped.

'Exactly, Meggie. You got there in the end, didn't you?'

Chapter Eighteen

The next night I give Megan an extra-large dose of Nytol, disguised by an even larger glass of the Koskenkorva. She has developed a bit for a taste for it.

Earlier that day I was busy washing up. We took it in turns to clean up the kitchen after each meal and today I was rostered on for good-husband duty. Our sink is ceramic and deep – the sexy estate agent called it a butler sink. The plug is no longer attached to the bit of metal chain. It's the kind of thing you should fix; the chain serves a specific purpose, allowing you to run the water out without fishing into the soapy depths. I had filled the sink with suds and begun the noisy task of washing up. I could see her standing outside the window, sucking on a cigarette as if her life depended on it and watching a series of small clouds labour across the pale blue sky. Although I had wanted to rip the disgusting thing from her fingers, I cut her some slack. This was a trying time for all of us. I waited until she walked back into the house before I dropped the highball glass into the water.

As expected, she came rushing to my aid like a well-trained poodle, to find a cut on my finger dripping crimson into the sink so full of watery soap it was almost overflowing. She plunged her hand in to remove the plug. I went to grab her hand away from danger, then feigned horror when she withdrew her hand to show me a slash on the fleshy heel part of it, about two inches long.

I apologised profusely and sat her gently on the sofa with a tea towel wrapped round her hand.

The gash was ragged and fairly deep. I probably should have taken her to the hospital for stitches. But in the midst of a pandemic you don't want to overwhelm an already stretched-to-breaking-point health service. Or at least that was how I convinced poor Megan to suck it up and douse the flame of the pain with paracetamol and a healthy slug of delicious Koskenkorva.

So now she is knocked out, I unwind the bandage from her hand and score the wound with the tip of the sharpest knife in the kitchen. I feel the muscles of her hand contract slightly. Even asleep, the body responds to pain stimulus. Crimson beads begin to form, and I carefully hoover them up with the tiny pipette that came with a brand of oral mouthwash for exceptionally bad gingivitis. I have always had great teeth and gums, but I thought it might be bad form to buy a random pipette from Amazon. Preparation and caution are the cornerstones of any plan.

I carefully swab away the excess blood and bandage her hand. Carry her to the bedroom and change her into the shorts and vest she uses as pyjamas. Finally, I squeeze a little toothpaste on to my finger and use it to massage her gums. She will wake up with a sore hand, a headache and the taste of toothpaste, as if she had taken herself to bed. None the wiser about my little vampiric extraction.

The night is dark, the sky loaded with cloud that blocks out the moon and the stars. I am driving fast, but not so fast as to attract attention. The car is technically not mine, but no one will report it stolen. It belongs to one of my neighbours, who hasn't left the house at all since the virus started circulating, not even to go to the shop or the pharmacy. A fact I only discovered because I am a good citizen and belong to the street's Facebook chat group about who might need help with groceries or going to pick up prescriptions. Community-spirited. That's what they say about Chris Hardcastle. Always one of the first on the street at eight on a Thursday evening to clap for the doctors and the nurses risking it all on the frontline. Always happy to pop round with milk or bread if a neighbour has been left in the lurch by one of the supermarkets. I have even helped a handful of parents to make sure their kids are set up to do their schoolwork online. 'Such a lovely man,' all the mums say about me. 'Good lad,' say the dads, 'always up for a quick beer too.'

How many of them could I fuck if I wanted to? Probably four out of the six I see most often. Wives that is. Probably at least one of the husbands too, although personally I'm not really into all that. Definitely Candice. She groped me at her Christmas-Eve-Eve-Soiree – her term – last year, pushing me into the darkness of the utility room while her husband handed out drinks to everyone, her palm rubbing me through my trousers. Sharon who looks twenty-five but is actually pushing forty. Kate is probably a good bet, with her bouncy ponytail and yoga-honed physique. Maybe Dina, although she's not really my type; unless she lost a couple of stone. Mabel is thirty years my senior, and although she has tried to grab my bum in the past, I assume it was entirely in jest. Then there's Yasmin, who turned sixty last year. Her husband is eighty-six. They have been married for thirty-six years.

Yasmin's husband has COPD, diabetes and heart disease and is at least five stone heavier than he should be. Yasmin is four foot ten and weighs just under seven stone. She is her husband's sole carer. Megan thinks she has it bad being married to a man who is trying to protect her from going to prison for murder. Megan doesn't know how lucky she actually is. Yasmin has talked more than once about 'When it's all over', and I don't think she means COVID.

I have tried to help Yasmin, bringing her groceries, and making sure there are some treats to help her through. A bottle of Koskenkorva, some nice chocolates, bubble bath. Last time I was there I grabbed the spare set of keys to their car while she was cooing over the goodies.

The garage they keep it in is down a side street, not visible from their house. It takes me just under three hours to drive to my destination and back. I pull over half a mile from the garage to inspect the car, wiping down the sides where small specks of mud from the dirty lane have marked the paintwork.

A man out walking an aged spaniel finds a phone under a tree. There is a smudge of blood on the screen. No fingerprints though, as the police discover to their disappointment an hour after it is brought in. They plug it into a computer and hack into it using some specialised software that the public is very wary about, accusations of spying flying around.

But still. The phone belongs to Leah Patterson. The picture on her cover screen is her and a man who most definitely isn't Tom. It is actually some random photo I pulled off her Insta; I think he might be the husband of her writer friend with the breastmilk fetish. Anyway, they were at a party and he has his arm round her waist and his eyes on her cleavage. Anything to help muddy the water. Leah's messages are full of exchanges with Tom in which she begs him to leave her alone. In which he accuses her of having a relationship with someone else. The last one she received from him says: *Either I have you or no one will*.

Megan and I watch the TV as they report on the finding. Tom Eagleton has been arrested on suspicion of causing harm. They tried to charge him with murder, but the judge had decreed it was too early and there was no evidence that Leah had been killed. This part wasn't reported on the news; I had to hack a few emails to get that snippet.

There is a further update on the nine o'clock news. Tom Eagleton has now been charged with the murder of Leah Patterson. Hair and blood have been found in the boot of his car. A shovel caked in mud was in his garage. There were no clean sheets in his closet, nor towels for that matter. His bathroom stank of bleach.

People think *corpus delicti* means there must be a body. It's not a reference to a literal body though, it means 'body of evidence', and there is more than enough of it to charge Tom without an actual body. Not just to charge him, either. With everything I have been putting out there during some nightly excursions, not all of which the police have actually uncovered yet, he will be convicted by a jury of his peers and face a mandatory life sentence. Although it might be fun to leave a little bit of a body for them to find. A few fingers maybe? Enough that they will know she is dead, but without enough of a body for there to ever be a tie to Megan.

I was lying when I told Megan that Tom was just an insurance policy.

The call comes in about two hours after Tom's charge has been televised. Poor show from the police really.

'I'm so sorry, Mrs Hardcastle,' the officer says to my wife. 'We should have called earlier. We have charged your sister's boyfriend with her murder. We are sorry for your loss.'

I take the phone from her hand. 'This is Mr Hardcastle.'

'The husband?'

'Yes.' I am curt. This is all terribly unprofessional, and they are acutely aware of it.

'We are sorry that no one contacted your wife before.'

'We saw the news. My wife had to find out that her sister might have been murdered on the nine o'clock news.' My voice is cold: low and level, like I am trying to keep the lid on the simmering pot of my anger.

'Yes, well. We are sorry. We will ensure that you are kept abreast of any future developments.'

'Please do,' I say and hang up.

'But he's innocent. . .' Megan says quietly. It is the first time she has spoken all evening.

'No, Megan.' I tuck my finger under her chin so she is forced to look at me. 'He fucked my wife.' Her eyes flick away from mine. 'I couldn't let him get away with that. Could I, Meggie?' I lean in to her, my lips grazing her earlobe, my voice no more than a whisper. 'Don't think that this is the worst of it either.' I kiss her neck. 'Now, let's go and have a nightcap, shall we? It's getting late.'

The Koskenkorva burns my throat as I sip it slowly, watching Megan gulp hers down. I top her up again. I have chores to do this evening and knowing she's safely tucked up in our bed will give me one less thing to worry about.

Do you know how long things stay frozen in a chest freezer if there's a power cut? It depends on how much is inside, and whether you keep the lid closed. I have a wonderful memory of being a boy and the power going out at home. My mother was in hysterics. My father laughed at her. The freezer had been stuffed to the gills: the result of years of special offers, the hoarding of leftovers, and pack sizes meant for a family of four when one of your children is so fussy she will only eat cheese on toast. If you keep it sealed, the temperature will be OK for almost forty-eight hours.

I, of course, was desperate to be shot of all the random ice-damaged chicken Kievs and the lemon ice pops that were always left over, and so I kept creeping into the garage and cracking open the lid. There was an insurance claim, and one day the local frozen food van pulled up on the driveway. The freezer was duly loaded with treats and goodies like it was Christmas.

But anyway, the experience made me cautious. I'd moved the freezer from the cabin to the summer house when I'd realised that Megan was planning to disappear and become Leah permanently; I couldn't risk her getting rid of the body and losing my advantage. But the dodgy electrics in the summer house had been making me nervous and the further we went with this, with Tom being arrested, the more I figured Megan might actually crack and do something stupid. Like confess to murdering Leah. So I'd found a better home for the freezer and checked it every few days, just to be sure. So once Megan was flat out on her back, snoring that strange snuffle both twins were guilty of, I crept out of the flat in my jogging gear. Thankfully there wasn't a curfew here, so jogging in the middle of the night could be explained by night working if anyone thought to question me. Not that they did; the streets were dead. Besides, I was only going one street back. To the garage of my poor old neighbour who hadn't been able to leave the house since all this COVID stuff began. Who was probably right now being ministered to by that beautiful diminutive wife of his who counted the days until he passed on and she could live again.

Yasmin was thrilled when I told her I'd make sure to jog past the garage on my daily runs, to make sure that everything was all in order. 'A weight off my mind,' she had said, patting my hand and offering me another slice of cake. 'And any time you just need some space,' she had added, 'feel free to go there. There's an old sofa and a power socket if you want to plug in a radio or something. I know it's not easy living so closely with someone at the moment. I promise I wouldn't dream of disturbing you.'

I had grinned at her and thanked her for being a lifesaver. 'Is it bad to want time away from my spouse occasionally?' I had wondered out loud.

'Not at all. I would give anything for it.' At that moment, her husband had rung the little bell he used to let her know she was required. 'Duty calls,' she had said as she stood up.

Although I am in my running gear, I am instead sitting on the slightly mouldy sofa and eating a bag of tortilla chips. With Yasmin's blessing I have created myself a bit of a haven in this cavernous space. The garage would be big enough for two large cars, but Yasmin's husband has a small Aygo that takes up less than one third of the floor area. She told me he used to have a Bentley – an old one mind – and a Mercedes for a while, until his business hit a rough patch and he had to sell it.

The rest of the space is more than big enough for the humming chest freezer, raised off the floor on a pallet to make sure it doesn't overheat. That's a really common flaw with chest freezers, overheating and melting the wiring. I won't take the risk. The sofa faces away from it. I mean, I can't exactly relax looking at the freezer in which the body of my dead lover lies, can I?

I have made sure she's hidden under a layer of random frozen goods: peas, sweetcorn, that kind of stuff. Just in case Yasmin does come in here to have a little poke around. Although if she does, I will just offer to find space for her husband in there too, and I'm pretty sure we could come to an agreement.

I brought my laptop with me and it is balanced on a box in front of me, playing a rerun of an old comedy show my mother liked. The loneliness of lockdown gets to us all in the end. I hadn't thought about my parents much before all of this. But now that I couldn't see them, I wished desperately to be back in my childhood home. Stupid for an almost forty-year-old isn't it, to long for the warmth of his mother like a clueless boy?

A noise behind me causes me to swing round. She stands in the door, dressed in black leggings and a hoodie.

'Megan, what the fuck are you doing here?' I move towards her, expecting her to flinch and pull away.

Instead she smiles. A lazy feline smile. 'Oh, Chris.' The 's' drawn out. There is only one person who has ever said my name like that. 'Did you *really* think I was Megan?'

Part Three
Leah

Chapter Nineteen

I look at him and narrow my eyes. 'You're a fucking idiot, Chris.'

'Megan? What are you doing?'

I laugh. 'Megan's dead. Lying right there. You never even realised it.' I am staring at the humming freezer. He is staring at me. I grin and take a little curtsy. 'Did I do a good job? All those acting classes over the years. I think they finally paid off.'

'But. . .'

'But what? You always thought you were so clever. Pegged yourself as this big genius.'

'I saw you. At the cabin. . .'

'Oh, sweetheart.' I smile. 'And that was only your first mistake. Like putting Nytol in my drink, for Christ's sake. Did you really think I wouldn't be able to taste it? You got sloppy and you fucked up, Chris.' I made sure to lengthen the 's' in his name.

I can see him starting to sway a little, unsteady on his feet. He's probably feeling like he's spent too long on a boat, lost his land legs, nausea and queasiness creeping up on him. I kept the doses small at first. The poison builds up in the system though, the rates in the blood steadily increasing over time. Although I was drinking Koskenkorva laced with Nytol – which was actually only enough to make me a little tired, you'd need a whole bottle to knock someone out cold like I was pretending

229

to be – he was drinking Koskenkorva laced with something much worse. It's a funny poison. You feel OK, then if your heart rate goes up too high, the effects begin to accelerate. If he took deep calming breaths and maybe sat in sukhasana for a while, he'd be fine. But of course he's panicking. His lovely well-laid plan has just turned to shit in front of his stupid face, and he has no idea what is happening. For a control freak like Chris this is the worst thing in the world. Well, actually that's about to come, but he doesn't know that yet.

I have planned this moment for a long time. Thought about how I might bring down a man who is at least thirty kilos – that's almost five stone if you're better with old money – heavier than me. The drug is one that no one will think to even test for it. So, it will need to look convincing that I could have over-powered him even if he'd been fully compos mentis. I had a few ideas that bordered on the avant-garde: a croquet mallet could have been fun, or even a Juicy Salif lemon squeezer – you know the one that looks a bit like a tripodal spaceship? – but eventu-ally dismissed them. Kept it nice and simple. A metal wrench, the type that you find in every man-who-doesn't-DIY's toolkit. Heavy enough to really hurt, too light to actually be of much use but at least I could swing it with ease.

His mouth is goldfishing as I swing the wrench at his head. The drugs have dulled his senses and he's unable to process the shine of the metal swinging towards him before it's all too late. He crumples – and I don't mean that figuratively, it's actually rather fascinating to watch a fully grown man fall into a literal heap – to the floor before a sound can pass his lips.

The backpack I left just outside the door contains everything I need. I drag him a few feet and use a pair of handcuffs to secure him to a floor bolt. I think it was put in to chain a motorbike to, but it works just as well for a human. Then I set to work. It'll be better to set the scene while he's unconscious – and yes, I have checked he's breathing – and then once he wakes up, we can have a little chat. I pour the contents of the backpack on to the cold stone floor and begin.

'Morning, sleepyhead.' My voice is singsong, almost chirpy. 'Did you have a lovely rest?' I watch the realisation sink into his handsome features, his hand fumbling for purchase but thwarted by the handcuffs. 'Oh, don't move too much. We wouldn't want you to hurt yourself, would we? Not like you hurt me, oh brother-in-law of mine.'

His eyes suddenly flash open, and I smile as he takes in the scene I have set.

In one corner a bucket emits the rancid stench of piss and shit, as if someone has been forced to use it for a while. A long chain, the kind you would buy from a hardware store if you were into some pretty weird stuff, snakes from the motorbike bolt towards the back of the garage, where a wad of rags is streaked with dried and fresh blood. I am wearing a pair of gym shorts and a grubby-looking vest, the same ones I've been wearing during home workouts for over a week. They smell pretty ripe. My hair is tangled and pulled off my face in a rough plait, a plait that screams of inexperienced fingers. The flesh on my right ankle is swollen and bruised around the cuff I have attached to myself and then to the long chain. My nails are bloody and there is quite a lot of his skin buried under my nails from where I tried to fight him off me in my attempt to escape.

His mouth hangs open in abject shock.

'Surprised, Chris?' I laugh and pick up his phone, which I took from his pocket earlier. 'Now then, in a few minutes I'm going to call the police and have them come to rescue me.'

'You think they'll believe this shit? Megan, Leah is lying in that freezer with your fingerprints all over the body.'

'No, Chris.' I shake my head slowly. 'In that freezer is the body of your wife, Megan. My beloved sister. Who you killed. And then you kidnapped me and held me hostage. You forced me to pretend to be Megan, threatening to kill me if I didn't do what I was told.' I allow a tear to snake down my cheek. I hope it makes my mascara run even more.

'But. . . but. . .'

'But, but, but! Use your words, Chris, you're not five!'

'But. . .'

'But what, Chris? This isn't how it was meant to be? This isn't the plan?'

'They won't believe you.'

'Which bit exactly do you think they won't believe?'

'I'll tell them you're Megan. That you killed Leah. That you're framing me.'

'But I'm not Megan. That's where this all went wrong for you, Chris. When you saw something and made an assumption. You placed your bet and you lost, big-time.'

'I know you, Meggie. Leah wouldn't—'

'What? Put up with your shit?' I'm standing over him now. I want to hurt him, punch him in the face, make him feel some of the pain he put me through. But I won't give him the satisfaction. I step back. 'I needed time. I was just going to slip away. Before. Have Megan just disappear. I've been working on it since the cabin. Megan was going to vanish into the night, and everyone would think she'd done a runner. Hannah would come forward and say you were having problems. There might be a bit of suspicion of foul play concerning her creepy husband, but in the end. . . well, no body, no foul, right? Corpus delicti. You said it yourself.'

I turn away from him and pull the shorts up so he can see my bare arse cheek. 'But then you did this, Chris.' You can still see the red welts. I think they'll scar a little. 'You lost control. I can't forgive you for that. So now, you will go down for the murder. With hostage-taking and GBH added to the mix for good measure. Who do you think the police are going to believe? Some wild story that I'm really Megan, but I've been pretending to be Leah since I killed her, and now I've staged the hostage-taking and whipped my own backside with a belt?' It's beautiful to watch his face fall. 'Or will they believe that you killed your wife, and then kidnapped her sister, who you tied up in your neighbours' garage? How many people will step forward and say you are a sick fuck, Chris? Even your mum offered to help me escape from your clutches.'

'You won't get away with this.'

God, I wish I could be there when the police finally charge him with murder and kidnapping and assault. 'When this is done, Chris darling, you will never see daylight again. I'll make damn sure of it.' I tap three nines into his phone.

'Meggie, please.' He's turned from arrogant dick to pleading husband, the change almost impressive. 'I love you, don't do this.'

'Megan is dead, Chris. You killed her. With your sick and twisted lies and cheating. And now you're going to pay for it.' I tap the green phone icon and the call goes through.

'Please help me!' I half screech into the phone before they even ask which service I require. 'He's trying to kill me. . . like I think he killed her. . . help me. . . I'm in a garage on Green Avenue, just off Harvey Road. I don't know the number, but it has a red door.' I let out a blood-curdling scream and slap myself around the face, hard enough to leave a red mark. Hanging up, I turn to Chris. 'That'll bring them running.'

'You bitch,' he whispers as I swing the wrench at his head once more.

There are a few moments, waiting for the police, when I'm a bit concerned I might have swung a little too hard that second time. I can't see his chest rising and falling.

But then blue light pulses under the door of the garage and things go crazy. I have wrapped myself in a blanket and tucked myself into the corner far away from his prone body, pulling out individual strands of my hair to make my eyes water and my nose run, and someone comes over and wraps me in one of those space blankets that runners or people who get lost and stranded up mountains use. You'd think it would make a crinkly noise like tinfoil, but it's almost soft, like fabric. A paramedic leads me out to the ambulance waiting to whisk me away. I can see faces pressed against their windows, residents wondering what on earth is happening on this sleepy suburban street. I cover my face in a way that a victim would, pulling the space blanket tighter around me.

Another paramedic runs to Chris. Please let him be alive.

'Is he. . .' I ask the police officer who is now sitting beside me inside the ambulance.

'You lamped him pretty hard.' There is pride in her tone. 'But not hard enough.'

Relief. He'll live to face his punishment.

'At first, he told me he would kill Megan if I didn't do what he wanted.'

'What did he want?' The detective is sweet and soft-voiced. She has brought tea and biscuits to the discreet hospital wing in which a doctor has assessed the – not very euphemistically described – damage I received at the hands of Chris.

'Money. At the beginning it was all about the money. I. . . I. . . well, I'm kind of well off.' There is an apology there, a recognition that I brought this on myself by being successful. Much better than have her resent me. 'But then. . . well. . . something changed, and he started to talk to me as if I was Megan. I don't know what happened. He drugged me and took me to that. . . that place. . . then he chained me up and. . .' A primal noise escapes from deep in my throat. I almost scare myself with the force of it.

'You don't have to talk now. Just rest and we'll talk again later.' She's kind and so I sip my tea and bask in the sensation that someone has my back.

Later I will tell them every last detail. I'm almost looking forward to it.

***

There are one hundred and one myths that surround identical twins. Some have a basis in reality, and some are such complete horseshit it's almost funny.

Myth one: we share the same DNA.

When my father's sperm met my mother's egg – not something I particularly like to think about, to be honest, but there we are – there was only one of us. Over the next few days, as the cells began to divide, the ball spontaneously cleaved into two. No one knows why this occurs; there is no genetic link, no societal or cultural phenomenon to explain it. The rate of identicals is the same the world over, in every population group. Most people therefore parrot the 'same DNA' mantra. It's not quite true. We are clones of each other, yes, but our DNA goes through subtle changes over time, constant micro-mutations that can be identified. However, the technique is rather sophisticated and generally only used in cases where murder convictions rely on DNA evidence to ensure that the wrong twin isn't inadvertently executed or imprisoned for life.

Myth two: we share some kind of psychic link.

Most twins are close. Most will hold hands while they sleep in their bassinets as tiny babies. Most will finish each other's sentences and, at least while they are young, enjoy the same kinds of activities. Some develop a special language that only the two of them can understand, to the chagrin of exasperated parents. But I have never known what my twin was thinking. And for that I am thankful. Can you imagine being psychic if your twin is a psychopath?

Myth three: it is difficult to tell us apart.

Most twins are easily identified, and when placed side by side you can see a huge array of differences. My sister and I are more identical physically than most; there's a convention in America that tries to find the most identical pair and we would smash that. But even though to the naked eye we look the same, it is easy to tell us apart. Dental records for example, if we didn't both suffer from such a deep-seated phobia that neither of us had ever been to the dentist. We fed off Mum's own fears and she'd been almost relieved when we refused to go. Just thank God we hadn't needed braces. Scars and birthmarks are good giveaways. Medical history too – if you could trust we were always who we said we were, of course.

Our fingerprints are completely different, as dissimilar as if we weren't twins at all. But here's the thing. You would need to know which set of prints belong to Leah and which belong to Megan, a base reference as it were. Are yours on file somewhere? Only if you committed a crime or had to be taken out of an equation at a crime scene, or there's another good official reason for them to be. All I need to do is prove that I am Leah and this will all go perfectly. And guess who recently went to Las Vegas and gave the US Border Force a lovely copy of her prints?

Actually, there is one way, but only we would know it. There was an old man in Turkey who covered the dots our father tattooed on us with a pretty flower design. There are a different number of stamens used to conceal the dots. You'd have to look pretty darn close though. And you'd have to know who has which number. Chris knows Leah has one more than Megan to denote her being the elder. But will he remember if Megan had nine and Leah ten, or if it was ten and eleven? I very much doubt he will, and it was really very easy to add an extra two little dots using a broken biro and one of the pins from the noticeboard we would pin takeaway menus to in the kitchen.

I don't know how well you know Chris by now. Has he bragged yet about how he doesn't need to sleep much? How he's super productive because he only has a few hours each night? It's all true, but damn! He sleeps the sleep of the eternal dead for those hours. You would need to drive a steamroller through the house to wake him up. Never have I seen anything like it. Although it did give me the ultimate window of opportunity to devise my own plan and find the chinks in his armour. There was always one thing that Chris was terrible at: seeing his own vulnerabilities and faults. There is no way he ever dreamed I would find a way to outsmart him. That it would be him in a little cell and not me or Tom.

My biggest problem had been finding a way to physically overpower him. I'd debated using the Nytol to knock him out, but you can really taste it if you take more than a little sip, so I needed something else. Yasmin – the neighbour who Chris plays knight in shining armour for – has a well-stocked medicine cabinet from which I was able to pilfer some interesting things when I popped round with a cake I'd baked. Chris had said her husband wasn't a well man and, judging by the veritable pharmacy in her bathroom, he hadn't been kidding. Amazing that the cure for one can be poison to another.

There is a long journey ahead of me. This is all far from over. But it will all work out in the end. Because there is something about Chris that when you finally get to know him you see, something that marks him out as one of God's fuck-ups.

When this goes to trial – and of course it will, he's hardly going to plead guilty and take the life sentence without a fight – any juror worth their salt will gradually see his true colours being revealed, and then they will decide that yes, this is a man who could do the things I've accused him of.

Chapter Twenty

'Where is Megan? Have you found her?' I have asked these questions over a hundred times since the police found me, and they have yet to actually give me an answer. I keep my eye on their reactions though, to make sure it is not me they suspect. There is no chance that they haven't found the body. I mean, it was right there in the room. It's not like they wouldn't have had a peek inside the freezer. I'd made sure that the thin layer of frozen goods – bags of peas and sweetcorn and the like – covering her had been moved aside just enough that even a cursory glance would reveal her.

'Where is Megan?' I ask once more and watch the flicker of pity cross the man's face. Yep, they have definitely found her.

'Can we take your statement first, Leah?' His voice is gentle, the way you would talk to a slightly unhinged great-aunt at a wedding sitting legs akimbo as the older children laugh that you can see her underwear. I nod, shoulders sagging as if I can feel the weight of the answer he might give me. I follow him down the corridor to the interview room.

The victim suite – actually I doubt that's its proper name but I'm assuming the room, decked out like a plush lounge, is never used to interrogate suspects – is bathed in soft light from a few strategically placed lamps, the comfortable furniture muffling the sound of my story finally being told in full.

The nice detective from the hospital is here again, but this time she has her boss with her. At least, I assume he is her boss. And possibly her lover, going by the stolen glances and secret smiles. Although heaven forbid that you could listen to the stories told within these walls and then want to go home with someone who heard the same ones; I would think the only way to stay sane in this job would be to totally divorce work from home.

'This is DCI Rosenmeyer interviewing Leah Patterson on Saturday, the sixth of June, 2020.'

'And this is DS Fonteyn in support,' the female detective adds, leaning in to the recorder to ensure that her own part in this is placed on the record.

I would be pissed off at his rudeness, but the resigned way she leant forward tells me this is something she is forced to do every time. I think there will be parts of the interview that I will only tell her directly. Make sure she stays involved every step of the way. We women have to look out for each other, after all.

'So, Leah.' DCI Rosenmeyer – or Jimmy, as he has previously instructed me to call him – gives me an encouraging smile. 'Can you tell us what happened? Start right back at the beginning.'

'When is the beginning?' I ask.

'When do you think it is?'

I pause. Was it when Chris approached Megan on the train that first time? When they had married? When he started an affair with his wife's sister? When one twin ended up dead? In my head I have practised this speech one hundred times into the darkness as Chris lay comatose next to me. I always started my story on the first day of lockdown. But that's not really where this all began, even in this fucked-up version I'm spinning. So, I leave my careful script to one side and begin to just talk.

'My sister and I have always had a fractured relationship. You hear so many stories of twins, so much crap about soulmates and two halves of the same person and best friends for life. Do either of you,' I wave my hand in the direction of both detectives, 'know what it's like for the world to think you are only half of a person? That your sibling is just another part of you, and you of them in return? To live your life praying that when someone asks, "Which one are you?" they won't be disappointed when you tell them?' They both shake their heads. Not that the odds were favourable to either being an identical. 'It can cause friction.' I flash a small smile. 'Nothing major, but the normal sibling rivalries get amplified. Competitions intensify. Megan and I had got to a point where we didn't really speak much. I think we'd both spent so much time trying to be different, to be our own person rather than one half of a whole, that we had ended up too far apart to see eye to eye.'

'So, you and Megan weren't close?' DCI Rosenmeyer – I can't think of him as 'Jimmy' – asks.

'Not at all,' I reply. 'We hadn't really spoken in years. I wasn't invited to the wedding, she never introduced me to her husband.'

'You didn't know who he was when he kidnapped you?' DS Fonteyn (she's asked me to call her Vicky) pipes up.

'Well. . .' I pick at my nails – easy when my DIY French manicure is so chipped – and take a few moments before I answer. 'The thing is, I did know him. I just didn't know who he was. In relation to Megan, I mean.' They both look confused. 'I met Chris in the bar of a hotel about a year ago,' I go on. 'He told me he was there for a meeting. That he was single. I don't think I need to elaborate.'

'You spent the night with him?' Vicky looks wide-eyed, as if I am a friend recounting a particularly scandalous liaison. Which I kind of am, and I need her to continue to think of me like that.

'I didn't know who he was. I wasn't seeing anyone at the time. We spent a couple of nights together. Continued to see each other after that. But it wasn't a relationship or anything. More of a. . . err. . .' I think of something shameful from my real past – the time I went swimming in a bikini I hadn't realised was totally see-through when wet – and feel the bloom of a blush light up my cheeks. 'Well, more of a physical thing. Dating is so tough these days. . .' I implore Vicky, who sneaks a peek at DCI Rosenmeyer, confirming my suspicions and revealing that, yes, she also thinks this dating lark is rather hard.

'When did you find out who he was?'

'He. . . he. . .' My voice breaks as I force the tears to well. 'He turned up on my doorstep on the night we went into lockdown. I thought he just wanted a. . . well, you know. . .'

'Booty-call?' offers DCI Rosenmeyer. Vicky shoots him a glare. Booty-calls are obviously a bone of contention in whatever their relationship is.

'Yeah. But. . . I was seeing someone by then. Someone I had come to really like.'

'Tom Eagleton?'

'Yes. So, when Chris came to the door, I invited him in. Just so there could be no weird argument in the street. You know, nosey neighbours and all that.'

'You let him into your house?'

'Of course. We'd had a thing. I thought he just wanted a final fling before he went home and locked down for however long it was going to be. I made him tea and was going to let him down gently, tell him to go home. Then I was going to ring Tom and see if it wouldn't have been too forward to ask him to come and lock down with me.'

'And then what happened?' I fear I am losing DCI Rosenmeyer's interest.

'Then he knocked me unconscious and the next thing I knew I was waking up in his house and he was calling me Megan.'

'He called you Megan?'

'Then he showed me their wedding pictures and a hundred other things to prove exactly who he was.'

'Did he want you to *be* Megan?' Vicky asks.

'He wanted my money.' I shrug and spread my hands, palms down, on the desk. 'He told me he would kill Megan if I didn't hand over everything to him. I don't know how he knew so much about my balances in my various accounts, but he'd obviously done a lot of research.'

'So, what did you do?'

I will tears to form in my eyes and swallow a few times. 'I thought it would all be OK. I thought you would come for me.' I watch as the detectives exchange blank looks. 'But you didn't.' I let out something akin to a wail. 'I waited and hoped and prayed, but no one came.' They continue their blank looks of incomprehension as I sob into the tissue Vicky passes me.

'No one knew you were missing,' she says eventually.

I take a deep breath; this is starting to challenge my acting prowess and I can feel myself getting tired. I don't know how actors do it, filming harrowing scenes over and over without fatigue setting in and causing them to stumble over their lines. I turn my attention to DCI Rosenmeyer; I think it is fairer that way.

'You should have known.' My voice now carries a hint of anger, a flash in my eyes. 'I guess I just wasn't on your priority list.'

'Now, now, Leah.' DCI Rosenmeyer breaks the concerned detective routine for a few seconds. He has probably been told to try to sweep this under the carpet.

'I raised the alarm and you left me. To fend for myself against a psychopath.' Even I don't know if I'm meant to be distraught by the outcome or angry as hell at their incompetence. I am therefore treading the thin line right down the middle, and I'm surprising myself at how genuine I seem.

'We couldn't track you.' He is speaking in the way you would to an injured animal, when you are not sure whether it will curl into a ball or rip your throat out. 'There were too many layers of encryption and location muffling. You could have been anywhere.'

'Sorry?' Vicky is still looking blankly at the two of us. 'What are you talking about?'

There has definitely been some kind of cover-up here. I imagine it's all a bit embarrassing for the police for it to come to light that the missing woman – who has finally turned up but not in the clutches of the innocent man they arrested – was actually flagged as the potential victim of a hostage situation by her very expensive bank weeks ago.

DCI Rosenmeyer sits back in his chair and squirms a little.

'I think it's best if Leah tells us her side of the story. Let's get it all out in the open and we can go on from there.'

'So you don't have to admit you failed me?' I ask. His face is impassive. He is probably worrying I will sue them. I talk to the kinder face of Vicky instead. 'I had security on my accounts, my main ones anyway. A code to enter in the case of a hostage situation. It's one of the premium services my bank offers to high-value clients. Turns out it was a waste of the fifty-grand fee I pay every year though.' I am chagrined about it.

'There was no way to trace you. He had set up the system to never let anyone pinpoint your location.' DCI Rosenmeyer is matter of fact.

'But you knew I had triggered it and still. . . what? You arrested my boyfriend thinking he'd done something?'

'There was evidence of foul play on his part.'

'That Chris had concocted. For Christ's sake.' I let my voice rise as a very real anger courses through me. 'I could have been killed. And all you would have done is blamed an innocent man for it.'

Now, I'll be honest. It had actually helped me that the police could never pinpoint the hostage warning. It gave me the time to plan this all properly instead of acting in blind panic. I've always been a little lucky and never so much as now.

'Leah – Ms Patterson – we are incredibly sorry for the failings that you believe occurred and we will investigate more fully, but you will be aware as well as we are that if Chris hid the location of the laptop into which you entered that code, it would be near impossible to trace.'

'Near impossible is not impossible,' I reply curtly.

'Look,' DCI Rosenmeyer says, 'I don't blame you for being mad, but let's stay on track. Please? We still need to hear the rest of it.'

'OK.' I sigh. 'So, my bank requires you to input a keyword before the retinal and fingerprint scans. I told Chris the code was Tarquin. It was actually Oberon, so I knew it would flag to the police when I entered it. The banking system says it's accepted the keyword but then comes up with an error message that it can't read the retinal scan and tells you to contact them. To someone trying to coerce the money from you it looks like the error is with the bank. In theory, it is genius. But when I couldn't send the money, he went ballistic. Told me that he would make sure I lost everything I cared about. While I waited for rescue, he began to tell me that he would fake my death and get the money from my estate that way. And that he would keep me hostage for the rest of my life, tied up with no hope of escape.'

I look at Vicky and then at DCI Rosenmeyer. 'I want to talk to you alone,' I say to her. He clears his throat and gets up, almost running to the door. I don't think he wants to hear the next part.

Vicky holds my hand as I tell all the details. The way he called me Megan over and over again. How terrified I had been. She pats my hand and tells me we can take a break for a while. Brings me sugary tea and a huge slice of cake. It's carrot cake with thick frosting. She says her mum makes cakes for the squad, which is kind of weird and sweet in equal measure.

'Did he. . .' She clears her throat before continuing, her voice gentle, 'did he force you to. . .'

I shake my head. To be honest I am kind of surprised that all he ever did was touch me in the kitchen that time. Did that make him feel good about himself? I bet the smug little bastard thought he was being some kind of gentleman.

'We'll get him. I will do everything I can to bring the fucker to justice,' Vicky tells me.

'Thank you,' I whisper in reply through a stream of tears and spit and snot.

Chapter Twenty-One

'There is something that is puzzling me,' DCI Rosenmeyer says softly. We are back in the interview room after a brief break for lunch. 'We have a note here,' he taps the thick file in front of him, 'that Megan was interviewed by the police at the Belsize Park station in relation to her sister's disappearance. To your disappearance?'

'That was me,' I reply, picking at the tissue in front of me. I had wondered when they would find the hole in the story. Better they are weighed down with the obvious, the parts of the narrative I can control, than they go digging around some of the things I have less confidence in.

'You?'

'Chris told me he would kill me if I didn't do it.'

'But we would have protected you, you just needed to say when you were at the station.'

'He was with me. He told the police I was having some problems, that lockdown hadn't helped my mental health issues. My paranoia and depression.'

'Does Megan have a history of issues?'

'No. But no one questioned him. He asked if he could come into the interview with me. I wasn't under arrest, or suspicion or anything. I was just helping with inquiries.'

'I see,' DCI Rosenmeyer says like he doesn't see at all. 'But you had forgotten this. When we took the rest of your statement.'

I wipe the back of my hand over my nose. It is one of those actions that produces a natural recoil in the viewer, forcing them to look away from you. 'It's hard,' I say. 'So much happened, so much I have tried to forget. . .'

DCI Rosenmeyer clears his throat. He doesn't want to get into another conversation about the more personal aspects of my ordeal. Because that's what we are now calling it. An ordeal.

'So, just to be clear. . .' He taps the sheet in front of him. 'You came into the police station of your own volition—'

'He threatened me,' I correct.

'I meant,' he clears his throat again, 'that you came in without it being at the request of the police.'

'The missing person report appealed for people to come forward. I'm her sister.'

'But you didn't know anything about her disappearance – or at least that's what you told the police at the time.'

'Wouldn't it have looked more weird if her sister never contacted the police at all? Despite it being on TV? What would you have thought if you were the officer in charge of a missing persons case and their family just ignored it like it was nothing?'

'I would go to their house and interview them,' DCI Rosenmeyer says.

'Exactly. Chris pre-empted what you would do. He couldn't have you anywhere near the house, could he?'

'But. . . could you not have given one of the officers a sign, some kind of signal that you were being held against your will?'

I take a deep breath and place the palms of my hands on the table in front of me. 'Three things, Detective. Number one; Chris is a psychopath. A violent, unpredictable man who can be sweetness and light one moment, and then pinning you by the throat the next. If he had thought for a moment that I was trying to get one over on him, what do you think he would have done? He had told me, at this point in time, that Megan was still alive.

'Number two; I had raised an alarm through my bank. I was half-expecting some kind of special forces squad to suddenly rappel in through the windows of the house at any moment and for this whole sorry mess to be done with. But that didn't happen, did it? And yes, eventually I realised that you weren't going to come for me, and that I would have to rescue myself, but I was still hopeful at this point.

'And number three; there was a signal. Jesus Christ. I told the officer all about how Leah would pretend to be me. I couldn't have been much clearer in what I was implying. Chris beat me with his belt that night, it was so damn obvious. And I was wearing the fucking watch. The one that Tom bought me in Vegas. I had hoped that someone might see it and realise. Stupid, I know, but what else could I do?'

'What's the significance of the watch?'

'I couldn't exactly wear a T-shirt that said "Hey, I'm Leah, by the way" could I? But I thought someone might look at the watch and realise it wasn't Megan's. It has registration documents with Jaeger-LeCoultre. I figured you'd be looking out for a ten-thousand-dollar watch. For something that Leah had posted about on her social media. Wouldn't it be an identifying item?

'When I was reported missing, wouldn't you have at least tried to piece together what I was wearing at the time?' I'm exasperated now, my voice raised.

'Alright, let's calm down a bit, eh?' He shows me both palms.

'Sorry,' I mutter. 'It's just. . . so. . .'

'Infuriating? Irritating? Yet another symbol of gross incompetence in a system designed to keep you safe but that fails continually?' Another man has entered the small room while I've been ranting, without me hearing him. I see a suited man in his early fifties.

'Well. . . yes,' I say curtly.

'We understand you are upset, Ms Patterson.' He is almost chiding me. 'But that kind of attitude won't help anyone, will it, hmm?'

I want to slap the smug, supercilious look off his face. 'Who are you?'

'I'm here at the request of the chief of police. Let's just say that I work in a department that is committed to ensuring the public continues to feel safe and secure when they go to bed at night.'

'You're a PR guy?' I hate PR guys, all spin and bullshit. Unless, obviously, it's my bullshit that I need to spin.

'I'm here to offer you an apology for the errors that have been made. Please accept our deepest regrets and assurances that all accusations of police mishandling will be dealt with internally. However, I must inform you that there will never be a public acceptance of any failings and should you seek one, we will be forced to take action.'

'What the hell does that mean?'

'It means we're sorry. But you need to keep quiet.'

'Or else what?'

'I'm sure we can think of something, Ms Patterson.' He spins on his heels and is gone.

'So. . .' DCI Rosenmeyer starts, 'now that things have been cleared up a little bit, let's move on shall we? So, Chris forced you to go to the police. OK—'

He is interrupted by Vicky entering the room. Her skin is ashen and her eyes flick to mine only briefly, unable to hold my gaze for longer than a second. She doesn't need to say anything; I can read her body language perfectly. She has been sent to tell me they have found the body.

'It's Megan, isn't it?' I whisper.

She nods. 'I'm so sorry.'

'Is she. . .'

She nods again. 'Yes.'

'Where?'

'There was a chest freezer.'

My hand flies to my mouth and Vicky steps back a few paces. Then the image of my sister's face, forever frozen into the same shocked expression as when the bottle first struck, comes to the forefront and I taste bile. Somehow, for the first time I think, the realisation that my sister is gone finally hits home. Perhaps it is the involvement of someone from the outside, staring at me with the abstract compassion police officers and other people employed to impart the worst of news to families and friends are trained in. My sister is dead. She is never coming back. No matter how much I hated her, how many times I had sworn that I would kill her, the anger and the irritation and the sheer exasperation of her. She had been a part of me for ever and now I am all alone.

I sink into a chair, my head between my legs to try to stop the room from spinning. But it continues to turn, round and round like the waltzers we had loved as little kids, screaming for the man to spin us faster and faster as our teeth chattered in our heads and candyfloss churned in our guts.

Vicky is talking but I don't hear what she is saying, until the words 'blunt force trauma' bring me back to the present. It sounds so clinical, so. . . surreal. I ask her to repeat what she just said.

'We believe the cause of death to be blunt force trauma, a single blow to the head with something heavy, wielded with significant clout. We can't tell exactly when unfortunately, because of the. . . err. . . method of storage.' She winces as she says it. I had been hoping that freezing would leave them unable to accurately pinpoint her date of death, and it seems I was lucky.

'Was it Chris?' I ask eventually.

'That's what it looks like.' Of course it does. My fingerprints were never on the body. It was February and absolutely freezing, so I was wearing gloves like any sane person standing outside would be. I did, however, pluck a few hairs from Chris's head and place them in the freezer with the body. Just in case there was any doubt that he had touched her.

'Poor Megan. . .'

'It looks quick. Single blow to the head. She didn't suffer.' She is quick to reassure me. She probably wants to stop the keening from my lips. Hell, *I* want to stop the keening from my lips.

Half an hour later, I am being led down a brightly lit corridor, a chill on my face. It isn't what I was expecting; I must have watched too many American dramas set in the modern subterranean morgues of inner-city facilities. I thought she would be on a metal gurney, draped in a sheet, a luggage label attached to one toe. I had prepared myself for the full cliché.

But the room is separated into two, one side with a few leather-upholstered chairs in front of a large plate glass window serving as a divider. On the other side, the walls are painted a light-diffusing magnolia. There is a small pale oak dresser with a single candle and a bouquet of flowers in a simple white vase. It is peaceful. She is lying on a gurney, but it is white plastic not metal, and she is covered by what looks more like a tarpaulin than a sheet; it covers from her neck down past her feet. Only her face is visible.

Inside that part of the room it is cold enough to keep her body frozen, you can feel the cold through the window. Vicky's hand is icy in mine as she squeezes it encouragingly.

'You don't need to say anything except to confirm if you believe it to be Megan.'

This is obviously a waste of time. There is no one else it could be, unless there was a third, a triplet we never knew about. Gosh, that would be something, wouldn't it? But I promise there were only ever two of us. Mum would have succumbed to her demons a whole lot faster if there had been three.

'It's her,' I say softly.

We head back to the interview room and Vicky clicks on the tape once more.

'Can you just confirm her full name for the record.'

I take a deep breath. This recording will be played in court, I am sure of it, and so I want to get it exactly right. 'This is Leah Patterson. I confirm that the body I was just shown is that of my sister Megan Hardcastle, née Patterson.'

The area of the police station where I have given my statements is obviously set far away from the cells where they keep the real criminals. It's a bit of a shame though. I would love to have seen his face as they brought him in in handcuffs. As they read him the list of charges I have levelled against him. Charges they will prove, and collect corroborating evidence of, over the next few days. I want to look him in the eye and see the knowledge that he is absolutely fucked. And that there is nothing he can do about it.

Instead, I watch the news on TV. It is the lead story, something violent and shocking to break the constant COVID reporting that otherwise dominates.

The reporter stands outside the hospital and says that Chris has been arrested on suspicion of homicide and kidnapping and has been treated here for a head injury requiring ten stitches. I really did hit him hard.

The shot switches to outside the red-doored garage, where a team of hazmat-suited individuals crawl over the space searching for evidence with which to nail him to the cross. The cameraman manages to get a zoomed-in shot of one of them picking up something green with a pair of oversized tweezers. It is a sweater in the softest green cashmere. They move a few inches and pick up a scrap of burgundy silk that used to be a pair of panties. As they pick them up the light glints off something hidden underneath.

It had broken my heart when I smashed the heel of Chris's shoe into the face of the Jaeger-LeCoultre watch Tom had bought. Although it escaped almost unscathed, a testament to craftsmanship and quality. There is a scratch on the face that will be easy to fix if I can ever get it back from evidence.

The screen cuts back to the hospital as reporters and photographers jostle for space, waiting for Chris to be escorted to the police station for questioning.

He looks angry. Angry and wild, like an animal caught in a trap. A big stick-on dressing runs across his forehead and down towards his left ear. It looks like a sanitary towel. He will hate this footage that makes him look like a violent fool. He has been dressed in surgical scrubs, faded green ones; I'm assuming they took his clothes to search for evidence. My blood is on them. My hairs. Some spit and snot for good measure.

A dozen microphones are thrust into his face as the police try to manoeuvre him towards the waiting car.

'Did you kill your wife?'

'How long have you had her hidden in your freezer?'

'Why kidnap your sister-in-law?'

I can see from the set of his mouth that he is desperate to tell his side of the story. But even Chris isn't stupid enough to blurt out his version of things on TV. He would sound like a lunatic.

This is all going perfectly.

Chapter Twenty-Two

After I had identified the body and watched the news of Chris's arrest, the police left me alone for a while, suggesting I have a little nap as it had been hours since I last slept. I took a blanket and pillow from them and tried to get comfortable. I think I'd managed a whole ten minutes before they woke me up again.

This time nice Vicky isn't in the room. DCI Rosenmeyer is accompanied instead by a very stern-looking man who looks like a cantankerous grandfather faced with a shitty nappy to change.

He barks his name and rank as he sits down in the seat opposite me: 'Superintendent Kurt Von Halen.' No pleasantries.

'Uh, Leah Patterson,' I reply, glancing at DCI Rosenmeyer in confusion. What's going on here? DCI Rosenmeyer refuses to meet my eyes.

'So you say.' Von Halen cuts to the chase.

'Sorry?'

Von Halen sighs theatrically and picks up the sheaf of files in front of him. 'You claim to be Leah Patterson. But you are an identical twin, are you not?'

I lay both palms flat on the table in front of me and tilt my head. 'Sorry, Mr Von—'

'Superintendent,' he interrupts.

'Sorry, Superintendent Von Halen. Are you suggesting that I'm not Leah Patterson?' Incredulity emanates from my every pore.

'Well, you can understand why we might be suspicious.' Pompous shit.

'I spent weeks as the hostage of a man who killed my twin sister. A man who chained me up, even beat me. And you think I'm lying.' My voice is rising, and I watch DCI Rosenmeyer sink a little into his seat. 'I am beyond insulted.' Am I laying this on too thick? I need them to shut this line of questioning down without a hint of real suspicion.

'It is usual in cases such as this to ascertain the true identity of all parties.' Self-righteous prick.

'How many cases like this have you seen, Superintendent Von Halen?' I ask.

'Well. . .' His facade is beginning to crumble. 'I have seen my fair share of domestic cases, spousal abuse, even a handful of homicides.' I think he wants some kind of medal.

'And so, in your learned opinion, I might not really be who I am?'

'We just need to be sure, that's all.' His confidence has evaporated.

Now that I have the upper hand, I take a deep breath. 'Look. . .' My voice is back to its usual pitch and I watch his shoulders drop a little as the tension begins to drift away from him. At least now he doesn't think I'm going to sue for defamation. 'This is a difficult time for everyone. What do you need from me to prove who I am?'

'Well, normally photo ID, but obviously that doesn't help here.'

'My bank account is secured with biometrics. Fingerprint and retinal scan.'

'That would work.'

It takes Superintendent Von Halen ten minutes to get my bank to send the retinal scan and fingerprints they hold on file, the ones I had added to my account for additional security two days after I got back from Vegas. More than enough to confirm my 'real' identity to them.

'Thank you, Leah,' Von Halen says as he leaves the room. 'And apologies for the inconvenience. It's just that we have to make sure every box is ticked. I don't want that bastard to walk free on a technicality.'

'Neither do I.' I offer him a sad smile. 'I want justice for my sister.'

'And yourself.'

'Yeah. . . that too.'

Later that day, the officer in charge of the original missing person's case comes to see me. Well, not the actual officer, her superior. DC Larry Johnson starts by apologising for Officer Milly's failings when I pretended to be Megan at the Belsize Park station. I feel bad for getting her into trouble; she seemed nice. I hope she doesn't end up getting fired.

DC Larry Johnson tells me that they thought I was dead. I laugh bitterly. 'I thought I was going to die,' I tell him, eyes burning into his until he looks away.

'Well, there was evidence that led us to believe that your boyfriend was involved and so we arrested Mr Eagleton a few days ago.'

'Tom had nothing to do with any of this.'

DC Larry Johnson is squirming in his seat. 'We had a tip-off. That you and he had an argument and he threatened you.'

'Jesus.' I say. 'Do you think Chris— I mean, did he try to set up Tom?' I have decided to play dumb. To not let on that I knew what Chris was trying to do. This will be easier if I keep things as simple as possible.

'That's what it looks like.'

'But that wouldn't be enough to arrest someone, surely?'

'We found videos. On his laptop. Of your house.'

'Tom's laptop?' I sound shocked and uncertain.

'Planted by Chris. We found the same files on his system too.'

'What kind of videos?'

'I think it's probably better if you don't think too much about it. Plus, there were messages on his phone, text conversations that sounded like you were breaking up with him and were scared he wouldn't let you go.' Did Chris message Tom as if he were me? That bit is news. I only half listen as DC Larry Johnson carries on talking. 'A dog walker found a mobile phone, with blood on it.'

I show him the palm of my right hand. The thin scar. 'He cut me and used this little syringe to suck up the blood. He thought he had drugged me and that I was asleep, if that makes it any worse?'

DC Larry Johnson nods and takes a photo of my hand for his own case records. He stands up to go. 'You've been very helpful, Leah, thank you.'

'What about Tom?'

'He was released a few hours ago. Can't really hold him for your disappearance when you're sitting right here, can we?'

I need to see him. To tell him I'm sorry he got caught up in all of this. To make sure that he's alright. That *we're* alright.

Oh God, what did Chris do? I'd had no idea he'd swapped the phones. But I should have guessed. Stupid, stupid, stupid! As if Chris would have let me continue to be in contact with Tom.

I am gripped by panic. Because what if? What if after everything, I don't make it home? That there is no happily ever after. With Tom. Because thinking of him has been the only thing that kept me going through all of this. But what if he doesn't want me?

DS Vicky Fonteyn comes to tell me I can go home. She finds me red-eyed and still sobbing as I think about what Chris might have said to Tom, and if Tom would even want anything to do with me now. Especially after he was arrested, and the things he was accused of. She assumes my state is the culmination of my sister's death, and what Chris did to me, and the sheer momentousness of the whole thing. She offers to drive me home and I accept.

She doesn't take a marked car and drives me home in her own. A turquoise-coloured Vauxhall Corsa that smells faintly of smoke and wet dog. 'Sorry,' she says, her arm sweeping around the car. 'DS salary isn't so great, and my dog stinks.'

I smile and laugh. It feels so surreal to be here, in such an ordinary car, among the detritus of a stranger's life. 'Would you like a fag?' she asks me. 'I don't mind if you smoke in the car.'

I take one greedily, pulling deeply and relishing the smoke drawing into my lungs. I close my eyes and allow the heady woozy sensation to engulf me. It's over. Whatever happens. Whatever happens with Tom. I have done it. I am free.

After Vicky has undertaken a full sweep and made sure there is absolutely definitely no one hiding in the house waiting to jump out, she calls Tom for me.

I am making coffee for us in the kitchen and she comes to find me after they have spoken. Someone has been through the house and taken a plethora of fingerprints. There is sticky black residue on the kettle and the fridge door and so many other surfaces. I have tried to scrub it off with a sponge scourer but to no avail.

'Nail varnish remover,' Vicky says as she stands in the doorway watching me picking at the marks on the sugar tin. 'Best thing for it.'

I wait for her to tell me what Tom said. I feel like a twelve-year-old again, waiting for my sister to run back from telling a boy I fancy him.

'He's seen the story on the news,' says Vicky. 'He's on his way over now. I assumed that was OK?'

I nod.

'I can stay, if you'd like? If it would make you feel safer to have someone else here?'

'How did he sound?'

'Distraught. Sick with worry about you. Desperate to make sure that you're OK. Angry at himself that he didn't save you.' She smiles at me. 'He sounds lovely.'

As it turns out, Tom gets here while Vicky is still drinking her coffee. The doorbell rings three times in quick succession and she opens the door, then stands to one side as Tom barrels into the house towards me and then I am in his arms and we are both crying. 'Thank God, thank God, thank God,' he keeps saying under his breath through a mouthful of my hair. Then he pulls away and notices Vicky, who has come in and is now standing next to me.

He throws his arms around her. 'Thank you, thank you,' he says as she blushes deeply.

Vicky leaves five minutes later, and Tom and I move to the living room, his hand either in mine or on my waist the whole time as if he doesn't want to let me go. We lie on the sofa and he gathers me to him.

'I thought I'd lost you,' he whispers, his eyes locked on mine. 'I love you.'

'I love you too.'

We stay like that for over an hour. Neither of us speaking, just bathing in the glory of our togetherness. Then I kiss his neck, then his lips, gently at first, then more and more greedily. He pulls away a little and looks at me, concern swimming in his eyes.

'Did he hurt you?' he asks gently.

I wish I could tell him the truth, my heart breaking a little at the look on his face, but I can't find the words.

Tom's phone vibrates in his pocket and the moment is broken. 'My sister says to turn on the news immediately. But only if you're OK to see him?'

I nod in reply. We switch on the TV and sit side by side. Chris's face fills the screen, that lazy vulpine smile I grew to hate so much.

'In the face of overwhelming evidence,' the newsreader is saying solemnly, 'Christopher Hardcastle has been formally charged with the murder of his wife, Megan Hardcastle, in addition to the kidnapping of Megan's sister, Leah Patterson. Earlier today, all charges against Tom Eagleton, Ms Patterson's boyfriend, who had previously been arrested in connection to her disappearance, were dropped. Christopher Hardcastle has been remanded in custody, pending his trial. Given the severity of the crimes he is accused of, and the volume of evidence against him, there will no consideration of bail at this time.'

Tom slips his hand into mine. 'We'll get through this, Leah, I promise.'

Should I tell him the truth? The whole truth and nothing but the truth?

Part Four
Jeremy Crumpton

Chapter Twenty-Three

On my advice, my client has answered every question with a brusque 'no comment'. I need to get him alone to find out exactly what his side of this story is. Until then, I must let the police ask at least some of their questions. I have to admit that Chris has a level of self-assuredness that impresses me. The best clients are those who refuse to fall apart under pressure. Trying to defend a sobbing wreck who has allowed the process to get to them can become tiring very quickly, and quite frankly I prefer not to waste my time on those men.

It's always men. I don't mean that in a derogatory way, I'm a man myself after all. But my clients are unchangingly men. Most of a certain age, with a paunch and a receding hairline, accompanied by visions of grandeur and a staunch belief that the world *owes* them.

You might think I hate my clients.

You'd be wrong.

There is something incredible about taking a seemingly watertight case and ripping it apart to get the client off on some kind of tiny detail other lawyers would have missed. I always did love to solve puzzles. And I always loved being the most intelligent person in the room.

I will charge Chris a fortune for my representation. There is about fifty grand in his savings account and his family have offered up another quarter-million from their house equity. I will take it all and then he will thank me, because it is better than a lifetime in prison.

The police have charged him with first degree murder and aggravated kidnapping. Apparently, he killed his wife and hid her body in his freezer. Then kidnapped her identical twin sister and held her hostage, demanding she transfer her sizable fortune to him. She has told the police that he called her Megan and made her dress in her dead sister's clothes.

The case is sick and twisted and I am so in love with it already. Add in a handsome client – and he really is gorgeous, so step aside Ted Bundy. Who will Hollywood cast to play him, one day, when this is all over? Plus Leah, the twin he held hostage, is something of a celebrity. This case will make my career. I won't just be dining out on this story for years; I'll be guaranteed to pick up all manner of girls just broken enough to find the case exciting. Think of all the fun we will have!

Chris says he's innocent. Of course he does, they all say that at the beginning. I'm not sure he's realised yet that I simply don't *care* if he did do it. Although, if he did, I probably won't be inviting him to dinner any time soon.

And I'll keep him far away from my daughter, who just turned eighteen and seems to be developing a bit of a thing for bad boys. Her mum tells me it's just a phase and she'll settle down. But, to be honest, I think she's just got that gene that makes you sniff out danger and excitement in a way her mother would never understand. You have never met a woman who turned out to be as vanilla and downright dull as my ex-wife Melissa. We met at a party when I was twenty-two and three months later she told me she was pregnant. I did the right thing and asked her to marry me. I thought it was what Benny would've done. My father thought differently.

'She's hardly the kind of wife Benny would have found,' he had told me at the wedding reception, eyes ablaze with the cheap single malt he had been quaffing all evening.

'You should have just paid her off,' my mother said, 'that's what Lawrence would've done.'

My whole life I had done what Benny and Lawrence would've done, living with the spectre of my dead brothers, making sure that my parents were proud enough of me to diminish the pain of their loss. But this time I had got it wrong. I was furious. With them. With Melissa for not being good enough. With Benny and Lawrence for dying and leaving me to be everything to everyone. It was exhausting. I made a pledge to myself that night to live my life for me, not for them, not any more. Of course, though, in the end it turned out that my parents were right. My marriage was a very costly mistake and one I am still paying for, even a decade after the divorce. Fucking Benny and fucking Lawrence wouldn't have ended up in the same mess that I've managed to make for myself.

Would either of my brothers have made a career in the law? Or would they have become doctors or investment bankers or done some other important thing? Whatever they had chosen they would have made my parents proud. Perhaps this would be the case that finally showed them what I was capable of?

The interview suite is actually rather fancy, far better than a lot of places I've interviewed my bottom-feeding clientele over the years. The wooden table is admittedly some kind of reproduction, a veneer over cheap plywood, but at least the seats have actual cushions on them so my legs don't mould to the shape of hard plastic.

He sits in front of me, behind a flimsy perspex screen designed only to deflect the unseen virus, hands resting on the table. I have requested that he is out of cuffs, a little symbol of my trust and something I do for all my clients, and he seems grateful for the gesture. There is a smattering of stubble across his jawline that only makes him look more handsome, but his eyes are dull and you can see the tiredness on his face.

A proper mug is beyond the wit of the prison service, so I have brought him a latte from the coffee shop next door.

'Did you wipe it?' Chris asks, pointing at the plastic disposable lid.

It takes me a second to realise that he's worried about the virus. 'That's your concern?'

He shrugs. 'Safety first and all that.'

I feel like asking if he wants to put a fucking mask on too, but I need to keep things friendly. 'Of course I wiped it. Don't want to take chances, do we?' He smiles and takes a sip, closing his eyes as the warm milky drink slips down. He's cocky and unperturbed by the severity of his situation. I like that. It's easier when they feel invincible.

I watch him for a few moments, getting a feel for the man they have accused of some pretty outlandish crimes. Eventually, I put down my own coffee cup and pick up my pen. 'How about you tell me what really happened, eh?'

'I'm innocent.'

'You've said. Look, I just need to know your side of it, OK? Just in your own words what really happened.'

'Nothing happened, I'm innocent.'

I want to scream. Why the fuck can't people just level with you? Even if he tells me he did do it, and that he liked it, that he got off on it. Hell, even if he fucked the corpse, I'd still take the case. God, that would make a good story, adding a necrophiliac angle! Instead I take a long exhale and level my eyes on him.

'Look, Chris. I need to know what happened from your perspective. There is a freezer with the body of your wife in it, and her twin is claiming you held her hostage. Help me out a little, please.'

'It's not my wife's body.' It is a statement; he holds my gaze without flinching. I've seen enough lying men to know he is telling me the truth.

'What do you mean, it's not your wife's body? The twin has already identified the corpse.'

He smiles at me, a slow, languid smile. 'And she said it was Megan. But *she's* Megan and the body is Leah. Megan killed Leah and is trying to frame me.'

'Why?'

He seems taken aback by the question. I think he was expecting me to dismiss his claim out of hand.

'What do you mean, why?'

'Why would she frame you?'

'What better way to get away with murder?'

He makes a good point. 'But why frame you specifically?'

'It's always either the husband or the lover.'

'They released her boyfriend.'

'Tom? He was a new addition.'

'So she had another lover? Do I need to ask?'

He at least has the good grace to look a little embarrassed.

'So, you were married to Megan but having. . . what? An affair? With her identical twin sister?' Damn. I'm impressed.

'I'm not proud of it.'

'No, no, of course not.' We both know he was proud, once upon a time.

'Is that why she killed her?'

'Jealousy is a bitch.' He grins.

'Alright,' I say, taking a sip from my coffee cup before placing it down carefully. I pick up my pen. It's a Cross and I notice Chris's eyes swing towards it. I do have the ubiquitous Mont Blanc, of course; I bring it out when my clients are more obviously label-driven, and they are always either impressed or a little pissy that I charge them so much that I can afford to spend hundreds of pounds on a pen. But the Cross is a power play; it says I have taste beyond mere price. Every president since Reagan has used a Cross, at least until Trump started using a Sharpie. Chris's recognition of the brand tells me there is a lot more to this man than a pretty face. I push myself back on to the rear legs of the chair and make a show of getting comfortable. 'Let's level here. There is a lot of evidence against you. I'm not going to sugar-coat it. You are up shit creek and I am the only hope you have of a paddle.'

'Yep.' There's a flash of something in his eyes, a sense of kinship perhaps.

'So. You are saying that your wife, Megan, found out that you were having an affair with her twin, Leah.' He nods and so I continue. 'So, Megan killed Leah.' I wait for another nod. 'But, now Megan is pretending to be Leah—'

'She's lying—'

'Just let me finish, OK? So, Megan is pretending to be Leah, and framing you for murder while also claiming you held her hostage and that you were abusive towards her during that time.' At that last part I watch a dark cloud pass over his face. In a normal person, I would say it was shame. But I don't think Chris is normal. Nor do I believe he deals in shame. Oh, no. That black cloud was anger. Chris isn't used to losing.

'So, how do we prove it?' I ask.

'You believe me?' He sounds surprised.

I shrug. 'It isn't me we need to convince. So, why are *you* convinced it's actually Megan?'

'We're married. I know my wife.'

I have a sly smile on my face. Husbands always think they know their wives. I've seen enough to understand what a load of bollocks that sentiment is. I don't say it though. 'But she's never done anything like this before?'

'Murder? No.'

'I meant violence, blackmail, self-harm, erratic behaviour, you know, anything that might indicate she's unstable.'

'Her mother lives in an assisted care facility. She has a delusional personality disorder and extreme paranoia. There were signs of it in Megan, but she always tried to cover it up, make me think everything was OK. But. . . I always worried that one day she would snap.'

'What kind of things?'

'Mainly forgetting things or thinking things had changed when they hadn't. She accused me of moving the living room furniture around once, and she thought I might be poisoning her. Which, of course, I wasn't.'

'Violence?'

'She had a temper and held a grudge unlike anyone you've ever seen.'

I laugh. He has no idea of the totally fucked-up shit I've seen. My practice are specialists in domestic abuse and prenup agreements. That shit gets nasty very quickly.

'This isn't funny.' He shifts in his chair. That bad loser side might end up being a problem.

'No, it's not,' I agree. Remember to always placate the client. That is rule number one with my boss. He decides my bonus so I can't help but obey. He will also need to agree for me to front this with the press, be the person on camera, sweeping into court in robe and wig. Pure theatre. But stodgy old Mr Geoffrey Billington will have to sign it off and agree to hand me the limelight he could choose to take for himself. I should probably start buttering him up, even though this will take a long time to get to court, especially if Chris refuses to plead and wants a full trial. And I'm pretty sure that is where this is headed.

'So, you know it's Megan. But how to prove it?'

He narrows his eyes at me. 'Isn't that your job?'

He's got me there. 'Well, of course. But it's probably easier for you to tell me the one thing you know that would prove it. A distinguishing mark, a tattoo, something that is definitively Megan not Leah.'

'They're identical.' He looks at me like a teacher would at an errant pupil.

'Except twins are never really identical, are they?'

'Google the book Leah wrote and look at the cover.'

'I've seen it. I stayed up most of the night reading it. It has a picture of them. They are similar, I'll grant you.'

'How very magnanimous of you. Could you tell them apart?'

'If I knew them, I would expect I could.'

He smiles and cracks his knuckles. 'I doubt it. They are so alike they have each always pretended to be the other. Any time Leah wanted something Megan had, Leah would pretend to be Megan to take it. I guess Megan thinks it has some sort of poetic irony now.'

'But. . . piercings? Tattoos?'

'They have the same tattoo. To cover up the marks their dad gave them to tell them apart when they were babies. Leah had one dot on her ankle and Megan had two. Baby number one and baby number two. Now they both have flowers. The dots are amalgamated into the stamen.'

'So, let me guess, the tattoos are now identical?'

'Not quite. Leah had one more tiny stamen than Megan, to prove she's the older one.'

'So that's how you prove it.'

'You think Megan is stupid enough to forget that? You don't think she's already changed her tattoo to make sure she has the most?' There is a smirk on his face. 'She does have a scar though. A car accident when she was in her late teens. She told me about it once when she was very drunk. It's the only time she ever mentioned it, didn't want to tempt fate, she said.'

'So, you know she's Megan because you've seen the scar?'

'I wasn't looking.'

'Sorry?'

He shrugs and smirks again. 'It's under her hair on the back of her upper neck. I didn't look to make sure it was there. You need to find the hospital record. Match it to the scar and there's your proof.'

'You don't sound convinced.'

'That you'll find sixteen-year-old notes of a few stitches and maybe a handwritten police report of an accident buried in an archive somewhere?'

I'm getting bored now. 'Fingerprints?'

'Neither are on file.'

'She's clever.' I wonder if I'm stating the obvious and the look on his face confirms that I am.

'Cleverer than I thought. Guess I married into some right old mess, didn't I?' Chris's laugh is somehow both self-deprecating and an alarming window into the mind of a man who just may be a cold-blooded killer.

God, he's fascinating.

I take a break, grab a quick coffee and have a final scan through his file.

Chris Hardcastle is a year younger than I am. A former pupil at Edenbridge Academy. There is a chance we met once or twice, if he played rugby or competed in athletics. I imagine he did both. But he is not who I expected him to be. I had assumed that I would dig into his past and find a horror show, an abusive family, a life marred by tragedy and loss, childhood trauma, something at least. Anything that would give a hint as to why he might turn out to be a psychopath. But there is nothing.

Christopher Aimo Jeremiah Hardcastle was born on the second of November 1980. A Sunday. *And the child that is born on the Sabbath day, is bonny and blithe, and good and gay.* Chris certainly was bonny. Six feet tall with broad shoulders and a narrow waist, blond hair with a slight curl, piercing blue eyes, and the square jawline of a Ken doll. He had that casual demeanour of a man who has always been attractive: throughout his childhood, through adolescence, and into adulthood. A man who is used to all eyes in a room turning to him, used to the constant flirting of the women who crossed his path. As for blithe? Once upon a time it meant happy and carefree, but now it implies a level of callousness. Fitting for a man accused of such heinous crimes, who has professed his innocence with little regard for the reality that protestation implies. After all, if he is innocent, if it is really Leah who is dead – and at the hand of Megan – then his lover is dead, and his own wife has framed him for murder.

What did he do to Megan to make her do this to him?

Pushing open the door to the interview room, I find Chris sitting exactly as I had left him.

'So, will you do it?' he asks.

'Take your case?'

'Yep.'

I sit back in my seat and watch him closely. He still has the outward air of someone totally relaxed. But there is a twitch in the corner of his mouth, and he can't seem to stop his eyes from darting between my left and right as if he can't focus on either. The first week I was in practice, one of my mentors taught me to always watch the eyes. The dilation of the pupil is often a give-away, but more so is the flickering. It shows that he is nervous. Actually, scratch that. He's fucking shitting his pants. If I don't believe him, or if I choose not to take the case, he will go down for a long time. And prison is not a nice place for a man accused of murder and kidnapping, especially as he is accused of beating Leah. Strangely moral lot, most prisoners, and quite adept at taking punishment into their own hands if they think the state hasn't been quite severe enough. Someone will make him their hostage and thrash him to within an inch of his life.

I wonder how long to make him sweat. I could tell him I need to think about it. I could walk away and go and have a nice lunch and then saunter back along the river while he stews away. But here's the thing. If he's guilty then a challenge to get him off awaits me. If he's innocent though? If that whole thing about Leah being Megan turns out to actually be the truth and a truth I can prove? I'll be able to write a book, get a deal on the after-dinner speaker circuit, maybe even challenge that smug prick for his role as 'TV Judge of the People'. I look good on camera. I had once contemplated an acting career, but to be honest the law is much more secure. And a lot more lucrative if you're good at it. Acting only works if you have a lot of luck to add to the mix. Jeremy Crumpton makes his own luck.

***

The last time I lost, I was eight years old. I was playing Monopoly with my brothers: Benny was the eldest, an eleven-year-old chess prodigy; Lawrence was almost ten and had just taken his grade six piano exam. I was the baby, the brunt of my brothers' teasing and name-calling. 'Loser!' Benny had screamed as he chased me round the house brandishing the dog-eared Mayfair card at me. I had woken up the next morning to find my bed full of tiny green plastic houses and red hotels. One had embedded itself into my cheek and left a bruise.

Two weeks after the Monopoly thrashing, Benny was diagnosed with a rare form of leukaemia. He died less than two months later. Lawrence travelled back from the funeral with my maternal grandparents. A drunk driver slammed their car at a roundabout. My grandparents walked away with scratches and whiplash. Lawrence was killed instantly.

But my story isn't a tale of hardship and death and all the terrible things that can happen. I took the anger and the frustration and I channelled it. I was ten when I became the national under-twelve chess champion. The trophy Benny should have won was finally where it belonged, in pride of place on the mantelpiece of my parents' sitting room. 'For Benny,' my father had said as he straightened it that first evening, a tear in his eye. Then I gave up chess and began to practise for hours and hours at the large piano in the draughty hallway between the kitchen and the dining room. It took me until I was twelve to be good enough to pass my grade seven and to win a commendation at the county music awards. 'For Lawrence,' my father said as he hung the certificate in the downstairs loo with all the other Crumpton accolades.

I should have led a pampered and easy existence at Winslow School for Boys, safe from flushings and other mistreatment by virtue of two big brothers to protect me. Instead I retreated into academia. 'Benny would have won the maths prize in third form,' my father had told my mother as she spooned roast potatoes on to my plate one exeat weekend. I became the first second-former in the school's history to win the award. 'For Benny.' I was offered the opportunity to do some of my GCSE exams a year early: 'Lawrence would have done his early,' my father had said with absolute conviction. 'And got an A*,' my mother had added. I, of course, got that A*. 'For Lawrence.'

'Benny was amazing at athletics,' my father told me. This was a problem, as I was not as tall and slim-built as my oldest brother had been shaping up to be. I was still able to represent my school though. There was a bout of food poisoning the day before the try-outs for the team and many of my more talented peers found themselves unable to take part. No one suspected a thing.

Lawrence would have been selected for the exclusive exchange programme with the sister school to mine in Vermont. Every year, one particularly gifted student went to the US school and one of the Montpelier students came to Winslow. Competition was fierce. It was considered the highest honour and every student selected had gone on to Oxbridge and carved out a lucrative career for themselves. The initial selection was by exam, one sat by every student in my year group, forty boys crammed into the prep hall for the four-hour marathon with no breaks allowed, not even to go to the bathroom. It was meant to test stamina and to ensure there was no possible way to cheat. As if you could only cheat once you were sat inside the room! I left after an hour and a half, my fingers cramped into some kind of ugly claw from gripping my pencil so tightly. I was awarded the highest score ever known for the test. Ninety-four per cent. The headmaster called me to his office, and here I learned a particularly valuable lesson. Crying makes a lot of people un-comfortable. I was fourteen and I blubbered for over an hour, sitting on the small chair in front of his enormous desk.

'I need to get that exchange, for Lawrence,' I told him through my tears. It's amazing what the sob story of my poor dead broth-ers would do. I was selected for the programme. Who could deny a weeping boy trying desperately to make his parents proud in the shadow of his dead brothers? Crumptons are winners. At any price. Because nothing is worse than losing. Nothing.

***

'You will have to promise me something.' I tell my new client. 'You must be honest with me, every step of the way.' I lower my voice, channelling the old headmaster of my school who used to give the other boys, the ones who didn't understand the value of a well-paced tear, the absolute willies. I see Chris make an involuntary shudder; he had a similar headmaster, I presume. 'If, at any point, I find out you have lied to me, or omitted something – which amounts to the same thing – then I will drop you like a fucking stone. You got that?' He nods.

'Jeremy Crumpton does not lose,' I say.

Chris looks at me. 'I don't lose either.'

Chapter Twenty-Four

It's seven o'clock in the morning. On a Saturday. And my fucking doorbell is ringing.

I pull myself up from my bed, bleary-eyed, and throw my bathrobe on. I'm not used to being awake at this time. As I trudge downstairs, I can see the outline of a man through the window. I know who this is going to be.

A week ago, after I agreed to take Chris Hardcastle's case, I employed one of my company's best investigators, Pete. No doubt he has prepared a thick, hard-copy file on my client and his family. He is old-school, this investigator, and always refuses to just email the damn information.

'It's a bit early,' I say as I open the door and usher him, and the huge file he's carrying, inside.

He laughs as he follows me down the hallway towards the kitchen. I am in desperate need of coffee; the half-bottle of single malt I drank last night is knotted beneath my left eyeball, pounding away like an excited toddler with a new drumkit.

Pete immediately opens my fridge and riffles through the meagre contents. 'You don't have any food.' It is part accusation, part disappointment. My heart sinks a little. No doubt he will pass this nugget of detail on to my mother. Pete is my mother's sister's stepson. My Aunt Lara only married his dad five years ago though, so it's not as if we've grown up together. I don't know if my mother has asked him to, or if he has done it off his own bat, but he keeps tabs on me and reports back on what I'm up to. I have no choice but to tolerate this interference. Partly because I don't want to rock the boat. Partly because he is a damn good investigator and has helped me to maintain my one hundred per cent success rate with my clients. That kind of track record is invaluable, and well worth the price of a little more of my mother's disapproval.

'Working too much to go shopping,' I say, trying to keep my tone neutral, to avoid the desperate need to explain myself.

'You need to look after yourself. What would happen to your poor mother, eh?' He doesn't finish the sentence, doesn't add *if she lost you too*.

'I'll go to the supermarket this afternoon.' I don't finish my sentence either, don't add *please don't tell her*.

'Coffee.' He flaps his hand at me. I slide a small mug towards him, full of steaming hot black sludge, so strong you could almost stand a spoon in it. He picks it up and grins over the rim at me. The smile shaves decades off his face, leaving him looking like an excited teenager instead of the haggard fifty-something ex-police officer he really is.

'What did you find?' The brief I gave him was to find something that pointed to Chris being the kind of man whose wife would want to frame for murder. As opposed to the kind of man who would murder his wife and kidnap his sister-in-law.

'Mr Hardcastle was a terrible husband.'

'What are we talking?'

Pete takes a deep breath and holds up his right hand, just his index finger pointing in the air. 'Number one, he was fucking her twin.' He raises his middle finger to meet the index. 'Two, he was squirrelling money from their joint account.' He raises another finger, 'three, he was jealous and over-possessive.'

'Says who?'

'Megan's best friend. Some girl called Hannah.'

'Would she be a character witness?'

Pete laughs. 'She wants to nail him to a cross. I had to tell her I was with the prosecution to get her to talk to me at all.'

'Shame. Anything else?'

'Chris was an escort.'

I stop drinking with my mug halfway to my lips. 'He was a what?'

'An escort. Well, that's a bit of a euphemism. More like a high-class call boy.'

'Did Megan know?'

'I highly doubt it. He gave it up a while back, before they met. But, from what I've found out about Megan, I doubt she would have taken finding out about his seedy past too well.'

'You think that was her motive?'

'I'm not saying it was her motive. I'm just saying that – narratively at least – it isn't too much of a stretch to say that she found out he had lied to her, perhaps even given her something nasty. There may be at least one person on that jury who would think that was a good reason for her to pin him for murder.'

'It's weak.'

'It's the best I could find.' Pete stands up and straightens his jumper over the small gut he appears to be developing.

'Let's get breakfast,' I say, clapping him on the back. 'To celebrate.'

A look of confusion crosses his face.

'You found nothing to make the jury think he's a murderer. I don't have to prove Megan is framing him. I just have to cast doubt that he killed Megan. And if *you* can't find anything, then no one can.'

Pete smiles and shrugs his shoulders. 'Does that mean you're paying for breakfast?'

'That depends.' I can tell he's been holding out on me, that he has another ace up his sleeve.

'I found his Cloud server. From when he was escorting. He kept a lot of videos.' He pulls out a small USB stick from his pocket and slides it along my kitchen counter, his eyes fixed on mine.

'Who?' I am almost salivating.

Pete breaks into a wide-mouthed smile. 'No one who will help you get Chris off. But you might be able to get into that club you've always talked about. I don't think Mrs Chalmers would want that video to see the light of day.'

I place my hand over the USB stick. Mrs Chalmers runs a very exclusive club just off Covent Garden, a place you need a certain pedigree to even cross the threshold of, let alone to enjoy a Gibson and appreciate the charms of the entertainment. Last year, she declined my application. I don't think she will this year.

Jeremy Crumpton always wins. Eventually.

'There is a lot of evidence that doesn't go in your favour.' I can hear myself clipping the words, the lid on my anger barely staying sealed. I have finally received the initial findings from the prosecution. It is bad.

Chris sits back in his chair and picks up the cup of coffee I brought him. I want to wrench the cup from his fingers and throw the contents in his face.

'I told you not to lie to me.'

'I haven't,' he says, and sips the latte.

We are less than twenty-four hours before the initial hearing. I swallow, trying to quell my frustration at the smugness of his square-jawed face. 'There is DNA evidence on the body. *Your* DNA.'

'Planted by Megan.'

'Your fingerprints are all over the freezer, on the frozen sweetcorn and peas, on the body.'

'I moved the freezer. To make sure that Megan wouldn't do anything stupid.'

'I can't say that in your defence, though, can I? You'd be admitting to covering up the murder. Plus, your prints are all over the chain Leah was shackled with, and there is a lot of evidence of harm against her.'

'That's why she knocked me out the first time. So she could press all those things against my fingers.'

I throw him a withering look. 'How *convenient*.'

'I thought you believed me.' His voice sounds small. Child-like.

I close the file and look at him. He is wide-eyed, one step away from tears. Crocodile tears. I know that face. It is the same face my daughter used when I refused to buy her a brand new car last year, right before she told me in a soft voice that sometimes she wondered if I would have been happier if she hadn't been born. She got her brand new Audi A3, with a custom paint job and the soft-top that folds away at the touch of a button.

'I need you Jeremy,' he says as he spreads his hands out on the table, palms down. 'You're the only hope I have.'

I am being played. I know it, and Chris knows it. I just hope he can play the jury this well.

Chris pleads not guilty during his initial hearing. It's a small affair; making court 'COVID-secure' entails spacing everyone out so it's essential people only. The judge calls me to her chambers after and asks me what the hell we are playing at. She pushes me to get him to change his plea and take a deal.

'It's a no-brainer, Mr Crumpton, and you know it.'

Even if it were, I still wouldn't recommend he changes his plea out of sheer bloody-mindedness. Who the fuck does the bitch think she is to talk to me like that? 'My client is innocent,' I say sweetly, hands in my pockets so she can't see how much her condescension angers me. My fists clenched.

'Is that so?' She's openly baiting me. I get this kind of vibe from most of the female judges, to be fair. Too many years of trying to prove themselves makes them prickly and defensive against a well-dressed male defence lawyer. But it's not misogyny that's the problem in the legal system, it's misandry. Even if she, and all those other progressive types, keep banging the old 'down with the patriarchy' drum. The system is designed to stack the deck very firmly in favour of the women, always upholding the poor darlings as victims of male depravity. Mix victim culture with ball-breaker judges and female prosecutors who think that all men – professionals and criminals alike – are out to get them, and you have a perfect storm for the overrun male-only prisons. This bitch isn't doing much to change my opinion.

'Chris is innocent, and I'll prove it.' I stand firm, I will not let her intimidate me.

'Spill it then,' she says.

This is a breach of convention. She cannot ask me to reveal my hand at this stage in the proceedings.

'I can see you are dying to tell me.'

She's not wrong, to be fair. 'So, just tell me what you're going to use as a defence.' She shrugs. It's not a big deal, her eyes say. 'A professional courtesy,' she adds. 'Just please, for the love of all that is holy, do not tell me that you are going to claim diminished responsibility, or temporary loss of control, or any one of the other bullshit things lawyers like you come up with to excuse the behaviour of the men you represent.'

'You underestimate me, your honour,' I reply. 'He's not innocent because the charge should be downgraded to manslaughter. He's innocent because there is no murder to try. Megan isn't dead.'

She laughs as she stands and takes a few strides towards the window, where a tall thin bottle of mezcal and four crystal glasses sit on a silver tray. I note that it is the brand 'Ilegal' – having it on display has become something of a running joke around chambers, where the offer of a drink is normally prefaced with a comment about 'having a spot of the illegal stuff'.

'Well, now I really have heard it all.' She motions towards the mezcal and I nod. 'So, if Megan isn't dead, why is there a body in my morgue?'

'The body is Leah Patterson.'

'The sister your client kidnapped?'

'The identical twin sister that you allege my client kidnapped, yes.'

She pours us both a large measure of the clear liquor and passes me one. 'Here's to a fun trial,' she says, clinking her glass against mine.

'May the best man win,' I reply, hitting my glass against hers with more force than is strictly necessary.

Chapter Twenty-Five

TEN MONTHS LATER...

There is one thing that has been bugging me since the start. Leah's bank account was underpinned with a state-of-the-art system that used biometric scans via webcam to confirm identity. Normally it would use facial recognition, but Leah's used retinal scan data. An identical twin can, obviously, fool facial recognition, but retinal scans are unique. Leah's account had a mechanism by which you could put in a flag word and then the system would 'lock you out' when you did the scan. It was used to create a flag for hostage victims, a way of raising a silent alarm that something was wrong.

But here's the kicker. It only sends a message if the retinal scan is successful. If just anyone activates the system, it won't work. Which means that it was Leah sitting in front of the retinal scan.

It took my intern Jemima almost a week to find the footage. The only image was one captured by a small camera above the posh cafe three doors down. A woman going into the Knightsbridge branch of Pullman Bank. Jemima found an employee of the bank who was willing to offer some advice on opening similar accounts and the kind of security measures put in place. Jemima used her trust fund to deposit over a million in cash into an account to prove the system. I went with her, posing as her bodyguard. I like a bit of role play and I'm not afraid to take a more subservient position if the situation calls for it.

'So, if I'm kidnapped, I just tap in a code and you report it?' Jemima is playing dumb, her eyes wide, winding a strand of honey-blond hair around her fingers with their manicured nails.

'Yep,' the man says. He too seems a little dumb, and has zero decorum regarding looking down her blouse. 'As long as it can verify it's really you. Otherwise we just get a load of false issues and the police get mad and stop responding.' I think I want to slap him to make him focus on something other than Jemima's tits.

'Like a fingerprint scan?'

'Generally facial recognition. Just using the camera on your phone or laptop.'

'I'm never sure about facial recognition. My uncle says it's rife for the hacking.'

'It's foolproof. Unless you're an identical twin, and then your twin could hack you. But we can use a retinal scan. In fact, we had a client recently and the system saved her life.' He is growing more animated.

'Really? OMG, what happened?'

'Well, she came in right before the first lockdown, so early March, and upgraded her security. Said she had a bad feeling about her sister going after her money. We added the retinal scan then, just to be sure. It flagged up when she was being held hostage.'

'Oh, my. So the police found her?'

'Well,' he shifts a little in his seat. 'Not exactly. There was a bit of a balls-up with some location muffling, but we've learned our lessons now. No, she saved herself actually. But there was a bit of a hoo-ha, and she used the retinal scan as the final proof of her identity to the police.'

Per Chris's timeline, Megan killed Leah in mid-February. If Chris is telling the truth, she could have altered the account details so she was able to 'prove' she was Leah. Very clever indeed. Not that it matters though; it would just be 'Leah's' word against his. Same as the fingerprints on file with the US Border Agency from the trip to Vegas. I need to find something more concrete.

I have also tasked Jemima with trying to track down the medical records from the accident Chris told me about. The one that gave Megan a distinctive, if subtle, scar on the back of her neck. Jemima may have to trawl through the archives of the hospital though; they were still using paper back in 2004 and the NHS is notoriously poor at record-keeping. I have a vision of swishing my robe as I cross the courtroom towards Megan in the witness box, medical records in hand as I prepare to unmask her in front of the judge and jury. Obviously, it wouldn't really happen like that, but sometimes it's fun to imagine a little piece of theatrics.

I can prove that Leah is lying about not having seen Megan for months. Or at least I can prove they were both in the same area at the same time back on the seventeenth of February. This is the day that Chris tells me Megan killed Leah and became both of them. There is CCTV footage of both their cars on the same stretch of road, and a crystal-clear image of Megan's number plate in a car park just down the road from the cabin. Where it stayed for five days before being collected. Five days during which Megan was pretending to be Leah in London.

'There is one thing, Chris,' I tell my client as I visit him in his little cell while he waits for his trial. He nods for me to continue. 'Assuming there is sufficient evidence to have you acquitted of murder and kidnapping, there will still be a charge brought against you by the state. You need to understand that, OK?'

'What charge?'

'Probably perverting the course of justice. But it could be aiding and abetting. You did know about the murder, and helped Megan to cover it up.'

'So, what's your plan?' he asks me. I know he wants to ask what kind of penalties he might face as opposed to murder, but he can't bring himself to contemplate the idea that he might serve any time at all.

'Find a compelling reason why you didn't report Megan back in February. Or find better proof that doesn't simultaneously show you knew there was a body in that freezer.'

His eyes are a piercing shade of blue in the bright overhead light. 'Just do whatever you have to,' he says in the end.

Derek is with my firm on work experience. I think he belongs to the sister of one of the partners, but I wasn't really paying too much attention. Anyway, he is very tall, weighs about as much as my ex-wife's miniature pinscher and apparently has a perfect memory.

I put him to work looking though every photograph taken at the Hardcastle house, those from Leah's house, and the social media accounts of the two twins and their extended families.

'Find me something that suggests a crossover,' I instruct him. I don't hear from him again for two days. I assume he goes home in the evenings, otherwise I think the partner's sister would make a fuss. I also assume he goes out to get himself a sandwich or brings a packed lunch or something, but whenever I peer through the window into the darkened office he's stationed in he is there, and he is laser-focused.

Jemima is in my office, sitting on the corner of my desk in a way that gives me the merest glimpse of her lacy underwear, when Derek knocks on the door. Jemima immediately crosses her legs and her panties are lost from sight. She raises an eyebrow at me. 'Rain Man's here,' she stage-whispers as she hops off my desk.

'I found something, sir.' Derek is holding a small stack of papers close to his chest.

I stand up and beckon him over. He's sweating gently; there's a sheen across his forehead. He stumbles a little as he approaches. Jemima stifles a giggle behind her hand. I will write her up for it later. You can't take the mickey out of people *in* the office, it's just not professional.

'Talk me through it,' I instruct as I take the stack from him.

He clears his throat, licks his lips, then clears his throat once more. None of it helps; his voice is reedy when he starts. 'See that picture?' he says, pointing to a photo that he's laid on the desk. He clears his throat a final time, which seems to do the trick. 'It's from Leah's bathroom in Belsize Park.' I nod and motion for him to continue. 'See that, there in the corner by the toilet? It's a brand-new package of toilet roll. Doesn't seem like anything at all.' He is warming up and there's something almost endearing to his earnestness now it's being channelled into something I want.

'Well. The brand is rare. The company was only set up in November 2019, and there was a distribution issue when the supermarket they were partnered with reneged on the deal. So, this company had a big warehouse full of the stuff and needed to shift it.'

I worry that he's going down a rabbit hole now. 'So. . .' I say.

'The company offered an online special through a Facebook campaign – one hundred packages for fifty pounds.'

'Bargain,' Jemima deadpans and rolls her eyes. 'But who cares?'

'Why would a multimillionaire buy bulk discount toilet roll?' Derek asks with glee, clearly thinking that he may just get one over on this bitchy woman who has been taking the piss out of him.

'I assume you have an answer?' I reply.

Derek takes a page from the top of the stack and almost makes a 'ta-da' gesture. 'She wouldn't. But Mrs Valma Hardcastle of Tunbridge Wells loves a good bargain.' The page he has revealed shows a grinning older woman with a huge pile of toilet rolls in the background. A Facebook post liked by all her friends at the WI, or whatever it is that Mrs Hardcastle does for fun. 'Chris's mum.'

I look at the printout. The post is dated December 2019. I smile.

Jemima leans over my shoulder and taps at the page. 'I don't get it. So what if Chris's mum bought a job lot of loo roll?'

'How would it end up at Leah's place?' I use my teaching voice and turn round to look at her. Her cheeks are starting to pinken as she struggles to find the link I have made and even the work experience boy has figured out.

'Chris was having an affair with Leah. He probably gave it to her.' She doesn't sound convinced of her own argument.

'Does your boyfriend bring you gifts of loo roll?' I ask, and the pink on her cheeks blazes to a vibrant red. We don't talk about her boyfriend, some chinless wonder her daddy wants her to marry. He's the reason it's only a quick handjob she's giving her boss, although I think after the gusset-flashing earlier, I might be getting an upgrade to a blow job. She won't let me touch her though; that's cheating in her book. I don't argue with her logic.

'Of course not,' she says hurriedly.

'So, how else might it have got there?' My teaching voice now a little more patronising than before.

'Umm. . .'

'Because Megan took it there,' Derek interjects, bored. 'Remember that week before lockdown when you couldn't buy toilet roll or hand sanitiser for love nor money? She probably just grabbed a pack from home.'

'I still don't get it.'

'If Megan took toilet roll to Leah's house, it proves Chris's story that Megan was pretending to be Leah.'

'Oh,' she says as the penny finally drops. 'But it's not really proof, is it? I mean, we couldn't use it in court.'

It's circumstantial at best. It might throw the tiniest sliver of doubt into the minds of the jurors, which might be enough but most probably would not.

'Plus,' she adds, 'Chris could have planted it.'

Damn. She's right, of course.

I'm still not sure why I told Jemima I'd come. Well, except that I want to meet the chinless wonder of a boyfriend, look him in the eye, shake hands with the man who has no idea how his girlfriend is playing him. She has booked the terrace of some bar in Stockwell, somewhere that had once been a bit of a dive before COVID had shut it down. But some enterprising young hipsters had bought the place and spent a small fortune making it COVID-secure. More than just spacing the seating out a bit, they'd strung some fairy lights around the traffic bollards used to carve out an area that was previously a public footpath, and whacked out some little tables to create the so-called terrace area.

Then they started a trend called 'Pandemic Chic'. Cocktails named after previous outbreaks: one with a Jägermeister base called Black Death; a modernisation of sangria they called Spanish Flu; there was even a Bloody Mary garnished with pork scratchings instead of celery, named – yes, you guessed it – Swine Flu. The staff all wore full hospital PPE: gowns, masks, face shields, hair hidden beneath surgical caps. The whole thing was macabre. People flocked to the place.

I'm late. On purpose. I don't want to be there for the flurry of awkward arrivals as everyone tries to do that stupid elbow bump. I think I might be too late though. Jemima has been drinking Black Deaths all night and her tongue is stained a deep blueish-purple like a bruise. She is stumbling towards me. 'Jeremy!' She pauses to get the attention of a gaggle of similar-looking women in their late twenties, all aristocratic features and overly dyed hair. 'My boss is here!' And then she launches herself at me. Luckily her boyfriend – Chester or Boris, or some other such name, I don't really care – intercepts her and pulls her away to sit her down before she makes a complete fool of herself.

One of the friends, she seems a little more sober than the others at least, comes over. 'Jeremy?'

'Eh, yes?'

'I'm Charlie.' She extends her hand to me and for a split second I wonder if she's expecting me to kiss it, but then she pulls it back in close to her body. 'Forgot about social distancing.' She grins and playfully slaps her own hand. 'Naughty!' There is something there, hidden beneath the haughty veneer, like she knows a secret that she's itching to tell. 'You'd better buy me a drink.' She turns and begins to walk over to the bar in the far corner.

I follow because I don't know anyone else here and to be fair, I am very much in need of a drink. Plus, Charlie has the kind of arse you only get from a vigorous horse-riding hobby and I am enjoying the view as I walk behind her. She stops suddenly and spins on her toes to face me.

'Jemima said you were a perv.'

'Sorry?'

'You were looking at my arse.'

'Can you blame me?' She is wearing a very tight red dress.

She leans in and whispers in my ear, 'I'm not mopping up Jemima's sloppy seconds.' So Jemima has been talking. Intriguing. I thought she'd be too afraid the chinless wonder would find out. 'Oh, sweetie. I know *everything*. But your secret is safe with me.' Does she really think I would give a shit if people knew Jemima had wanked me off a few times in the office? I thought she might actually have something more interesting to tell me, or at least would tease me for a little longer.

I order us both a drink, red wine for me and a Bird Flu for her (a gin fizz made with egg white – whoever had come up with the cocktail menu had obviously begun scraping the barrel by this point in the proceedings). 'Cheers,' I say, tapping my glass against hers gently to avoid spilling any of her concoction with its foamy head like a pint of Guinness.

'You know who he is, don't you?' Her eyes have narrowed as she stares into the crowd, her lips only millimetres from the rim of her glass.

'Who who is?' I ask.

'The one who keeps Jemima from going to bed with you properly.'

'You sound jealous.'

Charlie throws her head back and laughs. The skin of her décolletage is so pale it is almost luminescent in the glow of all the fairy lights. 'Jealous? I wouldn't let him anywhere near me.'

'Is he that bad?'

'He has no chin.'

'I'd noticed.'

She puts her hand in front of her mouth and sniggers into it. 'But when you have a daddy like his, you don't need one.'

I am going to have to bite. 'OK. So who is he?'

She leans in, so close I can smell the spliff she smoked before she came out for the evening, our lips almost touching, her eyes boring into mine. When she tells me the dynasty he belongs to, part of me wishes she had kept quiet.

The chinless wonder is the son of the most powerful man in British media. No wonder Jemima doesn't want our involvement advertised. I'm almost impressed. He could be a very useful ally.

I buy Charlie another cocktail, then another, then another. She has a constitution stronger than the horses she rides. When she goes to the bathroom, a guy sidles up to me at the bar. 'You Jemima's boss?' he asks.

'Yes. Jeremy Crumpton.' I extend a hand before realising he has gone for the elbow bump. It's awkward. I hate how it makes me feel like a socially inept fool.

'How can you do it?' For a split second I think he means Jemima and me. 'Defend someone who you know is guilty,' he clarifies.

I take a large gulp of wine and look him straight in the eye. He's younger than me – of course, everyone here is younger than me – with floppy light-brown hair and an accent from somewhere north of Milton Keynes. His suit is off-the-rack but brand new, his shoes shined to perfection. 'Let me guess,' I say and take another drink, 'Durham?' The chosen university of those not quite good enough for law at Oxbridge, but with ambition despite their lack of privilege.

'Edinburgh,' he corrects me.

Even worse. A man with ideals.

'Oh.' My reply drips with unspoken meaning. What I think of young lawyers like him. Men like him.

'Don't you have a conscience?' he asks. 'There are criminals walking free because you got them off.'

I take a step back and give him the full body scan, letting him know that I am taking in every detail of who he is and how he presents himself to the world. 'Let me tell you something.' I manage to avoid the temptation to call him 'boy'. 'I'm a defence lawyer. My job is not to judge. That is why there is an *actual* judge in the courtroom. My job is not to determine guilt or innocence. That is why there is normally a jury. No, my job is to ensure that everyone, no matter who they are, where they come from, or what they are accused of, is given a fair trial. That there is someone to ensure that their side of the story is told, to make sure no evidence against them is fabricated or illegally obtained. My job is not – as you so eloquently put it – to "get them off",' I did the air quotes, watching as he winced a little bit at the ferocity of my argument. 'No, my job is to make sure that the innocent are not unfairly, or unjustly, fucked over by our judicial system. That the innocent do not have their liberties curtailed. That the innocent do not have their lives destroyed by vindictive and unfounded proclamations of their guilt. That is why I do what I do.' I enjoy watching him squirm. 'You may not think it a noble endeavour, or an appropriate calling for a gentleman – sorry, that's the phrase my father likes to use, but no one ever satisfies their parents, do they? – but it is the very cornerstone of the British legal system. One which I am very proud to be part of, thank you very much.' I turn to walk away from him and there's a smatter of applause behind me.

'You were fantastic,' Charlie breathes into my ear. 'Get me another drink.' It's a command, not a request.

'What do I have to do to get you drunk?' I ask her.

'I told you I don't do Jemima's sloppy seconds.' There is a glint in her eye. She's enjoying the attention. 'But there is something that might win you some points.' She smirks but I have already seen through her.

I sigh. 'OK.'

'Tell me about him.'

'Who?' But I know who.

'Your client.' Her eyes are alive, and she is chewing her lip in a rather distracting way.

'What do you want to know?' I am nonchalant. It's not like I haven't already used this conversation to take two other girls home.

She leans in, her lips brushing my neck. 'Everything.'

Charlie and I have a lot of fun that night.

The next morning, as she waits for her Uber to pick her up, she instructs me not to tell Jemima.

'Why not?'

'She made me promise not to fuck you.'

'Oh?'

'She doesn't approve.'

I can't say I'm surprised. 'Our little secret then.'

She's been good, the one who calls herself Leah. As far as I can tell, she's not broken character once since Chris's arrest.

She posted on her social media accounts that she was thankful for the support of everyone over the years and then in the wake of this incredibly difficult time for her. Added a heart-warming tribute to her sister and a harrowing few lines about her ordeal at the hands of a killer. Then she shut them all down, saying she wanted a sense of a normal life, away from the spotlight, and requesting people respect her privacy at this time. *#AChanceToHeal.*

That red-haired man has all but moved in from the looks of things, but the pair seem to spend little time out and about, even with COVID restrictions lifting. They sometimes stroll up to Hampstead Heath, but that's the main extent of their outings. Three weeks ago they rescued a little dog from a local shelter. According to the security company I had running the operation to watch her, the dog was called Lily and had been horribly abused by her former owner. I'm not a dog person, so I skimmed the rest of that part of the report.

The woman has not set foot south of the river since she came home. None of Megan's contacts in Guildford, or at work, have been approached. Everything points to Megan being dead.

Chapter Twenty-Six

Derek, the awkward work experience boy, likes cats. Of course he does. He probably should have returned to school, or university, or wherever he is meant to be, by now, but he's still hanging around. He looks nervous as he knocks on the open door of my office. With only a few days until the trial, I'm in a shitty mood and he shrinks back as I tell him to get the fuck inside and close the door.

'Sir. . . I. . . errr. . . I think. . .'

'Just spit it out, Desmond.'

'Derek. Sir. . .'

I'm impressed that he corrected me. He's already much bolder than he was a few months ago. I break out one of my special smiles. 'I'm just kidding with you, Derek. Pull up a seat and tell me what you've got.' As I talk I am reaching for the bottle of Glenfiddich and two glasses on my desk. Confusion clouds his face for a second but then he sits. He knocks it back, without even the flicker of a shiver. Perhaps I can make something of this boy after all?

'Leah had a cat.'

I look at him without speaking, silently willing him to continue.

'He was a Nebelung, a kind of long-haired Russian Blue, or at least I think he was. I mean he was a rescue so there's no exact way of knowing, but he looks like one.'

Still I say nothing.

'The forensic report said there was cat hair on the clothing the body was dressed in.'

'And?' I ask. There is more to this, I can tell.

'Not just the odd strand. Have you ever had a cat?'

'We had a dog, when I was little.' A dog that Benny had begged and pleaded for. My parents rehomed him two days after Benny passed. They said he was a painful reminder. Did they send me to boarding school for the same reason?

'Close enough. You'll know the hair gets everywhere. And Nebelungs are terrible moulters. The clothes were covered in the stuff.'

'So. . .' Although I am warming to the boy, I do wish he would cut to the chase a little faster.

'So, Megan didn't have a cat. Where did the fur come from?'

'Do you know the answer or was that rhetorical?'

'Megan's friend, Hannah? Her mum has a Nebelung.'

'So, you're telling me that is where the fur came from? Hannah's mum?'

'No, I'm telling you that Megan gave the cat to Hannah's mum.'

'When?'

'Late February. He had a turquoise collar. See this photo from Leah's Instagram?' He slides a sheet of paper over the desk towards me. I'm not a cat person but this one is kind of cute. The turquoise contrasts nicely with his light grey fur, slightly mottled like the ash in a grate from a fire long since extinguished. Derek slides over a second sheet, another cat photo. 'This is from Hannah's mum's Facebook.'

'You think. . .'

'That Megan gave Hannah's mum Leah's cat. Yeah.'

'Have you spoken to her?'

'Well,' he says and offers an almost apologetic smile, 'she claims it was a stray.'

'Microchip?'

He shifts uncomfortably from one foot to the other. It seems to be dawning on him that this isn't the slam dunk he'd imagined it was. 'No,' he finally says.

'So how can we prove it?'

'We could get a DNA match on the fur?'

It's actually not a bad suggestion. But if Hannah's mum claims it's a stray, I'll need to get a warrant to obtain a sample. Somehow I can't see Judge Elspeth Metcalfe, with her fancy bottle of mezcal, siding with me on the need to grant one though. I can just hear her condescending tone as she berates me for bringing something with such a *'flimsy hypothesis'*.

Derek flinches as I throw my glass across the room. It shatters into pieces like a rainfall of diamonds. 'FUCK!' I scream. So many pieces of the puzzle and none that I can actually use. Either Chris was the unluckiest man in the world, or Megan was cleverer than any of us had given her credit for.

I think it is time I went to see the one person who might just know the truth.

The Jonas Institute is a hideous place. I will make my daughter promise me that she will never, ever let me live somewhere like this. Oh, it looks nice from the outside, a huge manor house nestled in the shadows of the North Downs, just outside Dorking. The grounds are full of trees laden with fruit, so much so that the boughs are drooping towards the ground with the weight of their bounty. The gravel driveway crunches under the wheels of my Lexus, and for a few moments I am overcome by a sense of serenity. One subsequently shattered by the screaming of the stark-naked man who is running at full pelt towards my car. He is chased by two huge men who look like they belong on the New Zealand rugby team instead of the white nursing scrubs they are wearing. I stay in the car until they have tackled him and bundled him towards a smaller two-storey building to the left of the main house. A building whose windows are covered in bars.

The reception area smells of cabbage and piss and sweat and abject despair. Thankfully I have to wear a face mask anyway.

'Mrs Patterson does not receive visitors,' the woman on reception tells me curtly.

'It would be very helpful if I could see her.' I flash my winning smile, which normally opens doors. This time, concealed behind my pale-blue fabric face mask, it fails me utterly.

'She does not receive visitors,' the woman tells me again. 'Too many of your type over the years have come sniffing around. Even more so these past few months.'

'My type?' I ask.

'Journalists and the like.' She waves her hand at me like she is swatting a fly. 'Nasty little lot who want a piece of the circus.'

'I'm not a journalist. I'm a lawyer. I could get a court order to speak to her if I need to, but that just seems like an unnecessary faff, doesn't it?' I try my best 'come on and be reasonable' voice, but she remains impassive.

'Get a court order if you need to. But it won't do any good anyway. Barely spoken a word since her daughter's murder. Such a waste.'

'You won't let me have just a few minutes? Even if I ask very nicely?'

'You can't come in the house.' She shrugs and turns away. 'I'll send her to find you outside,' she throws over her shoulder.

I walk laps around the grounds, waiting and watching. One eye looking for a woman who might be the twins' mum, the other ensuring no naked lunatics can creep up behind me. In the end I am so preoccupied looking for crazies that I almost dismiss the woman who is shambling in my direction, painfully thin and looking a decade older than her fifty-five years.

'Mrs Patterson.' She offers me a hand. 'You were looking for me?'

There are deep lines on her face, scoured into the skin of her forehead as if she has spent all the years of her life wearing a permanent frown.

I decide to just be honest with her. Something tells me not to bother trying to play games. 'It's about Leah. She visits?'

'Megan, you mean. She's the only one who comes.'

'That's Leah, Mrs Patterson,' I say gently.

'My daughter visits with her lovely new boyfriend. So much better than that husband of hers.'

'Mrs Patterson. That's Leah who visits.'

'Those girls always thought I didn't notice when they swapped or pretended to cover for each other. They used to do it all the time, from when they were tiny to almost full-grown adults. Now,' she waggles a finger towards me, 'I might not remember what I had for breakfast' – she pauses to giggle, and I see a flash of the stunning young woman she had been once – 'but I know my daughter. And that man knows it too.'

'Man?'

'The lovely boyfriend.' She sighs in exasperation. 'He loves my Megs. That husband used to call her Meggie and it made my skin crawl. Always knew there was something off with that one.'

'And what does the new one call her?'

'Not Meggie, that's for sure! Now, if you'll excuse me, there's meatloaf for lunch and I don't want to miss out.'

For a few moments I let myself dream that I could put Mrs Patterson on the stand and make her swear on the Bible that it was Megan who was standing in the courtroom. But the judge would never allow me to call a witness who barely knew what day of the week it was, and the jury would dismiss her testimony as the ramblings of a batty old woman. My trip has been another waste of time from the case's perspective. Megan really is turning out to be far cleverer than I'd thought.

There has been a last-minute change. The Crown Prosecution Service had given the case to a lawyer who I knew to be something less than fully able. And that was being generous. But he went on an 'essential business trip' to one of the smaller Greek islands and brought a new variant of the virus back with him; there was an item on the ten o'clock news that called him a 'carrier' after twenty people on his return flight home had also been diagnosed. He hadn't known he was pre-diabetic, although the extra thirty pounds he was carrying was pretty obvious. Idiot had refused the vaccine. With his health hanging in the balance, a new prosecutor had been sourced. Luke Berryman. I should have known it would be him. We have never come face to face in the courtroom, but his reputation precedes him. One of those 'the law was my calling' and 'I just want to make the world a little safer' types. He looks honest and harmless, like butter wouldn't melt. Juries trust him. Judges love him. I fucking hate him. Behind that holier-than-thou exterior is the heart of a man who will stoop to any depths to get a conviction.

'Bad?' Chris is sitting opposite me, his face like a mask as he watches me stroke the cover of the file lying on the table between us. Yesterday I received the last submissions from Luke, the final details of the case he was planning to bring against my client.

And the final nail in the coffin. Luke Berryman is requesting for the jury to be sequestered for the duration. Some crock of shit about them not being 'unduly influenced' by the media circus. Everyone knows that when a jury is sequestered, they are much faster in their judgement; even at the best of times, they're keen to get home to their lives. But after the year we've had, and with restrictions finally easing, the jurors will not appreciate being locked up again.

Derek is standing at the door to my office, but he does not look nervous. He looks me straight in the eye as he says, 'Jemima is dating the oldest son of Nathanial Dolan.'

'I know.' I motion to the chair in front of me and notice his gaze flicker to the Glenfiddich behind me. It's only one o'clock in the afternoon but who am I to judge? I pour us both a large measure and wait for him to tell me the next part. He has a plan, I can feel it.

'The *Gazette* could publish Chris's story. Now. Before the jury is sequestered.'

'You know I can't tell the press his defence strategy – I'd be disbarred. And they wouldn't publish it without confirmation of the source.'

'Nathanial Dolan might. If you had something to trade.'

The tone of his voice suggests I do, in fact, have something to trade. I top his glass up.

'Nathanial Dolan wants to join Mrs Chalmers's establishment.'

'And you would know this how?'

He shrugs. 'I'm quiet. People forget I'm there. They talk, and I listen.'

'And how do you know that Mrs Chalmers may be something I can offer him?'

He blushes, a sudden raspberry bloom across his cheeks. 'I saw the. . .er. . .video.' Then he smiles at me.

'Fuck!' There is pride in my voice. He's right. I grab my suit jacket from the back of my chair and run from the room. 'Jemima!' I bellow as I pass the door to the small office she shares with another junior staff member. 'We're going to the pub. Right now.'

So, what do you do when you have a load of evidence that you can't use in court, but which is the only way to ensure your client has a hope in hell of winning at trial? Because whatever he did, whatever crimes of poor judgement he committed when he lied about his past to his wife, or when he started an affair with her sister, he is not a murderer.

First things first, I need a way in with Nathanial Dolan.

'I'll tell him about us.'

'You wouldn't.' Her eyes flash with anger.

'Wouldn't I?'

'You'd get in trouble.' She takes a sip of wine. An act.

'Jemima. Who do you think will care?'

'You bastard.'

I spread my fingers out across the table and grin at her. 'Yep.'

'Will it work?'

'It can't hurt.'

'You bastard.'

In two days, the jury will enter the courtroom for the first day of the Hardcastle trial. From that point on they will not be able to read or watch the news, they will relinquish all contact with the outside world as they are shown the facts of the trial, to ensure they are not unduly influenced. But until then, they are an audience I can still reach. With the help of a certain chinless wonder's rather chinless father. And the newspaper he publishes to millions upon millions of people every day.

Jemima takes out her phone.

I realise I am crossing my fingers behind my back.

It has taken over a year to get to trial. A year in which my client has sat in a holding cell waiting for his moment to tell his version of events. I will be honest though, the prison look suits him. His skin is pale, almost translucent. His pallor speaks of lost liberty and a man imprisoned needlessly.

He has lost weight too, although this has only served to chisel his features further. We debated for an hour last week over whether he should be clean-shaven or sport a tidy beard. In the end I told him to shave. Beards could cause suspicion among some of the jury, and the lack of facial hair accentuates those cheekbones. The suit I have bought for him is half a size too big. He looks like a man almost broken by the allegations against him; but still someone the ladies will fall for and whom the men would quite like to have a drink with.

'How do you rate my chances?' he asks as we wait to be called into the courtroom.

'Jeremy Crumpton doesn't lose, remember,' I tell him before taking a huge glug of the hyper-strength coffee in front of me. I don't think I've really slept for months as my team and I built the case. But we've done everything we can and now it's just the final hurdle.

***

Will the Real Ms Patterson Please Stand Up?

The headline screamed from the front page of yesterday's *Gazette*. Accompanied by a picture of Leah – or is it Megan? – sporting a look the journalist had described as 'conniving'. A photo of Chris, taken by a long-range camera as he was transferred from prison to a holding facility ready for the trial, made him look like a man on the edge of despair, face pallid and drawn. A victim. Falsely accused by a scheming, lying woman who would stop at nothing to destroy him.

The journalist had been creative in his use of terms like 'sources close to Mr Hardcastle suggest' and 'friends of the falsely accused have intimated'. Quite frankly, it was a masterpiece. Not enough concrete fact to ever be tied to information leaked directly from my firm, but enough juicy titbits to plant doubt with the jury. When Leah enters the witness stand and claims Chris killed Megan and kidnapped her, at least a handful of jurors will be more interested in which sister she really is than in the evidence she will give against my client.

Will it be enough? I don't know. The article also included a request for anyone with information about Megan's accident all those years ago to contact the *Gazette*; there was even the offer of a reward. I have to hope someone comes forward. But in the meantime, there's a bounce in my step as we walk towards the courtroom.

Part Five
Megan

Chapter Twenty-Seven

'Will the Real Ms Patterson Please Stand Up?'

The headline was ridiculous. But not as ridiculous as the swagger in Mr Jeremy Crumpton's walk, like a dressage pony carefully picking up each hoof with coquettish flair. He really thinks he's won. If only he knew what was coming.

The eyes of the jury linger on my face. Are some of them wondering which twin I really am? Perhaps. Let them wonder. None of that matters, not any more. The case has already been decided, despite the efforts my husband and his superstar lawyer have gone to. I feel bad about the amount of money Valma will have shelled out at her husband's insistence they must protect their only son from a lifetime in jail. She thinks he's guilty. It's etched so clearly into her features. She raises a hand to me, a tiny wave across the chasm of the courtroom. I don't wave back but it breaks my heart to watch her face crumple at my hostility. I wish I could give her a hug and tell her it'll all be OK, that her evil prick of a son will remain in his cage.

The court is adjourned a few minutes before five p.m. I watch the jurors file out, off to enjoy the short ride to the small Holiday Inn down the road, with its tiny gym and a bar they aren't permitted to use. I hope the trial is short, for their sakes. Given that the whole defence rests on the idea that I am actually Megan, it's over before it's even begun. Chris and Jeremy just don't realise it yet.

A faint hint of Jeremy's aftershave reaches me as I follow him down the corridor, the tap of his slightly heeled shoes echoing off the bare concrete walls. I catch up to him before he presses the button for the lift to take us to the underground car park and, as expected, he is gentlemanly in his insistence I get in first, an extended arm and a slightly sleazy smile. I refuse, staring at him until he gets inside. I turn my back to him; the prosecution's key witness shouldn't be seen to be talking to the lawyer for the defence.

I have thought about this moment for months. It was always going to come down to Chris's word against mine. And the trump card he still hopes to play. That *Gazette* article appealed for information about an accident that took place over sixteen years ago, one that left its mark on the girl they cut from the wreckage. I trust Jeremy is watching as I lift my hair away from my neck, the action of a woman who has spent too much time inside a hot stuffy room and who just wants to feel the cool air on her skin. The lights are bright and the scar almost buried in my hairline glows silver. I don't turn round as I stage-whisper, 'I think this is what you've been looking for.' In my right hand is an envelope. I wave it slightly, until I feel Jeremy slip it from my grasp.

I listen to the rustle of paper as Jeremy removes the sheet from the envelope. The yellow part of a triplicate form, a hospital release note dated 10 September 2004. The night I went to get my sister a packet of cigarettes from the petrol station down the road. She had a car, but I did not. I didn't even have a licence. 'Just take mine,' Leah had told me. 'You can always say you're me if you get caught.' I had agreed. Like I always did.

The door slides open into the dim shadows of the car park and I walk away, raising one hand to wave at Tom, who is already sitting in the BMW coupé, waiting to take me home. My pace is slow. Jeremy is only a few steps behind me.

He waits until he is sitting inside his own car and the closed door muffles the sound. But not enough that I can't make out the frustrated scream as he reads the name on the hospital form.

Leah Patterson

Printed in bold type, the name taken from the car registration papers and the driving licence in my pocket that night.

Tom kisses my cheek. 'Is it over?' he asks.

To be honest it will never be over. I see her everywhere I look and hear her name on the lips of everyone I care about. I will forever bear the weight of the loss of her.

My perfect twin.

Read on for an exclusive extract from
Sarah Bonner's brand-new novel

Her Sweet Revenge

Available in Spring 2023
Pre-order now!

Chapter One

HELENA

My mother-in-law is already holding court in the dining room when I arrive to meet her for lunch. Just like every other Tuesday, regardless of anything else I might have going on. God forbid if I were to ever miss the bi-weekly torture session Geraldine subjects me to.

'You're late,' she calls as I walk in, voice booming across the space. I glance at my watch – it's one minute past – and my heel catches in a gap between the flagstones causing me to stumble a little. 'Drunk?' she asks, and her minions titter into their hands.

When I say I'm meeting her for lunch what I really mean is that I'm having lunch in her general vicinity. There are at least a dozen other women here, all wives of important people. Or at least people *she* considers to be important. The Grange is a very exclusive private members club, with a stringent set of rules around who can – and more importantly who can-not – sip a cocktail at the large mahogany bar, eat a steak in the damask flock-wallpapered dining room, or stay in one of a handful of bedrooms each equipped with its own claw-foot bath. My husband's family have owned this club for decades.

'You have something on your dress,' Geraldine wrinkles her nose as she gestures to an almost microscopic piece of fluff on my ribcage.

I pluck it off as I go to sit down and place it carefully on the napkin at my side. 'Probably from the lining of my coat.' I hate myself for explaining. I hate myself even more as I hold my breath to wait for her next criticism.

'You should be more careful if you're going to wear black.' Her tone is clear: black is not appropriate for lunch. Black is for funerals and the weddings of women she loathes.

'I came straight from a meeting with a client.'

She takes a sip of her water before she replies. 'Yes, well I suppose it is *admirable* to have a hobby.' Translation: she does *not* think it's admirable. She is just making sure she gets in her usual dig about me having a career. Taylor wives do not have careers. They have charities they support, husbands they look after, and – most importantly – children they coddle. And you thought 1950 was a lifetime ago. 'But next time, please ensure you are dressed appropriately for lunch. There are important people here and I do not wish for you to embarrass me fur—'

Her last sentence is cut short as she notices the waitress hovering next to her, the large glass of wine in her hand dangerously close to sloshing over the brim as she bobs and weaves to avoid Geraldine's gesticulations.

'Just put the glass down you *stupid* girl,' Geraldine snaps. I catch the waitress's eye and offer a small smile of encouragement. She looks terrified. I can't say I blame her. My best friend calls Geraldine 'Smaug' – not to her face though, obviously – because she thinks she's a wealth-obsessed dragon. Geraldine is *also* a stuck-up class-A bitch and she's rather prone to firing any member of staff at The Grange she deems 'not up to par', despite the fact she's meant to leave the day-to-day running of the place to the manager.

As lunch continues, I find myself desperately trying to ensure conversation around the table remains in a territory I'm at least vaguely comfortable with, such as the weather or the new coffee shop opening in the next village along. Edward and I have been married for almost six years now, so I'm well practised at staying away from anything political to avoid an inevitable argument, but I'm also trying to steer clear of anything baby related that might trigger Geraldine to bring up the subject of her lack of grandchildren. At least the food is incredible, and I have to confess I love cracking the burnt sugar on top of the world's smallest – and possibly most pretentious, in a really quite fabulous way – crème brûlée.

After the dessert plates are cleared, I excuse myself and duck out the side door of the dining room. Geraldine believes it is the height of rudeness to 'check one's telephone in polite company', but I'm waiting on an important email from a potential investor. I'm ecstatic when I see the invite for a lunch meeting next week to 'discuss the finer details'. My dream might actually happen and I practically prance around the corner to ensure I'm out of sight before I call to confirm. I almost fall over the waitress who is sitting on the floor, smoking.

'Shit! Sorry!' She leaps to her feet, grinding her cigarette butt with the block heel of the ridiculous shoes Geraldine insists the female staff wear with their uniform. 'I . . . err . . . I was just . . .'

'Hey. It's OK. I promise I won't tell.' I give her a smile. 'But get one of the barmen to show you the spot on the roof. It's a much better place to hide from Smaug.' The name flies out my mouth before I really think.

'Smaug?' She mouths the name back at me, but her eyes are dancing as she suppresses a giggle. 'Like the dragon in *The Hobbit*?'

'My mother-in-law,' I confirm with a raise of both eyebrows.

'Ouch.'

'Yeah. Complete cliché, I know, but in this case it's true. The whole mother-in-law-from-hell thing. I'm Helena by the way,' I extend my hand to her.

'Ella,' she says. Then her face crumples, 'I think she's going to fire me.'

'That might be a blessing in disguise.'

'Except that I have to pay my rent and this is the only job I could find. Maybe once I've saved a bit and I can buy a nice suit for interviews . . .' she trails off. 'Sorry. You don't want to hear my problems.' She lets out a shuddering sigh that should be melodramatic but instead seems . . . well, she seems vulnerable, as if she's balanced on a precipice and liable to fall at any moment.

'I could help you. I mean, we're probably not that different in size. And I have a wardrobe full of "interview suits"; I'm a stylist.' I say the last bit with pride, despite Geraldine's insistence that 'shopping for other people is rather beneath the Taylors – people shop for *us*'.

'Would you?' she stares at me, her whole face hopeful.

Looking at her is like looking into a mirror back to 2005. 2005 Helena took her youth for granted, accepted that her long hair would always be glossy without needing three hours in the salon, that her skin would be dewy – a term I hate, but it's so damn accurate when you're in your early twenties – and that her teeth would always be white and perfectly straight (no one tells you that your teeth move as you head towards forty and you find yourself googling how intrusive adult braces might be). 'When you finish your shift, pop round, we only live down the road, on the corner, just before the *Welcome to Ofcombe St Mary* sign. The Gatehouse, you can't miss it.'

'Thank you!' She launches herself at me and wraps me into a tight hug as if we've been friends for years. 'You're a life saver.'

Back inside the dining room, Geraldine leans in to sniff my hair the second I slide onto my chair. 'Fraternising with the help, were we? Well, I guess you can take the girl out of Torquay but you can't take Torquay out of the girl. But really, Helena, you need to be more careful around smokers.' Her expression hardens, her eyes piercing through me. 'Especially if you're going to start IVF soon.'

I stay silent, crossing my arms across my chest. It looks defensive but it hides the way I'm pinching the delicate skin on my inner arm, the bruising hidden by the bolero I'm wearing. It's the only way I can stop myself from hitting her.

'Oh, don't give me that sourpuss look. You're hardly the only person to ever do it. Moira's niece did.' Geraldine points to a small woman with blond hair so perfectly coiffed it looks like a helmet. 'Moira!' The woman looks ecstatic to be singled out. 'Your niece did the IVF, didn't she?'

'Oh yes. Six rounds in the end. Horrible process, but needs must.'

'See.' Geraldine hisses. 'She did six rounds. And you won't even do one.'

'Edward and I are looking at our options.' I tell her, wishing we could drop this ridiculous charade. I do not want children and neither does my husband; we've agreed that the Taylor name ends with us. Whatever the cost. Yet his mother refuses to believe us and continues to insist I must be having trouble conceiving.

'I just don't understand why you haven't made an appointment yet. I gave you the number of that specialist who Cecily's friend was seeing. *She* just had triplets.'

'I—' But my reply is interrupted by the sound of glass on concrete. A lot of glass. Ella is standing in the doorway of the dining room amidst a sea of glittering shards, a look of abject horror frozen on her face, an empty tray held vertically out in front of her.

'Oh, you *stupid* girl!' Geraldine exclaims. 'Look at this mess!' Geraldine turns away from Ella and rolls her eyes at her friends. 'At this rate I'm going to have to find yet *another* waitress.' She turns her gaze to me. 'As if I don't have enough to worry about.'

Geraldine doesn't fire Ella for the glass incident, but it's clear her days at The Grange are numbered. When Ella turns up at my house later that afternoon, frazzled and nervous, I vow to help her find something else.

'Why are you being so kind to me?' she asks.

I shrug. She'll probably assume it's to get back at Geraldine, and I admit that is part of it, but I just can't help but see myself in her. Once upon a time I was completely out of my depth, stuck in a place where the people around me treated me as if I were a second class citizen. Ella and I have a lot in common.

'Follow me,' I say to her, and lead her through the house.

Half an hour later, I've found the perfect skirt suit for her to wear to interviews; classy and demure but with a clinging skirt that keeps the look feeling young enough for someone who is only just twenty-three. The only problem is a blouse, as Ella is blessed in a way that I am not and so all of mine gape unattractively. 'How about I take you to this outlet place I'm a member of?' I offer.

'That would be amazing!'

Her enthusiasm is infectious, she's so different to most of the other people in my life. Geraldine and her geriatric mean girls. Edward and his 'rugger chums' – his term, not mine. Apart from Thea, all my friends are parents now, conversations dominated by school choices and screen-time limits. They've moved on from the baby phase, passed the toddler days, careering towards the tween years as I stay exactly where I've always been. I stand by the decision Edward and I made, but if I'm entirely honest I hadn't realised how much my life would diverge from the lives of my peers. Or that there would be some parts I *would* miss: no first words, first day at school, dance recitals, chess tournaments, their first love and first heartbreak. I've never told even Edward I was pregnant once, but it wasn't meant to be. I would have called her Thea after her godmother and she would have been fierce and fearless. She would have changed the world.

'You must be so proud of your business.' Ella pulls me back from the daydream. She's scrolling on her phone. 'This is UH-mazing!' She turns her screen to show me what she's looking at. It's my Instagram feed. 'You have like a hundred thousand followers. You're practically a celebrity.'

'Hardly,' I reply, but I can't help smiling, and busy myself preparing us a mojito. I try to avoid glancing at the alcove I use as a home office, the vintage roll top closed to hide the chaos of papers sprawled across it. And the hidden drawer stuffed full of the evidence of my notoriety.

'Tell me all about it.' Ella begs, taking the proffered cocktail, curling her legs underneath her on the sofa.

'There's not a lot to tell.'

'Really? I don't believe that for one minute.'

'Well, there is this investor who is interested . . .' I trail off. 'But it's early days and I can't really talk about it.

Ella applauds. 'Brilliant. I'm in awe of you. It must piss your mother-in-law off, seeing you with this big successful business.'

'Not quite . . . Geraldine is horrified that I suggest people wear *high street*.' I do my best impression and Ella snorts mojito as she laughs. 'Like where else do real people shop?' Geraldine only wears vintage DVF wrap dresses; she has a whole wardrobe of them. Geraldine's functionally bankrupt, essentially living on money borrowed against The Grange, but she's very good at keeping up appearances. The late Mr Edwin Taylor – my father-in-law – put all the cash assets in trust rather than leave them to his wife, or directly to his son. There is no Taylor money unless Edward produces an heir. Edwin revelled in making everyone's lives as shitty as possible when he was alive and he just couldn't help himself continuing his legacy in death.

I drain my glass, pushing the thought of him from my mind. 'Another mojito?' I ask Ella, not waiting for her answer before walking back into the kitchen and starting to prepare another cocktail.

'I'd love to, but I'd better run.'

I must fail to hide my disappointment because she adds, 'but I'll see you on Friday?'

'Absolutely,' I confirm and follow her into the hallway.

'Ooh, what's that?' She scoops a little envelope from the doormat and passes it to me. It is small, about the size of a postcard, *Helena* written on it in elaborate calligraphy. Did I miss it earlier, or was it delivered while we were sipping mojitos? I try to peer round Ella, but it's almost dusk, the trees silhouetted against the darkening sky, offering a perfect place for someone to hide. A chill runs down my spine; is someone watching from the shadows?

'Thank you, Helena.' Ella says, lifting the suit slightly. 'For the suit and for . . . well, for treating me like a person.'

I close the door behind her and look at the envelope in my hand, exactly like the others hidden in my desk. Inside is a simple white card, a single sentence written on it.

We all have secrets . . . but you're going to pay for yours

Acknowledgements

Firstly, a huge thank you for reading this novel. Megan was my constant companion during the craziness of 2020, and I am thrilled to be able to share her story with you.

Writing these acknowledgements in May 2021, just as restrictions are being lifted, feels very strange. I wrote this whole book in lockdown and have still not actually met most of you in real life. But what this period has missed in physical interactions has been compensated for by the huge network of individuals I have met online over this time. Thank you to all the other writers, book bloggers, reviewers and readers who have offered me their support and friendship; I am hugely appreciative to have found my 'tribe'.

A huge thank you to my agent extraordinaire, Hannah Sheppard, whose enthusiasm for the book blew me away, and who gave me the courage to write the ending it deserved. You have been the greatest champion an author could wish for and I am so thankful to be part of the DHH Literary family.

Next, thank you to Sara Adams, whose editorial wizardry brought the book to the next level. Working with you has been an absolute pleasure. Thank you also to the wider team at Hodder Studio; to Kwaku, Grace, Jacqui, Taliha, Kate and Callie to name but a few. And to Alex Logan and the team at Grand Central for helping to bring *Her Perfect Twin* to US readers.

A massive shout-out to my friends and former colleagues for your support, advice and generally for not telling me I was a lunatic for thinking I could write a novel. Special mention to Bronwen, Mo, Eamonn, Jennifer, Sally, Theresa, Wouter, Wendy, and everyone else who read the early drafts of my nonsense!

To Marie Henderson for offering me your feedback and words of wisdom right from the start of my writing attempts. Without you I doubt I would have had the confidence to write this book, let alone to send it out into the big wide world. I owe you a LOT of wine when we can finally go to Harrogate together!

Huge thank you to my family: to Bill for your sage advice, to Dad for always making me believe I could do anything, and to the Bonners for your support and encouragement. To Mum, you have been the most amazing alpha-reader and cheerleader. Thank you for reading every single draft and offering me your advice, comments and grammatical expertise; I couldn't have done it without you!

To my lovely husband for keeping me sane throughout the strangest year of our lives, and for giving me the freedom to chase my crazy dream of publication. And finally, thank you Lily, for insisting I take regular breaks for walkies and trips to the park. You're the best goofy furball in the world.

THRILLINGLY GOOD BOOKS
FROM CRIMINALLY
GOOD WRITERS

CRIME FILES BRINGS YOU THE LATEST RELEASES FROM TOP CRIME AND THRILLER AUTHORS.

SIGN UP ONLINE FOR OUR MONTHLY NEWSLETTER AND BE THE FIRST TO KNOW ABOUT OUR COMPETITIONS, NEW BOOKS AND MORE.

VISIT OUR WEBSITE: WWW.CRIMEFILES.CO.UK
LIKE US ON FACEBOOK: FACEBOOK.COM/CRIMEFILES
FOLLOW US ON TWITTER: @CRIMEFILESBOOKS